HOPE AND CHRISTMAS TREES

Jill Debra Green

LIGHTHOUSE
BOOK PUBLISHING

© Jill Debra Green 2021

Lighthouse Book Publishing
12 Dukes Court, Bognor Road,
Chichester, PO19 8FX, United Kingdom
www.lighthousebookpublishing.com

ISBN: 978-1-910848-50-0

British Library Cataloguing in Publication Data. A catalogue record for this book is available from the British Library

Formatted by Lucy Frankland, Lighthouse Book Publishing
Cover by Ellie Atkinson
Printed in the United Kingdom

Table of Contents

Chapter One 4

Chapter Two... 18

Chapter Three 35

Chapter Four 47

Chapter Five.. 66

Chapter Six 82

Chapter Seven 92

Chapter Eight 107

Chapter Nine 128

Chapter Ten 141

Chapter Eleven.. 152

Chapter Twelve 161

Chapter Thirteen 177

Chapter Fourteen 190

Chapter Fifteen 204

Chapter Sixteen... 219

Chapter Seventeen 228

Chapter Eighteen 248

Chapter Nineteen 261

Notes 271

Chapter One

"The unmistakeable David Bowie with 'Ashes to Ashes,'" announced the relentlessly perky radio breakfast show host, "and before that, Blondie's 'Call Me.' Gill and Nancy from Clayford and Amy from Victoria Green say it's 1979. Close, but not close enough, and Barry Richards – you're way off with 1988. Can *you* name that year? Text or call C2C Breakfast on…"

"Nineteen-eighty," Faith muttered flatly, her head in her hands, feeling the bitter memories begin to engulf her. Attempting to push the memory away, she listened closely to his list of upcoming Christmas events – the usual craft fairs, carol services and charity dinners across the county.

She took a deep breath, knowing the 'playing now' broadcast would be the sound that welcomed her to the building. "Come on, Faith," she chided, "get a grip," reaching to open the car door beside her.

"…the Christmas Tree Festival down in Applebury, something new to view from December," he chanted, "and finally it's the Christmas number one of…you tell me!"

The commercially sweet voices of the St Winifred's School Choir oozed from her car radio for a split second before she hit the 'off' button. Faith New, star of C2C Daytime Radio, sat back in her seat. "Pull yourself together woman," she scolded out loud. Rather than risk a scene in the radio station, she breathed back her tears in the safety of her car, re-living the horror of the year that shaped her life.

Faith, at that time known as Sarah-Faith Browne, attended an expensive boarding school. Her parents, seeing every expense as an investment in her future, had agreed to her joining the small band of privileged girls on the Easter Holiday ski trip.

Fifteen-year-old Sarah-Faith, intelligent, naïve and starry eyed, fell in love. It had seemed that Jacques the ski instructor – so handsome, so much older and so passionate – was in love with her too. She was certain. If she had not believed it to be so, she may not have consented to something so unknown and unexpected, and, if she were honest, so unpleasant, on her last night at the resort. She felt their love would last for ever. Her heart was broken when she returned home at the end of the ski trip. It broke again as, returning to her Hampshire boarding school, she discovered that she was not Jacques' only 'petite cherie.'

Of course, the other girls, more knowing, giggled over their romantic flirtations with every Jacques, Joules and Armand. Looking back, Sarah-Faith Browne was not surprised that her parents believed she had hidden her pregnancy, but it had only dawned on Faith that she may be pregnant when her new school skirt would no longer fasten at the waist. She had no plan for the future, except some adolescent fantasy that her parents would pity her broken heart, condemn her seducer and care for their grandchild.

Home for half term in November, she tearfully confessed her condition and within hours was seated at the dining room table between her enraged mother and her silent, devastated father. She had let them down, her mother screeched. She should be ashamed. She was ungrateful, irresponsible, wilful, wanton,

5

immoral, degenerate, difficult, and disappointing. An object of disgust.

Mrs Browne marched little Sarah-Faith to the family doctor the very next day. No one asked her whether she wanted the baby, in fact no one asked how she had become pregnant in the first place. The doctor's sneer as he jotted down 'father unknown' was enough to tell her that the only crime was hers and this was her deserved punishment. Between the doctor and Mrs Browne, it was agreed that this immoral, immature, fifteen-year-old child did not have the capacity, intellectually, emotionally, or practically to care for a baby. Thus it was written on the documents she was forced to sign.

In the following frenzied, furious weeks, she found herself in a maternity unit a long way from home. In the earliest hours of Christmas eve, with no pain relief and no support beside a few barked commands to control herself when she cried in pain, Sarah-Faith gave birth to a daughter. The apparently pitiless midwife was called to attend another birth almost immediately after Sarah's delivery, leaving mother and child alone for a short while. Despite the brutal ordeal of birth, Faith was overwhelmed with love for the tiny, dark-haired scrap in her arms. Alone, afraid, and evidently despised by every adult in the place, she held her daughter close, pouring every ounce of love into her in that precious hour.

"May you be happy, may you be loved, may you be safe, my little Angel." She whispered.

A nurse wheeled the baby from the delivery suite 'for a check-up.' "I want to keep her!" she cried," Tell them I am keeping her."

*Back on the ward, they said she should put the baby's needs before her own, that she could not give the baby any sort of 'decent' life, that the baby deserved a mother **and** a father. That she would soon forget and start again. That she should be a good girl. That it would be illegal to try to find her daughter now. That she had already signed the papers.*

She never held her child again.

*They gave her medication to dry up her milk and said that the doctor had taken the baby to a **respectable** couple who could give her a decent life. The implication being, of course, that Faith was neither decent nor respectable.*

She cried. She was told to pack her bags. That afternoon, Mrs Browne pulled up at the back door to the maternity unit, pushed her sobbing daughter into the car and drove her home.

"You can stop your noise young lady"

"I miss her, Mum!" cried Sarah-Faith. "I love her!"

Sarah-Faith's mother pulled the car over. She turned and slapped her daughter across the face. "HOW DARE YOU! What you have done is unforgivable! Your father and I have sacrificed our lives to give you the very best education money can buy. And you threw it all away. You disgust me, you slut!" she snarled. "No," she said calmly, restarting the engine and pulling out into the traffic. "You will go back to school, complete your education and make up for the damage you have done. You will forget this whole sordid affair and our lives can go back to normal."

"But Mum!" cried Sarah-Faith. "Mum, she is my own daughter, how can I...?"

"You are not to speak of your grubby little secret to any one, EVER!" her mother shouted, cutting across her daughter's plea. "None of this ever happened, do you understand? You are to forget you had a child. You never had a daughter, it's as simple as that."

Sarah-Faith wept the deep heaving cries of grief. At the loss of her daughter, the loss of her own childhood and the loss of any trace of love for her mother and father.

"Oh, for goodness' sake, Sarah-Faith, shut up!" shouted Mrs Browne. She flicked the radio on, to drown out her daughter's heartbreak. It was the Christmas number one, ironically 'There's No One Quite Like Grandma.'

Like a limbless man learning to walk on prosthetics, Sarah-Faith returned to 'normal life' as instructed. She studied hard at school, gaining a reputation for being aloof and antisocial. University, away from home, allowed her time to develop a personality very different from the polite, reclusive girl her parents saw. Sarah-Faith had wrapped all that shame, confusion and terrible, terrible, grief in a bubble, buried it inside herself, along with her capacity to love or trust another human being. Sarah-Faith's only motivation in all her endeavours had been to ensure that she never had to rely on anyone but herself again. Peers and tutors alike would describe her as confident, mature, single-minded – maybe even ruthless.

She found herself a job that required her to work the holidays, and rarely went back to her childhood home. Her father wrote regularly, but she would simply put the letters in the bin, unread. She invited her parents to her graduation only as the carefully planned final chapter in their shared story. The ceremony complete, her mother loudly informed her, and the surrounding crowds, that she had booked a table at the Savoy to celebrate Sarah-Faith's first-class honours degree, and the lucrative job she had secured on the strength of it.

"Thank you, but I have other plans" their daughter said.

Mr Browne, who had seen his cheerful, confident little girl become a withdrawn hard young woman, said tearfully to her, "Well done, Sarah-Faith, we're so proud of you. It was all worth it in the end." He gently touched her cheek then winced as she pulled herself away. It was as if he had struck her.

"Worth it?" Sarah-Faith hissed, in a low calm voice. "If you are referring to my 'grubby little secret,'" looking directly at her mother, "I believe it was never to be mentioned again." Her parents, startled by her reference to the long-buried family scandal, regarded her in uneasy silence. "You weren't so proud six years ago, when I was seduced into sexual activity long before I knew what it was all about, then, as punishment, coerced into allowing my child to be snatched away by strangers."

"I didn't know you were..." muttered her mother.

"Abused, effectively? Well, you never bothered to ask. I was a child, mother, a child. All you cared about was your plan for my success and covering up my 'mistake.'"

Mrs Browne began to object and was immediately silenced as her daughter continued. "And the way you let them treat me was a violation all over again, when you should have protected me." Furiously, she wiped away an escaping tear. "The worst part of it all, though, Mum and Dad, is that although I can never

*forgive what you did, I can never, ever, forgive myself.
I will carry the shame, guilt and regret for the rest of
my life. So, you win, I guess."*

*She dodged back as her father reached for her.
"No!" she insisted. "We made a bargain six years ago
and I believe my part of the bargain has been fulfilled
now. To quote you, mother, 'You are to forget you had
a child. You never had a daughter, it's as simple as
that.'"*

*They watched their daughter walk away into a
future they would never share. Somewhere a jubilant
crowd of graduates cheered as they threw their caps in
the air. That same day, in a legal transaction, Sarah-
Faith Browne became Faith New.*

Now, nearly forty years later, Faith would see
young women and try to trace in every one the features
of herself. The few relationships she had started had
fallen apart. She had never married, never had a child,
and had never forgotten the child she had to surrender.
Faith had never tried to trace her child. She sometimes
hoped her daughter would look for her, but the
deliberately scant adoption records made that almost
impossible.

The song finished and Faith was mercifully
brought back to the present, repeating the mantra that
she had said so many times, "*May you be happy, may
you be loved, may you be safe, my Angel.*"

Faith carefully regathered her self-possession and
stepped from her car, shook herself into 'cool,
successful reporter' mode, and headed for the entrance
to County-to-County Radio Broadcasting Network,
popularly called C2C. The doors to the car park
swished open. Hope Taylor, the cleaner, was hurrying
backwards through the door, momentarily blinded as

she pulled her coat on and checked her phone at the same time. She bundled through the gap as Faith walked in. Collision was unavoidable, and the file Faith carried flew into the air, paper scattering.

"I'm so sorry," Hope stuttered, scooping up the papers and standing to hand them back.

Their eyes met, Faith raised an eyebrow and, taking the disorganised bundle, merely turned sharply and continued into the building. Faith headed for her desk as the door to the station manager's office opened. Miles Carter, Head of Regional Radio Broadcasting, invited her in. He saw a woman at the peak of her career, dedicated, professional, respected. She saw a family man who had somehow hung on to the 'work to live' ethic, in spite of his reputation for uncompromising leadership.

Following her surprise decision to leave her high-profile journalistic career in London, Faith had moved to the county town of Sparchester and had presented the enormously popular daytime spot on their local station for some years. Her fearless exposure of corruption or injustice, coupled with a biting, humorous wit during phone-ins had secured a number of industry awards. She looked at him, questioning but silent.

"Faith," he said, with a smile. "What are you working on at the moment?"

"I'm looking at the local planning scandal—they want to build 300 houses on Motley Heath. The builder is a cousin of the town planner."

Miles pulled a wincing face. "Anything else?"
Faith sensed the prospect of a big supermarket draining the life out of another little town was inevitable, and no more a news story than the rise in

the price of bread. She mentally ditched that story. "I'm looking into the hospital bias towards Lambert's Taxis when patients need to go home. Maybe someone is taking a cut."

Miles looked equally unimpressed. "I don't know," he interrupted, pulling 'that' face again. "It's the run up to Christmas, can't we be a bit more…*optimistic*?"

"Optimistic?" Faith was perplexed. Their little radio station was known for its unearthing of scandal, forthright opinions and local campaigns.

"Yes." He went on, "Every station is grinding out the same old cynical, hopeless calamity."

"I think you mean outstanding investigative reporting," she retorted, referring to the awards she and her station had snatched from the other local and national radio stations. She saw the flinch of resignation in his face, disappointment that she may be, after all, too set in her ways for innovation.

"Faith," he went on, "things have changed. We are up against it, our audiences can google news the minute it happens, and get instant views and opinions from social media." He sighed. "We're in a recession – we need something to make people feel good, to make them feel part of something…"

"…and commercially?" Faith knew all this 'global village' talk was not the real point of Miles' speech. "Commercially, Faith, we need people to keep tuning in, we need advertisers and we need more than our old reputation to keep our station at the top."

"Are we in danger?" she asked. "Can they shut us down?"

"Shut us down, no," he responded. "But they can *slim* us down, centralise us and, well 'rationalise' salaries and staffing." He mimed quotes as he spoke.

"So, what you are saying is, scrap the truth and sell the –?"

"What I am saying," he cut her off, "is truth does not have to be angry protest. It can be a celebration of genuine, real life events, that make people feel happy." He scratched his head, trying to think of an example. "Like a Royal Wedding! Millions of people tune in for a Royal Wedding!"

Faith was genuinely concerned that Miles had lost his grip on reality. "I'll call the Palace," she said.

"I'm serious, Faith," he said. "Ever since you left the big time to work with C2C, people have tuned in to hear you, because it's you, but now every local daytime show is a carbon copy of yours. And the content is identical to every media outlet, be it TV, radio, online, or even newspapers."

Faith thought about the plan for today's show. Opening with the latest gripe against the government, then a scandal over a royal faux pas, a few items of local interest which followed the same polarising political themes, and then the closing 'light-hearted' item would be a critique of whether or not shops had their Christmas items out too soon. Even tomorrow, her 'Freaky Friday' spot was just another mocking exposé of nonsensical local rules or 'jobsworths' in the local community. She had to agree, the topics were pretty much a selection of 'current popular whinges' playing out across media outlets the whole world over. Which was the reason she had left 'the big time,' as Miles called it, hoping for a more civilised and indeed civil approach to reporting.

"Finding something that is going to drag people away from their addiction to 'happening now' catastrophe will be a challenge," he continued, "but it is essential we lead the field, not follow the pack. We need something new, something different—and you are the person to do exactly that!"

"Don't we need a focus group, market research…?" Faith felt the ice getting a little thin under her feet.

"Faith," Miles continued, "do you know what I do when I get home from managing this place, with all its bang up to date news, staff egos, budgets and other corporate jiggery-pokery?" Faith looked at him, amused. "I watch cars being towed on YouTube, or a couple of guys exploding fridges in slow motion, or some guy cutting down a tree in his back garden and destroying his shed in the process! The last thing I want is more bad news!"

Faith laughed. "I watch 'random singer joined by star,' or 'music coach reacts to,' or," she mimed terrible shame, "undercover boss." Just then, Megan, her show's producer, appeared. "What programmes do you watch at home, Megan?" asked Faith.

Megan, keen to appear on the ball, replied as she thought she should, "The latest live feeds from RT, FOX, CNN, Al Jazeera and…"

"Very commendable," Miles said. "Now, what do you really watch?"

"Love Island!" she yelled back as she hurried out. They laughed.

"You don't look convinced," Miles said to Faith, looking at her.

"No," said Faith, "I think you have a point. At least for *this* Christmas, we could stop scraping up all the filth from the bottom of the journalistic barrel. Maybe we could actually host a celebration of all that is good in community life."

"Now that would be different," said Miles, "and, I'll be honest, if it backfires, this could be an interesting career move for both of us." Faith nodded in agreement. "So, we have a choice, die the slow death of same old, same old, or risk it all on something radically different…" she searched for a word…

"Unashamed joyfulness, not systemic cynicism," suggested Miles.

"Bold authenticity, not hackneyed contempt," agreed Faith.

"Human interest, not self-interest," Miles continued.

"Career suicide, not cosy retirement?" groaned Faith, seeing her own feeling of hopeful recklessness expressed in Miles' face.

"Absolutely," he nodded.

"Definitely," she said at the same time.

A moment of paralysed silence followed.

"Oh well," said Miles, "it's only one Christmas. What's the worst that could happen?"

"Or even the best!" declared Faith. "Let's go for it."

****

Even at eight am, it was a thirty-minute drive from the county's main city to Hope Taylor's home in Applebury. The text from Agnes had asked for a few 'essentials' that were only available at the superstore across the road from C2C. It would be a miracle if she could get the shopping and then get home on time. Her phone buzzed in her bag. She ignored it and drove straight to the supermarket. Grabbing a trolley, she opened her phone to find the texted shopping list from her mother-in-law. She noticed the missed call from

Harvey's Garage, with a follow up text saying her MOT was due.

Hope flew around the supermarket following Agnes' list. Aside from the usual necessities, there were always a few of Brian's favourites to try to tempt him. Hope rang the garage as she packed her groceries, and arranged to drop the car in the next day for an MOT, negotiating a time that would cause least impact on the family. Paying with contactless, Hope pushed the trolley from the store. She had not exchanged a word with the cashier and could not even remember if they were male or female. Hope loaded the car, shut the boot and bumped the trolley onto the walkway behind rather than return it to the bay, saving a few precious minutes.

As she did so, she almost collided with a petite, stylish woman striding towards the supermarket. The woman started back in surprise, but received only a resigned grimace and exaggerated shrug from Hope in response. Faith watched as she jumped into her car and sped away.

Faith had gone for a brisk walk 'to get a decent coffee' she had said, but in reality, she needed time to consider the deal she had just cooked up with her boss. Scandals in the council chamber, strikes in the factories and tragedy and comedy in the well-to-do of the county, who really cared? In reality, the sensational stories of today were forgotten and replaced in days. Miles was right, it was time for something different. Something that included everyone, was joyful, an opportunity to show people at their best, and, if she was honest, their worst. In her experience, revealing 'good' people to be just as flawed as the rest of us was always a great ratings winner. Bad news and bad people were always good news for the ratings.

Faith was jerked out of her inner soliloquy by the harassed young woman almost swiping her with a shopping trolley, then flinging her arms in the air by way of exaggerated apology. Recognising her as the cleaner who had knocked her folder out of her arms this morning, she smiled at the woman's comedy reaction. She noticed as the car was pulling away, a 'bumper box' of Christmas cards and several rolls of gaudy Christmas-tree-printed wrapping paper rattling about on the parcel shelf.

Faith walked into Bella's, the tiny coffee shop. In the back of her mind, she remembered the catalogue of local events from this morning's breakfast show. "Of course," she muttered to herself, "the Christmas Tree Festival." It seemed as good a place to start her career gamble as any.

Chapter Two

Hope groaned as she looked at the clock on the dash. Every second was precious and she had already lost fifteen minutes. She arrived home as her husband Adam and eldest daughter, Rosa, were loading up the car. Adam would drop Rosa at the college bus stop, before heading for Taylor's Country Garden Centre, the family business. Hope gave them both a quick kiss and hug, straightened Rosa's scarf, and walked into the morning chaos of the kitchen. Lily was the only child at the table – the other two were in their rooms having abandoned the remains of their breakfast.

Lily was reading as she slowly, very slowly, ate her cereal. A comb and hairband lay on the table. Hope began forming Lily's blonde hair into a braid.

"Five minutes, Lily!" Hope warned, closing the book.

"Mummy, I haven't finished that bit!" Lily objected.

"You also don't have your shoes on and we are leaving in five minutes."

With a tragic sigh, Lily went to find her shoes. Hope scooped the crockery from the table, disposed of the waste, stacked the dishes in the dishwasher and wiped the table. No sign of any child now.

"Time to go!" she yelled up the stairs.

"Callum! Briony! We are going! Now!"

Callum came running down the stairs, "I brushed my teeth and you didn't have to tell me!" he boasted.

"I can see that," frowned Hope, scrubbing toothpaste from his face and shirt with a tea towel.

Callum lingered beside his mother as she knelt to buckle Lily's shoes. "Briony take Callum and get in the car, NOW!" she shouted.

"Shotgun!" shouted Callum, running to the passenger seat. Briony grumbled and whined – she was the oldest and should be in the front. Too tired to referee another fight, Hope bundled her two youngest children into the back seat and sped off for the school, as Briony, despite being thirteen and 'not even bothered,' turned and poked her tongue out at Callum.

Late again, Hope managed to find a parking space, although the woman behind her gestured and swore as she flung her car left to grab the precious space. She could hear the woman's profanity following her as she let her three children out of the car and walked with them across the road. Thankfully, the Senior and Junior schools were next to each other. Briony turned left with a wave, and Hope hurried Lily and Callum to the school gate ahead, just as the bell rang. Each class lined up and was collected by their class teacher. Hope waved at her children and turned to go. As she did, she heard her name called, and turned to see Miss James, Callum's teacher, walking purposefully towards her.

"What's he done now?" Hope thought, and noticed the other parents lingering in the hope of some sort of 'trouble.'

"Is everything alright, Miss James?"

"Oh fine, fine, couldn't be better."

Hope smiled and turned to go, but Miss James continued, "It's just, well," the woman coloured, "a sort of favour, really." The parents left, realising there were no 'rich gossipy pickings' about to fall to the ground. Hope looked enquiringly at the embarrassed young woman before her. "Applebury Church has organised a Christmas Tree Festival, as well as the Carol Service this year, and since you own the Garden Centre, we wondered if you would kindly donate a tree?"

Hope agreed – of course, they would be very happy. It sounded so very grand, 'owning' a garden centre. In reality, her in-laws' once-profitable Taylor's Country Garden Centre had been failing for years, pushed out by huge out-of-town concerns and shrubs and flora on sale everywhere from supermarkets to garage forecourts. Eighteen months ago, Brian, her father-in-law, had collapsed at work. He was rushed to hospital where it was discovered that he had suffered a heart attack. The sheer stress of watching his life's work crumble before him, despite various costly attempts at innovation, had literally nearly killed him.

Hope's husband, Adam, had stepped in to run the business and found the truth to be far worse than Brian had acknowledged. Adam, who had his own accountancy business, now ran the garden centre seven days a week, and did his 'real job' in the evenings. Adam worked hard to rescue the family business from ruin, while his mother, Agnes, worked hard to rescue her sick husband from the depths of despair. Hope just worked hard.

She ran back to the car, which was blocked in by a carelessly close Audi. The owner was conspicuously gossiping with a group of parents, leaning on the back of the car, as if she had nowhere else to be. Hope beeped her horn and gestured for the woman to move. She was met with a sarcastic smile and a look of disdain as the woman returned to her conversation.

"Well, I *do* have some where else to be," muttered Hope. She snatched into reverse gear and edged back, not too carefully, then swung out, missing the parked car by a hair's breadth. Looking in the rear-view mirror she could see Miss Audi glaring after her in astonishment.

Arriving at her in-law's house, Hope threw the back door open with four bags of shopping in her hands. "Agnes!" she called, "shopping's here!"

Agnes appeared, smiling broadly to see her. "Let me help," she said, taking the bags on to the kitchen table. Every day Agnes thanked the good Lord for her daughter in law and blessed the day she met Adam. The only child of mature parents, Hope had the values of a past generation. It seemed that Hope took everything in her stride and simply stood up, brushed herself down and carried on after each successive blow, determined to 'keep calm and carry on.'

Agnes hesitated. Hope looked tired, almost grim. "You're so busy, Hope," she faltered, "I can postpone the appointment, they will understand," with a flick of her head and a roll of her eyes she signalled that her husband was in the next room.

Hope shook her head "No, you go on to your hairdressers," she said. "I'm sorry I'm so late, the school asked me for a free Christmas tree for some competition the church is doing. I couldn't get away."

"Oh yes!" exclaimed Agnes. "It's our church and it's a Christmas Tree Festival, not really a competition. The whole town is involved. There will be all sorts going on, a talent show, a craft fair…"

"I hope you said yes," interrupted Brian from the sitting room.

Hope ran in and hugged him. "Of course, I did. Your grandchildren would expect no less than one of Grandad's trees at the great Applebury Christmas Tree Festival!" Brian frowned, but his eyes smiled.

"Oh, that's such a good idea," said Agnes, putting on her coat, "and remind Adam that we *always* supply the biggest one to the church." She glanced at her little gold wristwatch. "I had better get going!"

"No hurry," said Hope, looking back at Agnes. "You take your time; I'm not working until twelve-thirty."

"Maybe Callum and Lily could pop in after school?" Agnes asked hopefully.

Hope explained that Briony would take them home and she would be home by the time they got there. Brian and Agnes used to have the children regularly, but since Brian had become so unwell, he found their visits tiring and the children found Grandad snappy and hard to be around. To Agnes' great regret, she saw rather less of her grandchildren than she wished to. Agnes kissed Hope on the cheek. "Well, maybe next time," she said, and rushed off for her hair appointment.

Hope put the shopping away and made a cup of tea for her and Brian. She piled a few biscuits on to a plate, carried them all through on a tray and sat in the chair beside him. "Cup of tea, Brian?" she asked.

"I don't need looking after, you know," he sighed. "I'm not an invalid."

"I beg to differ old chap," smiled Hope, "you *have* been unwell and you still need looking after."

"I just feel so useless," he complained. "Especially at this time of year. Taylor's can be so busy and the Christmas trees just fly out of the doors!"

"Oh no!" gasped Hope. "I totally forgot to tell Adam about the free Christmas tree! I hope he's happy with the idea; I've said yes already!"

"It's not up to Adam," protested Brian. "*I* own the garden centre and *I* say it's a good idea. In fact, I think it would be in the spirit of Christmas to give a tree to the pre-school, the juniors, *and* the seniors. *You tell Adam I said so!*" Brian's colour was rising with his temper.

Hope, afraid he was putting strain on his heart again, quickly held up her phone. "I'll call now," she said, finding the number for Taylor's Country Gardens on her phone.

Brian listened as Hope apologetically explained about the tree, then that his father had insisted on Taylor's giving away three of their best trees 'to raise publicity.' Adam's tone grew louder and more exasperated, so she stood and walked into the kitchen, shielding Brian from his son's reaction to this latest 'business suggestion.'

"Hope," Adam said, "we are running on credit here. I was hoping the trees would spin us a profit and help dig us out of the hole."

"I'm so sorry, love," she explained. "I told Dad about the junior school, which I *did* agree to, then he took the idea further."

"And that's why the place is drowning in debt and looks like a jumble sale!" Adam despaired. He took a deep breath. None of this was Hope's fault, she had been nothing but supportive through the whole thing, even giving up the small sum her parents had bequeathed to her. "No, Hope," he sighed, "it's me who should apologise. Let's face it, there's worse things we could do than give away a Christmas tree to three local schools and the church. Sorry for snapping."

Hope smiled and he could hear it in her voice. "I love you, Adam," she said.

"And I love you, Hope," he responded.

They said their goodbyes and Hope returned to find Brian finishing the last biscuit on the plate. "All sorted," she chirped. "More tea?"

Brian handed her his mug. "You're a good girl." He grinned.

Adam Taylor had worked in his parent's Garden Centre since he could lift a bag of compost. Every weekend, each day in the school and university holidays, and even when he graduated and started his own career in accountancy, their loyal son would help out whenever the opportunity arose. If he was honest ` with himself, he did not have 'green fingers,' he did not love gardening, and he did not love face-to-face customer service, which required a lot of small talk and smiles. He did, however, love his parents deeply. Lately, in his troubled father, Adam could barely discern the hero of his childhood. His dear mother, always putting on a brave face, was devastated by her husband's collapse, and isolated by her determination to maintain his dignity and reputation in the community.

Looking around the place that morning he had seen the remains of his father's attempts at rejuvenating and restoring the old place. The problem was, Brian had swung from horticultural specialist centre, with ludicrously-priced rare plants, to the 'pile it high, sell it cheap' approach, which the supermarkets could beat hands down. Neither fish nor fowl, Taylor's Country Gardens had tumbled from 'all things for all people' to 'nothing for anyone' in less than ten years. Adam gazed hopelessly at the make-shift pallet shelving stacked with hideous yellow canary-shaped flower pots and garish garden gnomes. His eyes fell on the dirty laminated notice stapled to the wall behind them. 'All breakages must be paid for.' "If only!" he whispered to himself.

Seated at his desk in a corner of the office, he looked at the sales figures. The only department scraping any profit at all was the 'Cosy Café,' although revenue was considerably down from last year. The café had been run by his Auntie Pat for several years, but she had also stepped in to help throughout the store once it was no longer possible to employ more paid staff. Pat was a formidable woman, insisting on serving only 'good home-made.' Her repertoire was limited but satisfactory. Pat did not believe in paninis, flatbreads and chai tea. But she had, at last, mastered the coffee machine and at that moment plumped a frothy latte down in front of him, with a couple of slices of toast.

"Eat up, sunshine," she commanded, "then I need help with a few things – if you are not too busy?" Pat was the kind of determined woman who would get on and do a job herself, whatever the challenge. For her to ask for his help was as much a sign of her trust as of her need.

Adam clicked the mouse to save his spreadsheet, gulped down his coffee and followed Pat out into the main area of the garden centre. Tall displays of greetings cards and dusty postcards stood haphazardly amongst stacks of bagged compost. Just in the small area outside his open door he could see an old Welsh dresser piled with houseplants and circular tables, one laden with china mugs, the next with flower themed jewellery, another with gardener's hand creams, lotions and potions. These jostled for space with rails of garden tools, clothing, and novelty garden gifts. He knew it was a dreadful mess, but had no time and no talent for bringing order out of the chaos. He headed for the café, where Pat would be waiting with her list of chores.

Despite the many cafés in town, people still came to Taylor's for Pat's scones, cakes and home-baked savouries; and her afternoon teas were legendary. To get to the café, customers had to navigate their way through the main store, with its muddled displays, past a couple of blocked doorways leading to now defunct industrial-sized greenhouses, through the remaining 'working' greenhouse with its rows of annuals, and finally through the 'bargain basement' tunnel to find the café buried amid whatever seasonal displays were required at that particular time of year. This being early November, Pat had emptied and dusted the old shelves around the café. Adam collected last year's unsold collection of Christmas decorations and stacked the shelves, ready for the store opening at nine-thirty. For the rest of the morning he lifted, carried, stacked and shovelled, as directed by Pat.

****

After her retirement from teaching, Grace Wright had chosen to be a tutor at Livewire Learning Centre, an optimistically named subsidiary to the County College. Hers was a small class of those who, somewhere in some Department of Education file, would be labelled as 'NEET,' that is, Not in Education, Employment, or Training. These students who, due to lack of exam passes, had already failed to increase any school's income or prestige, were now part of the lucrative scrapheap scavenged by post-sixteen providers. A one-year course in 'progression,' 'skills for employment,' or some similarly nebulous qualification would see these young people through until they could finally leave the education system at eighteen, and then fend for themselves.

The management saw a bunch of faceless teens with a lucrative cash sum attached; the general public saw delinquents and drop outs; but Grace saw the story of each individual and respected their sheer determination to keep on trying, in spite of the demons they battled each day. By the time they had reached Grace's class, most had had more than one 'professional' involved in their life, from foster carer to social worker, child protection officer to probation officer, from support worker to therapist.

Each year Grace felt she was engaged in a futile attempt to wake these young people out of their dream of reality TV romance, YouTube stardom, or becoming a lottery millionaire, for a ten-minute rehearsal of 'real life.' This Thursday was 'job interview' day at Livewire Learning Centre. Each student, having completed a CV, and gone through various 'the job for me' quizzes, had to go through a mock interview with Grace or Greg, their teachers. The next step would be a real interview for two week's work experience, as soon as they could find an employer interested enough to take them.

Danny was the final 'applicant' of the day, and far more committed to the exercise than his indifferent classmates. Of all the students in his class, Danny Jones seemed more ready to launch into the adult world. At only seventeen, he gave off a sense of world-weary suspicion. He was scruffily self-assured, never rude, fiercely private, often late for class but worked hard after he arrived. Sticking with the scripted questions and answers that had been practised in class, Danny started with a handshake and conducted a very realistic, confident interview.

"You did very well, Danny," Grace encouraged him. "I was interested to see that you are looking for a labourer's job. You've often said you would like to work in forestry or as a gardener, but in fact your profile results say you are more suited to creative work."

"In my dreams, Miss," he said. "In real life I've got no qualifications and no money, so…"

"I have a friend who owns a garden centre, maybe you could do your work experience there?" Grace offered.

"Doesn't matter to me, Miss," he shrugged. "I don't like people and I do like being outdoors, so labouring will suit me fine. I just need a job that makes enough money to get a place of my own."

Not long afterwards, Grace was packing away and locking up. The students, having gathered their belongings, were each staring at their phones in the hallway, waiting for their transport to arrive. Rarely, a couple spoke to each other, but more often than not, they would send photos to the person right beside them. Grace mourned the lost art of conversation as she locked away the last of the files and switched off the smartboard.

"Miss?" She looked around to see Danny leaning nonchalantly on the door frame. "If you wanna find out about the garden centre, I don't mind," he said, and abruptly turned and went.

She smiled after him. There was a church meeting that very night, and Agnes Taylor would be there. Agnes Taylor of Taylor's Country Gardens. Grace would now be attending the meeting not only as church pianist but as Danny's advocate. She looked up at the heavens. "It's a done deal, I reckon," she declared.

****

The church building was in its most recent incarnation, having been originally a huge Victorian fire station. Extended and adapted for each new purpose, the place became in turn a meeting house, a nursery school, and finally a rather dubious artists' commune, until it became Applebury church back in the sixties. An enterprising young bunch of families, with the help and blessing of the big church at the top of town, had planted a church to serve the newly-built housing estate. The church grew as those young couples grew into middle age, as their children left to pursue careers far from their home, and the congregation, though smaller, was just as active and faithful as ever. When the pastor retired, in the late nineteen-eighties, they gathered to pray that the right couple would find their way to Applebury.

Mark and Debbie Thorne, with their two young boys, arrived soon afterwards and set about opening the doors of this church family to a wider and wider spectrum of the population. Now, over twenty years later, they continued to reach out and were actively involved in most of the activities taking place in the church buildings. Alive with genuine love and a wish to help anyone who needed it, Applebury Church had become the centre of the community, both geographically and socially. Today, Pastor Mark surveyed the dilapidated building, long outgrown. He found an increasing amount of his time was spent fighting the church trustees for even the most basic repairs. Most recently, they had suggested selling some of the carpark to finance repairs, or even selling the prime land to finance a rebuild on a more practical and less expensive site.

Applebury Christmas Tree Festival, with the theme 'Love@Christmas' had been another of Debbie's ideas. A way to bring people in to the church who would otherwise never step inside the door. "They come into the hall," she said, "but not the church. I want them to see the place so they don't feel scared of coming on a Sunday." Mark smiled at her. She was ever wanting to share the 'Good News,' always helping, encouraging and praying. "We can have the trees all down both sides and across the platform for the nativity."

Mark smiled at her optimism. "That would be about twenty trees," he said, "evenly spread out. Do you really think we'll get that many?"

She looked at him with an 'obviously' expression, and continued, "We set it up Thursday evening. Then Friday morning, have the all-schools end-of-term carol service in the church, then we set up for Saturday." She paused for breath, then unveiled the second part of her plan. "Saturday, we have our Christmas fair in the hall and get everyone to choose their favourite tree, then there's 'Applebury's Got Talent' in the evening in the church, and then on Sunday morning everyone comes to see which tree gets the prize! The price for admission can be a tin for the foodbank. We could have a donation box for the foodbank and a collection box for the…"

Mark spread his hands in front of himself to stop her. "It's brilliant, my love, but don't get carried away! How many are you expecting, and what is the prize? You haven't got a secret pot of cash somewhere have you, cos if you have…" He pointed upwards where she saw the familiar peeling paint on the suspiciously bulging ceiling above.

"Come on," she said, "we'd better have something to eat before the church leaders' meeting."

****

Agnes had arrived home, refreshed and beautiful, to find Hope had prepared a lunch for them.

"Only two places set, Hope – don't you have time to stay?"

"I have to be at Trevone Hall at one," Hope replied. "They've got a group arriving this evening."

Hope's 'real' job was on the 'changeover décor team' at the Hotel and Conference centre. Trevone Manor was a former country estate which, alongside its thriving five-star hotel and events service, had established a reputation as the best provider of corporate Christmas parties in the area. The hotel went to great lengths to 'individualise' the setting, and clients would usually book the hotel for a long weekend. Themes would range from 'Traditional English Christmas' to 'Corporate Colours' to, well, anything the customer demanded. Hope, who in her life before motherhood had been a window dresser in big London stores, was a respected member of the team. Her professionalism and high standards were commendable, but it was her creativity that made her stand out. Last year's fantasy writer's centenary convention had been delighted with the 'Hundred Unicorns' centrepiece, unaware that Hope had spent the previous week gluing Fimo horns to a bulk purchase of white china stallions.

This afternoon it was a quick change from cool, Scandi Christmas to Victorian festive overload for a group of American businessmen and their significant others. The place was transformed by three pm, ready for the vintage coach to arrive from the airport, and allowing Hope time to race home, arriving soon after her children.

Hope was mentally listing the next set of tasks as she drove home. Her evenings ran according to a strict regime: make the meal, feed the kids, clear away, stack the dishwasher, set the table for breakfast. Check homework is done. Fill the washing machine with today's dirty PE kits and school uniforms, empty the tumble dryer of yesterday's washing. Prepare tomorrow's packed lunches. Clean the kitchen (again), empty dishwasher. Put washed clothes in the tumble dryer. Put youngest children in bath then bed. Check Adam has a second cup of tea while he is working in the study. Read bedtime story. Check older children have done homework. Remove second load from tumble dryer. Sort. Iron school shirts and Adam's shirts. Put folded and ironed clothes in each child's rooms, hang Adam's shirt in the wardrobe. Usually she had finished by nine, and she and Adam sat together on the sofa where they both fell asleep, only waking to go to bed. "Maybe I am a robot," Hope thought to herself. "I feel like one."

She parked the car and hurried into the kitchen where she found her three youngest children at the table, doing homework. A picture of domestic harmony. She clutched her chest, dramatically. "A miracle!" she cried.

Briony and Lily smiled at her sweetly. Callum kept his head down, concentrating hard on his map of an Iron Age village. Hope switched on the oven, scrubbed and pierced six jacket potatoes, placing them in the oven. She opened the fridge for the cauliflower, block of cheese and…no milk. "I swear there was a six-pinter in there this morning…in fact I know there was."

Now the unexpected devotion to homework made sense. She looked at the three of them, who, having been looking at their mother, glanced away very quickly. She looked in the bin, no milk carton there. "Okay, where's the milk?" she demanded. "You can *not* have drunk six pints between you in half an hour."

"*Callum?*"

"Why do you always think it's me?" he cried.

"Well, wasn't it?"

"Mum, it wasn't his fault, it was an accident." Briony defended her doomed little brother. "He was getting us all a drink…"

"Milk and cookies like they have on the TV," beamed little Callum, hopefully.

Briony continued, "Only, he dropped the milk. We cleaned it up, though."

Looking closely, Hope could see a line of pooled milk puddled beneath the kick boards of the kitchen units, between the ridges of the floor tiles and pooled in the join between the cooker and the worktop. She saw the mop, soaked in milk standing against the wall

"Oh, Callum!" She wailed. "It will *stink* and there's no milk for breakfast now, or cauliflower cheese!"

Cauliflower cheese was Callum's favourite. "*I'm sorry!*" he wailed.

Hope grabbed his hand. "Come on," she said, her face like thunder, "you're coming with me!"

"Where are we going, Mummy?"

"To get more milk, of course. I can't even give your father a cup of tea because of you being so silly."

"But I want to stay here, and I was just helping, Mummy!"

"If you think I'm leaving you here to make more mischief you can think again." She was so angry and exhausted, she almost cried. "Briony! Get some kitchen towel and clean that milk up *thoroughly*! Lily! Grate that cheese and lay the table."

Chapter Three

Faith never took anything at face value. Her journalistic and broadcasting success was built on her innate instinct for duplicity and her ability to peel back the mask to reveal the real agenda behind any public act of generosity, sincerity or goodness. Faith had become a 'name,' respected for her utmost integrity and refusal to drop an investigation until the truth was laid bare. This commitment to 'truth at any cost,' led to her being respected by the elite in both the establishment and entertainment worlds, but shunned by many for fear of being her next target. This exposure of hypocrisy in high places had taken its toll on her psyche. On her 50th birthday, alone in her beautiful London apartment, she realised that she had become weary and cynical. She had no regrets over her working life, far from it, but had determined to shake off the glitter of 'Vanity Fair' and find some simple joy.

She moved south to a regional station where, she mistakenly assumed, there would be genuine goodness away from the corruption of London. However, she had found that wickedness, corruption and self-interest were thriving just as well in the rural idyll as in wicked old London Town. Thus, it was, as she researched Applebury Church and the instigators of this 'happy festival,' she realised she was waiting for the hidden agenda to reveal itself. She was mildly disappointed to find that there was no shadow on the reputation of Mark Thorne, his wife or his family. One of their boys was married and living in Hampshire, and the other was serving in the military. All very average, apart from their phenomenal effect on the population of Applebury.

She clicked on 'Meet the Leaders' on the Church website: Doug Wright and his wife Grace, both former teachers; Brian and Agnes Taylor, who were the proprietors of that run-down little garden centre just up the road from the church; and a short list of 'Trustees.' Normally, Faith would have asked Megan or one of her staff to arrange visits and other details, but the underlying fear that she was on a fool's errand remained. To have all the office staff giggling at her new 'feel good' assignment would be humiliating. She found the contact number on the rather old-fashioned website and called to arrange a visit the following afternoon.

Debbie Thorne was slightly shaken by her call from the celebrity radio presenter. She joined Mark in the church where he was repairing the joints of several unsteady chairs and dropped slowly to the floor beside him.

"You've gone pale, Debs, is it bad news?"

"Not bad news, but it is unexpected, and rather strange." Mark looked at her to explain. "That was Faith New from C2C, she has heard about the Festival and wants to know more about it."

"And?"

"Well, I told her what I could, who was involved, and that Taylor's are giving us a tree as always. The All-Schools Carol Service, Applebury's Got Talent," she ticked them off on her fingers.

"Did you tell her about the Christmas Craft Sale?" asked Mark, hoping a few extra sales might mean a few new chairs.

"I did," his wife replied, "and about the Sunday Service."

She held together the two parts of a particularly broken seat as Mark applied superglue to the joint. He stood this last newly repaired chair back against the wall, with the rest. "That should get us through to the New Year at least," he said. "Now let's get out of here, the fumes are making my eyes water."

They walked into the adjoining hall and Debbie put the kettle on for a cup of tea. "Applebury Christmas Tree Festival," she said. "It sounds rather grand. I hope it will not be a flop."

Mark wrapped her in his arms. "It will be wonderful," he said, "just like you. I hope you told her that!"

"You can tell her yourself; she's coming to see us tomorrow afternoon!"

****

Cosy Café's picture windows, overlooking the outdoor gardens and sales area, had an outstanding view across the late autumn hills and farmland. Adam sat with his Aunt Pat, sharing a cup of tea and a plate of broken cookies that would not make it onto tomorrow's menu. He had told her of the unexpected call from C2C, wanting an interview about their part in the Christmas tree festival.

"Well, of course I know about the Festival," Pat admonished him, "it was arranged at the last church meeting. Not only that, it was on the breakfast show this morning. 'Love@Christmas' it's called!"

"I didn't know you listened to C2C Radio, Auntie Pat," he said with surprise. "I thought you were more of a Radio 4 lady!"

"There's a lot you don't know about me, young Adam," laughed Pat. "I'm not just a golden oldie you know. I like to know what going on in the world."

"Have you heard of this 'Faith New' then?" asked Adam, who only vaguely recognised the name and had certainly never listened to the Faith New show.

"Faith New, is *she* doing the interview? Pat almost shrieked with excitement. "She must be planning something big. Faith New is *quite* a celebrity!"

Adam watched as Pat wrestled with the thought that Faith New, in the flesh, would be at the garden centre the very next day. "Apparently, she's doing a report on that Christmas Tree Festival at the church," he informed her. "She rang Mark and Debbie, and they told her about us donating the trees to the church and the schools."

Pat's eyes widened. "It's our chance to put Taylor's back on the Applebury map!" she enthused, clapping her hands together.

Adam looked around him. "Maybe, but look at the place," he said, indicating the hodgepodge of displays around them.

Pat surveyed the dodgy stands, wobbly shelves, and stock that had seen better days. She shrugged. "We can have a tidy up first thing tomorrow, but after that, she'll have to take us as she finds us!"

****

Hope had picked up the milk, still seething at Callum. She did not speak to him at all. He just sat there wretched and sorry. Rosa arrived home just after four-fifteen and her mother had already replaced the milk and prepared the meal.

Before Adam arrived home, around six, everything was cleared away, Lily was bathed and ready for bed, and the table had been set for breakfast. Hope gave him his meal on a tray, a quick peck on the cheek, and set off for her in-laws for the second time in the day. She took a deep breath before entering the pretty cottage. These days she never knew if there were calm or stormy waters to navigate. Hope knew how important it was for Agnes to get out, to carry on as 'normal,' particularly with Brian so unpredictable and increasingly less like himself.

"Hello both!" she greeted them. Agnes bustled out, a biscuit tin in her arms. "Have you been baking?" asked Hope.

"Just a few shortbreads," she replied. "I made a batch for Brian but he's not so keen, I thought I'd take the spare off to the meeting."

"Well, there's nothing quite so welcome as a homemade biscuit at a boring meeting!" said Hope.

Agnes looked mildly offended. "Oh no, dear, this one is going to be exciting. We are planning the Applebury Christmas Tree Festival! The church will be so busy the last weekend before Christmas." Hope was filled with love as she watched Agnes face light up. "It will be spectacular," Agnes continued. "I wish you and Adam would come back, it is really not the same without you there."

Hope bit back a sudden surge of anger. With a husband who was working himself to exhaustion seven days a week at their money pit of a failed garden centre, then working another three hours each night keeping his own customers happy, with four children to care for, working two jobs and spending her 'spare' hours with Brian so that Agnes could get a break, Hope had no time and certainly no intention of wasting a morning in church, thanking God for 'everything.'

She let out the breath she had been holding. "You had better get going, Mother T!" she advised, "or they'll start the meeting without you!"

"Oh, they fuss around with tea and coffee and the minutes for the first half hour," Agnes replied. "But yes, I had better be on my way. I'll see you in a couple of hours."

Hope walked into the lounge where Brian rested. The big old plush armchair seemed to emphasize his gloomy frailty. She walked to the window and watched as Agnes drove away, then pulled the curtains together. "Tea?" she offered. Brian nodded.

Brian was a gardener at heart, not a business man. Always open-handed and honest, he had been easily swayed by savvy sales reps who signed him up to all kinds of commission-rich, long-term contracts. On the self-interested advice of various consultants and suppliers, the little family garden centre stopped doing what it did best and 'diversified.' Now, with only a mountain of debt, piles of unsaleable stock and a broken body to show for the last forty odd years, this honourable man had watched his life's work fall through his hands. He had wanted to build a legacy; instead, he had ended up with a millstone of debt and failure that threatened to sink the whole family.

Brian, having wrapped himself in guilt, had become isolated. It was not just the illness that had sapped Brian's strength and emaciated his body. The man everyone had looked up to felt he was less than a child. Waiting to die. He stopped going to church on the pretext of ill-health but in truth, he could not face the pity of the congregation.

The day a visitor asked, "Didn't you used to be Mr Taylor, of Taylor's Country Gardens?" finished him. After all his attempts to set things straight, investing his own money and then, disastrously, his son's savings in the business, there had been nothing but a black hole. His prayers had been left unanswered, and now the man that used to be Mr Taylor believed himself to be no more than a burden. He was waiting to die, and hoped it would not be too long a wait.

Agnes arrived at the meeting and, as she expected, the elders and trustees were only just getting settled. There was tea and coffee in the green china cups and saucers that seem to be regulation crockery in every non-denominational church across the United Kingdom. She placed her tin of buttery shortbread on the table.

Mark thanked her, putting his arm around her shoulder. "How's he doing?" he asked quietly.

"Just plodding along, Pastor," Agnes admitted. "The life has gone out of him."

Mark nodded silently and gave her a little hug. "He'll get there," he said. "He will, we'll just keep praying." Mark's prayers had recently been as much for the healing of Brian's inner self as his body. He and Agnes took a seat at the table.

Item one on the agenda, as usual, was another request by Mark for funds to patch up the crumbling church building. Mark felt a part of this building – it represented the labour of almost half his life. Pastor Mark of Applebury Church. That was him. The constant rejection of his appeal for money to keep the place standing was, to Mark, a sign of their lack of faith in him and, quite frankly, a lack of trust in God.

"I'm sorry, Mark," said Doug, interrupting Mark's thoughts. Doug was a fellow elder and along with his wife Grace, a longstanding member of the church. "The congregation is large, but not wealthy, and once your salary has been paid there's only enough left for the bills and the emergency fund."

Mark was becoming angry, his face reddened. "I have built this church from nothing," he insisted. "When I came here, the only thing outside of Sunday service was the over 60's club and a few little old ladies in the prayer group. The congregation on Sunday is ten times what it was when I came, and the only reason revenue is dropping is because we are too full in the week to rent the hall out! It has taken *me* twenty-five years of hard work to put this place on the map, and I think it dishonours God when it looks so shabby."

Debbie, embarrassed both by him and for him, looked intently at the table in front of her. The elders respected and loved Mark. His preaching and pastoral work was the bedrock of their service to the community, but it was Debbie's friendly, accepting outgoing love and eye for opportunity had been the adding souls to the church, one by one. Agnes, seated beside her, squeezed her hand, a wordless 'I understand.'

"My mother was one of those little old ladies, Mark," said Agnes. "They prayed you into this church, and they prayed for you every day since you joined, as we all do. Maybe we should stop and spend some time asking God what *His* plans are for Applebury Church."

Mark was brought up short in the middle of his tirade. "I…" he took a breath. "I see the building falling apart as more and more people are coming through the doors. I still have faith that the Lord will provide," he said, "do you?"

"We should sell and move," said Doug, "it makes sense." The others nodded in agreement.

"*No!*" Mark dug his heels in. "Unless God himself tells me that we should sell up and sell out, then Applebury church stays exactly where it is, if I have to do the repairs myself!"

They moved on to more amiable conversation as they planned the Christmas Tree Festival and the meeting ended on a friendly, familiar note, since the members of this team had known and loved each other for many years. Nevertheless, the harsh words at the beginning of the meeting had left them all feeling ill at ease. Mark saw a bunch of intractable old retirees standing in the way of progress. They saw a tired, godly man, who had become wrapped up in a success he saw as his own.

After the meeting, Grace tapped Agnes on the arm. "I want to ask a favour," she whispered with a smile. She explained about Danny. Agnes was hesitant, but it was hard to say no to Grace when she was advocating for one of her students. Anyone overhearing the conversation would be convinced that only the most heartless person could refuse a life changing opportunity 'to the brightest, most hardworking, most misunderstood...' Agnes had no choice but to agree, and it was arranged that Danny should go to Taylor's Country Gardens with Grace the very next afternoon.

Hope finally went home, her mother-in-law having returned after the meeting. Adam was still working in his home-office, a tiny room off the main hallway. The two youngest children were sleeping soundly, and Rosa and Briony were tapping away at their phones in the lounge. The TV was on, but really as a kind of atmospheric wallpaper, since no one was paying any attention. Hope made a mug of hot chocolate for the four of them, handed the girls theirs and then walked back to Adam, still tapping away on a spreadsheet for 'JJ Cole, Jewellers,' one of his longstanding clients.

He looked up, smiling, and put his arm around her waist. "Home at last, eh, my darling wife?" She returned his smile, as he went on, "Callum was a bit upset when I got home," he said, "poor chap."

Hope felt her hackles rise, just a little. She had been a bit hard on the boy, and her conscience was pricking her. After all, he was only eight. But if there was a breakage or a mess, or a fuss, Callum was usually right in the middle of it. "Meaning?" she retorted.

Adam mentally backed off; he did not have the energy for a disagreement. "Oh, nothing at all," he said. "I just thought you'd like to know."

"Okay," she clipped. "Well, I have a pile of ironing to get on with." She marched into the living room and banged the ironing board open, flung the laundry basket down and started her final chore of the day.

"Mum," asked Rosa, "would you like me to do that?"

If it were possible to press the creases out of shirts with anger and resentment alone, Hope was demonstrating that skill. "No!" she insisted. "No, I would not, but if you are not listening to that Telly can you at least turn it off?" Sensitive to the brewing mood, both girls stood, switched off the TV and muttering excuses about finishing off homework, beat a hasty retreat to their room.

Totally insensitive to his wife's gathering ire, Adam crashed into the room. "I almost forgot to tell you, Hope!" he beamed. "I had a very strange phone call today, from C2C, the radio station!" He went on to describe the call from Faith New and her request to visit the next day. His wife's reaction surprised him.

"You turned her down, of course."

"Why would I turn her down?" he asked, puzzled. "It will be great for Taylor's Country Gardens. As Auntie Pat said, 'free publicity can't do any harm!'"

Hope looked at him in hopeless incredulity. "It will do a lot of harm if she gives a true picture of the state of the place, and then people will stop coming altogether," she observed. "Oh well, we might as well shut down sooner rather than later."

Adam went silent. Seeing his stricken face, she was overcome with remorse. "I'm sorry Adam, I am tired and grumpy. I should not have said that."

He gave her a hopeful smile. "We are going to straighten the place up first thing in the morning. But we cannot perform miracles," he said. "Neither of us are good at displays and stuff."

Hope finished ironing the last little polo shirt. She unplugged the iron. "Why don't I come in tomorrow night, and Saturday morning. We can give the place a good going over, ready for Christmas."

"Seems a bit pointless if we are going to shut down anyway," he moped.

His wife, never one to admit defeat, sat beside him and laid her head on his shoulder. "Well, let's go out in a blaze of glory at least," she declared. "If we're going, we'll go down fighting."

She went and collapsed the ironing board. "I will come over tomorrow evening after I have picked them all up from school, and see if we can make a plan of sorts. If it were up to me, I would gut the place and start again. Including that grungy old café."

Adam put on a face of theatrical terror. "Auntie Pat might have something to say about that!"

At that moment his redoubtable aunt was rifling through her wardrobe, trying to find something fit to be seen. She always wore a black tunic and leggings under her nylon overall in the café. But now that they were to be visited by radio royalty, she felt the need to dress for the occasion. Pushing aside her smart coats, funeral outfits, and barely worn 'special occasion' outfits, she found the perfect dress.

"Aha!" she squealed, "there you are, my sensible professional frock." She pulled out a royal blue, A-line dress, and hung it on the door of the wardrobe for the next day, then hunted and caught a pair of tights and her makeup bag.

Her phone rang. It was Hope. She told Pat of her plans. "I think we've all got so disheartened it shows in the state of the Garden Centre," she explained. "The whole place needs a good wash and brush up."

"I couldn't agree more," answered Pat, as she looked in the mirror, "we've let the place go. I'll see you tomorrow, dear."

Chapter Four

Hope thought about Taylor's Country Gardens as she made her way to C2C Radio studios. She had hardly been to the family firm in the last year, and she always came away feeling depressed and somehow dusty. It was no surprise daily customer numbers had dwindled to almost single figures. She realised that she felt quite excited to be planning a re-vamp for the old place. As she cleaned, vacuumed, mopped and dusted her way through the offices and studios, Hope imagined a makeover that was practically impossible, given their financial situation. She was finishing off with the last of the top floor offices. These 'big-wigs,' the directors, managers and star turns, were never in before nine and it was not even eight o'clock yet. She flicked off and unplugged Henry the hoover, picked up her crate of cleaning gear and hurried through the open door, colliding into Faith as she hurried into the office to start her day. Faith, a slightly built woman, fell back onto the floor. Hope, horrified, apologised. She had just all but rugby-tackled the station's most well-known name.

Instead of berating her, Faith sitting in a jumble on the floor, laughed heartily. "Has someone taken out a hit on me?" she laughed. "That's the third time this week!"

Hope looked at her more closely. "Was it you in the supermarket car park, too?"

Faith nodded, Hope helped her up and followed her into her office, checking she was uninjured. "Please don't worry," Faith reassured her. "Your Christmas wrapping paper actually gave me the idea for my next story."

"Really?" Hope responded, deciding that now was not the time to share her connection with Taylor's Country Gardens.

"Yes, I'm doing a piece on the Applebury Christmas Tree Festival," Faith said. "Have you heard about it?"

"As it happens, I live in Applebury," Hope replied. She introduced herself, shaking Faith's hand.

Faith looked at her, a slender, honest-faced young woman, with more than her fair share of thick, jet-black curls, tied up in a red bandana. "Good to meet you, Hope."

"Oh, my word!" Hope cried, glancing at the clock on the wall. "I'm so sorry, I have to get my kids to school." She rushed out, pulling the vacuum cleaner behind her, like a dog on a lead. She threw all her equipment into the cleaner's cupboard, rushed out of the building and into her car. Hope got Lily and Callum through the gates of the school with seconds to spare. She noticed most of the other children, in their lines, were holding bundles. A sequinned mesh wing poked out of an orange supermarket carrier, the Graham twins proudly carried a wooden manger between them, and a rather tall boy with an ornate paper crown on his head held a gold-sprayed cola bottle covered in stick-on gems. Hope went cold. She had forgotten the Nativity costumes.

Callum saw her dilemma. "It's all right Mummy," he reassured her, taking her hand, "it's just the rehearsal."

"Why didn't you tell me?" she asked, frustrated.

"Don't worry, Mummy," said Callum. "Next time I will always tell you."

Lily piped up. "I did tell you Mummy, and Callum did. If I told you once, I told you a *hundred* times."

Hope laughed inwardly to hear an echo of herself in Lily's words. Not finished, Lily put her hands on her hips, in an attitude of outraged injury. "I am an angel and Callum is a shepherd, we told you *and* we gived you a note!" chided Lily. "Just make sure we have our costumes for Monday!"

Hope knelt beside her children, Callum, quiet, comforting, taking responsibility, so much like his father. Fiery Lily, with that determined sense of justice, well, who knew where that came from! Hope hugged them both as she said goodbye. "Love you two so much," she said, "and I'm really sorry about this."

She had twenty minutes before she had to drop the car at Harvey's. The thought of Callum and Lily being the only pupils in school uniform was just too much. She rushed to the supermarket for an instant angel and an instant shepherd outfit. Before the garden centre turned their family life upside down, Hope had looked down on those parents who bought costumes, proud of her creatively handmade costumes for Rosa and Bryony's Nativity. I am such a hypocrite, thought Hope. Posting all the 'shop local' memes on social media, and then ordering all her clothes and gifts online. "Who has the time?" She said to herself.

She drove back to the school, ran through the gate and ran into the school foyer. "Callum and Lily Taylor!" she shouted, flinging the outfits, still on their hangers, at the receptionist. "Sorry, got to dash!" She raced to the Garage and, thankfully, was only five minutes late for her MOT. Luxury of luxuries, Harvey's Motors offered a 'while you wait' service. She could sit for forty-five minutes and drink free coffee.

She texted Rosa. *'Need you to babysit the littleys tonight, I'm going to help dad at the garden centre. sorry for short notice xx.'*

It was not likely that Rosa would have any plans. At sixteen she seemed determined to get her qualifications, and, so far, that seemed to trump her social life. Hope leafed through the rather limited magazines on offer. A disappointing selection of caravans, motorbikes and two-week-old news in the local free paper did not hold her interest for long. Instead, she laid her head back and shut her eyes for a few seconds, to plan the makeover of Taylor's Country Gardens.

As Hope waited for her car, Adam was already at work on the first part of her plan. If they were going to transform the place over the weekend, they would at least start with a relatively blank canvas. Adam had a skip delivered that morning and, filling a trolley load by load, he emptied the broken and damaged stock from the redundant greenhouse into the skip. Surveying the piles of tat his dad had bought wholesale in an effort to 'draw in customers,' he wondered if he should do the same with most of the things on the shop floor. Vivid lemon canary shaped flower pots, piles of wicker baskets, plastic garden gnomes, not to mention the absurd selection of 'specialist' garden paraphernalia and ornaments. Wherever he looked there was something that he knew would never sell.

Pat appeared with a box full of well-worn mugs and plates, and some faded and water-damaged old 'gardening expert' books. "I would suggest we give some of this to the charity shop," she said, "but I don't honestly think they would want it."

Adam's phone rang. "Mum?" he said, "is Dad alright?" It was unusual for her to ring him at work, especially on his private number.

Agnes assured him that she and Brian were well. "I have some good news, actually," she said. "Grace will be bringing one of her students to start a bit of work experience. I thought you could do with the help."

"Mum," he objected, "it's not possible at the moment. Christmas is nearly here and I don't have time to be supervising one of Grace's sulky teenage boys."

"Oh well, I'm afraid I've already promised. He will start on Monday. Give him a try, son, its only two weeks and it might help him out!"

"Mum, your kind heart is a bit of a liability at times."

"Yes, well, I'm afraid the deed is done. Grace is going to bring him in to meet you later today."

Adam looked at Pat as he spoke into the phone. "Mother, you are incorrigible!" Agnes laughed and hung up. Adam, fuming, explained the call to Pat. "Grace is inflicting one of her ne'er do wells on us just before Christmas. That's all we need at the busiest time of the year!" Pat's only comment was that she hoped he was a beefy lad who could shift a few pallets.

Back at the garage, Hope jerked awake with a snort, as Guy Harvey tapped her on the shoulder. "All done, Hope," he said. "Nothing to report."

"Sorry, Mr Harvey," she said, "I must have dozed off."

"Understandable," he said. "You and Adam work so hard since…" He hesitated. Harveys Motors had a

51

long-established reputation for reliability, honesty and expertise which meant Guy had at least a passing acquaintance with most of the population of Applebury. "How is Brian doing? He won't have any visitors you know. Absolutely refuses."

Hope saw the real concern in his eyes. "It's so hard for him," she agreed. "He can't seem to get better."

"Poor old beggar," observed Mr Harvey. "A man builds a business and works so hard it nearly kills him!" He shook his head in fellow feeling. "Give him my best when you see him, will you?" She assured him she would, then set off do the weekly shop and, hopefully, change the children's beds before school pick up time.

That afternoon Grace dropped off her work experience candidate at Taylor's Country Gardens, promising to return later to complete the necessary paperwork and drop Danny home. Adam was almost immediately sorry for his earlier words. Danny was about the same age as his oldest daughter, yet for some reason, Adam's first response had been to write him off as a waste of time. The boy was polite and seemed genuinely attentive, as Adam showed him round and talked him through his duties. Danny had seemed interested, although his remark that it was not very Christmassy was rather too frank.

They stopped in the 'bargain corner,' an area which served two purposes. Firstly, as a last resting place for all the unsaleable old mistakes now offered at a fraction of their cost price, and secondly to block off the entrances to the Victorian orangery on one side and the huge greenhouse on the other. The cost of heating and lighting both had become far greater than any income they generated, and Adam had simply shut them off, using the greenhouse as a rubbish tip for items that were past selling.

"We're in the middle of a re-stock at the moment," said Adam defensively, "clearing out all the junk and tidying up." He pulled a display of hideous canary shaped yellow flower pots aside and opened the door to the greenhouse. "I've already started in here."

Danny nodded, looking around as if to say it was about time he did. Adam, keen to get on, asked, "So do you think you would like to give it a go here?"

"Aren't you supposed to interview me, or something, Mr Taylor?"

"Well, I could do," Adam smiled, "but Grace has said you would be ideal, and you seem pretty switched on to me. Do you want an interview?"

"No, you're alright, thanks, Mr Taylor." Danny replied with a relieved expression.

Just then Pat appeared. "What are you hiding here for?" she cried. "*Our visitor has arrived!*"

Adam, already thrown by Pat turning up dressed for a wedding, was suddenly very nervous. "Here goes nothing!" He sighed, striding away.

"Mr Taylor!" shouted Danny, "what am I supposed to do? I'm here until three-thirty." Adam, his mind already rehearsing radio sound bites, floundered for a moment. "I could tidy up in there," Danny indicated the greenhouse behind him.

"Good plan," Adam replied. "Go into the greenhouse, see if there anything worth rescuing. The rest you can just dump in the skip out the back. Be ruthless!"

Danny began by dumping several boxes crammed with the dusty detritus of a failed business. Amongst them he found one containing several cans of spray paint. As he carried it past the acid yellow canary pots, he had an idea. Did he dare? *They are going to throw them out anyway*, he thought, *I'll give it a try*. Danny retrieved the cans of paint and one by one the hideous canaries disappeared into the greenhouse.

Faith, meanwhile, listened to the history of the neglected garden centre. Originally an old, near derelict country house, Brian and Agnes fell in love with the place, mostly because of the huge orangery which was part of the original building, and the fact that the place had its own pump and well. Both keen gardeners, they had bought it and restored it into a beautiful Garden Centre in the late Seventies. As Taylor's Country Gardens prospered, they added another, larger greenhouse to extend their growing season, employed a nurseryman, and took on several retail staff.

Seated in the quaint café, which in the 80's had been the very latest in modern design, Adam was disappointed to hear that Faith had driven past the centre several times but had always assumed it was closed down. She did not add, but thought nevertheless, that her tour of the centre had only added to her impression of a dying business holding desperately on to its outdated past. Adam spoke enthusiastically of Taylor's contribution to the Christmas Tree Festival, and their hopes for the future. She made a few half-hearted notes but the sorry state of the surroundings, and Adams anxious deference left her with an impression of general gloom.

Faith's attention had been drawn to the striking woman who evidently ran the café. Dressed as if she were about to attend the Royal Garden party, Pat had been extremely disappointed when Faith declined one of her cakes and settled only for a small black coffee. Having set Adam's and Faith's coffees down, Pat then set to theatrically wiping the tables nearest them, looking at Adam with eyes wide open, trying to communicate her own answers to Faith's questions. Pat's tactics were hard to ignore and Adam was having great difficulty in translating her surreptitious gestures and very obvious glares into any kind of sensible response to Faith. Faintly amused, Faith tried not to be distracted.

"Finally, Mr Taylor," she needed to wrap up this unexciting interview, "it seems that Taylor's is rather behind other retailers in regards to the Christmas season. Is that something to do with the Christmas Tree Festival, or..." she indicated the shabby Christmas displays around the café, "is *this* the Taylor's Christmas?"

Pat drew in a sharp breath. Adam gave up any pretence of this being a private interview. He pulled out the chair next to him. "Would you like to join us, Auntie Pat?" He explained Pat's relationship to himself and the garden centre.

Pat feigned surprise. "Really? Oh, that's so kind!"

"I couldn't help hearing your question," she addressed Faith, her tone tinged with suppressed fury. "What Adam *meant* to say is that the Garden Centre is looking a little empty at the moment as we are preparing for our *seasonal refurbishment* and Christmas opening." Faith went to speak but Pat went on, her dander well and truly up. "And furthermore, yes, Taylor's supports the Applebury Christmas Tree Festival wholeheartedly. In addition to the three trees we are already donating, we are offering a ten percent discount off trees bought for the festival." It was

Adam's turn to stare and gesture as he heard Pat give away a substantial proportion of their profits. "And *finally*, Taylor's is a traditional but trendy store, so *this*" she indicated the same Christmas displays, "is vintage and shabby-chic styling, thank you *very* much."

Adam thought she had entirely blown their chances of any good publicity at that point, but to his surprise, Faith stood and shook Pat's hand. "Thank you, Pat," she said, "it's so refreshing to hear someone that feels so passionate and loyal. I look forward to returning when the seasonal changes are in place." Faith wound the interview up quickly, there was no story here and Applebury church was next on her list. She left hoping there were richer journalistic pickings there.

Adam showed Faith to the door, returning to find Pat and Grace in the coffee shop, discussing the interview. Pat still buzzing with indignation. "I told *her* what for, Miss High and Mighty!"

Grace looked towards Adam. "So, how did it go?"

"Well, I think she was impressed with what we are doing for the festival, and she said the café had an authentic retro feel. She wasn't very well up on Taylor's, though. Pat's probably told you everything else you need to know."

"No, I mean with Danny! Where is he, by the way?"

Adam slapped his hand to his forehead. "I completely forgot!"

All three looked at each other. "Don't look at me," said Pat, "I haven't heard sight or sound of him since I came and got you for that rude woman's interview."

Grace, slightly concerned at this stage, asked, "Well, where did you last leave him?" They set off through the bargain tunnel and across to the entrance to the enormous greenhouse. Adam noticed at least half of the yellow canary pots were gone. Opening the door, the smell of spray paint hung in the air. "Oh no," thought Grace, "not graffiti, please not graffiti!" Instead, there was one of the old pallet shelves, filled with neat rows of canary flower pots. Only they were no longer canaries. Each one had been painted brown with a bright burst of red on its chest, beady black eyes and a yellow beak. Danny, seated on another pallet, was painting the yellow beak onto his latest transformation.

"Hello, Miss," he said to Grace. "I thought these were too good to chuck out, so I just made them a bit more Christmassy." He looked at Adam, concerned that he may have overstepped the mark. "I hope that's alright?"

"Alright?" Adam picked up one of the cheery robins. "It's amazing, what a brilliant idea! Well done Danny."

Grace beamed. "So, Danny, are you happy to come here for the next couple of weeks?"

"If you want," he said, nonchalantly, thinking he would like to more than anything else in the world at that moment.

"Definitely, we want." Adam smiled and walked forward to shake Danny's hand. "It will be great to have you on board!"

As Grace drove Danny home, he was surprisingly chatty about the possibilities at Taylor's. He asked her to drop him at the top of the road, not wanting her to see the place he called home. Pushing open the gate, Danny walked up the short path to his house. Energised by the joyful approval of his work and the keenness to have him join Taylor's, Danny almost skipped through the front door. The TV was blaring out some afternoon soap. "Dad!" he shouted, as he hung his coat over the banister. "Dad, I've got work experience next week!" He stepped into the lounge. Kit Jones lay sprawled on the couch, snoring. An empty bottle of cheap vodka lay on the floor by his slackened hand. Danny's smile dropped from his face. "Oh, Dad," he whispered.

His father slurred some expletive, shouted at Danny to get out, then fell back to sleep. Danny turned the TV off and rolled his father gently on to his side, securing a cushion behind his head and another behind his back to ensure he stayed in position. Tucking a blanket across him for warmth, Danny placed his hand on his Dad's back, counting the number of times his chest rose and fell. Finally, he filled a glass of water and placed it on the table by his father's head. He went to the kitchen – no milk, but there was some cereal in the cupboard and a jar of instant coffee bedside the kettle. Danny walked back into the lounge and checked on his Dad. "Do you want a coffee, Dad?"

The man woke partially. "I was watching that," he slurred, jumping up suddenly to switch the TV back on. Then, collapsing back into the sofa, he cursed at his son.

"It's alright Dad, I thought you were asleep."

"Dad! Roll onto your side," Danny said as his father lolled sleepily back onto the cushions, reaching for the vodka bottle. He held it to his lips, almost sucking the last few drops of precious vodka onto his tongue. "What are you looking at?" he bawled and threw the bottle at his son, finally crashing out completely.

Danny dodged back into the kitchen, made himself a coffee with no milk and poured himself a bowl of cereal. Sitting on the stairs he started to crunch his way through the dry cornflakes, then just poured the coffee into the bowl and ate it. Sometime later, he checked on his now sleeping father and did a familiar search through the house and garden. Three empties behind the bath panel, several hidden in the old shed under a pile of carrier bags. A couple in the airing cupboard and one in the back of the garden behind a bush. He went up to his room. Sat on his unmade bed and cried.

****

The Applebury church visit, as expected, was as unremarkable as the Garden Centre. As Faith arrived, a boisterous crowd of five-to-seven-year-olds looking forward to games, activities and above all, tuck shop, were swarming in to the church hall. A young couple were welcoming them, and another couple around the same age, or maybe a little older, were playing some song about grapes, melons and bananas which involved a great deal of spinning, hugging and clapping. Most children ran straight to the piano and joined in. A few preferred the 'quiet table' where there was a pile of pens, papers and art materials, where a couple of volunteer parents were helping out.

Mark, the Pastor, named the other adults who waved at her, and as the noise levels rose, he and Debbie took her through the big double doors into the mercifully quiet church. Like the hall, the place looked to be on its last legs. Huge, bright banners hanging along each wall could barely hide the chipped paint and old wallpaper beneath them. Looking up beyond the pitch-stained beams, Faith saw the ceiling had been discoloured from a patched-up leak. The building had neither the soft historic beauty of traditional church nor the electric techno-minimalism of a modern place of worship. Yet Mark and Debbie talked enthusiastically about their plans to expand, to do more, to help more, to love more.

Disheartened by the absence of any ulterior motive or even any unique point to this story, but determined to squeeze some sort of victory from the jaws of career death, Faith went home, wrote up her notes and tried to find some sort of hook to hang this story on.

****

Hope had prepared a slow-cooked stew ready for her quick exit once Rosa arrived. She and Briony would be able to keep an eye on the younger two and put them to bed while she worked on trying to sort out the garden centre. "I've got to pop out later," she said to the younger two. "Now, you can say up until seven-thirty, but then you *must* go to bed." Callum and Lily were so thrilled to be given an extra hour; they asked no further questions. Hope was already stacking the dishwasher as Rosa let herself in the front door.

"Hey, Mum," she smiled, "what's for tea?" Hope indicated the slow cooker as she put her coat on and kissed the two younger children. "Give my love to Auntie Pat," called Rosa.

Hope froze as a huge siren wail rose from the depths of the house. It was Lily. "I WANT TO SEE AUNTIE PAT!!" she howled, screamed, insisted.

Briony and Rosa looked at their mother, one in apology for saying the trigger words 'Auntie Pat,' and the other in horror at the thought of spending the next few hours with an angry, inconsolable Lily. Callum just looked in awe at his little sister's ability to go from nought to naughty in less than three seconds. He waited for the 'big trouble' that normally followed fusses. Lily would be sent to bed and he would have the TV all to himself until *seven-thirty!* Instead, his mummy just grabbed Lily's hand and said "Oh, come on then!" and pulled Lily to the car with her.

Callum said nothing, but after a few minutes of TV, he went to his room. Rosa could hear him playing with his action figures, and Iron Man was coming in for a pretty big telling off from Captain America.

Hope was more impressed with Taylor's Country Gardens than she expected. The place was clean and tidy and a lot less higgledy-piggledy than the last time she looked in. The first thing she did was open the door to the big greenhouse, the scene of Danny's earlier victory.

"Okay," she said, as they stood in the greenhouse. "We need to take all that dreadful bargain corner stuff and just put it on the tables in here for now. "We'll work out what to do with it later."

"I'll do that," said Adam, pleased to be doing something useful that did not require his exhausted brain to be creative.

"And now," she said, almost rubbing her hands together as she opened the door to the gothic style orangery, so fashionable when the farmhouse was built, "let's look at this place."

"Since I had to shut it off," said Adam, "it's been filled with dead plants and old garden furniture I'm afraid."

"It's such a beautiful structure," said Hope, "it's a shame not to use it. Especially this time of year."

"It'll be freezing," said Pat, zipping her fleece cardigan to her chin.

"Exactly," said Hope. "This is going to be our Winter Wonderland!"

Looking at the dried-out vines and dead trees in grimy pots, the dusty cross bars, the floor thick with leaves, and old wooden garden benches that had seen better days, Adam beat a quick retreat. "I'll get on with the bargain basement," he said.

First, Pat and Hope simply moved all the lifeless trees to the centre of the floor so that they could sweep the place clean. As they wiped down the benches and paint work, Lily, bored with her drawing, wandered in to watch them work. "It's a forest!" she said, pointing at the clump of withered, misshapen or downright dead trees plopped in the centre of the floor.

Hope took a second look. "Lily, you're a genius," she said, "do you want to help?" Lily certainly did. Hope grabbed a piece of chalk from the café blackboard, drawing an oval island at the centre of the orangery. "Lily, I want you to go and get me all the white flowers in little pots that you can find and put them in here."

Pat stood with her hands on her hips, waiting for her orders.

"Auntie Pat, have we got any of that spray on snow in stock?"

"We certainly have," grinned Pat. "In fact, if you're thinking what I'm thinking, you should go and have a root around in the big greenhouse, there are tons of damaged and unsold Christmas bits in there.

"Come on," Hope said, taking her arm. "Let's have a look."

Adam had already done a marvellous job, the bargain spot was stripped and bare, its contents now laid out in rows on the benches in the big greenhouse, an eclectic mix of the unsold detritus of ten years of bad buying choices.

Hope dumped a box overflowing with unsold personalised bottle openers, Christmas baubles and key rings onto one of the old benches

"All those Ethels, Mauds, and Earnests have really missed out on this lot, Auntie Pat!" she exclaimed. Box by box, anything that could be sprayed in white, gold or silver was restyled and repurposed. Even squished oasis rings, synthetic pine wreaths and artificial apples were transformed into magical winter foliage.

"Seriously?" Hope called out in despair, as she held up a fake standard holly tree and a trailing plastic ivy. "Fake plants in a garden centre?"

Pat held up a long garland of unnaturally dew-spotted roses. "I think these were from the wedding décor phase about five years ago," she said. "There must be yards and yards of them, and those," she said, nodding towards a pile of thirty or more wicker baskets, "were for bridesmaids."

Between the three of them, they carried everything set aside for the 'Winter Wonderland' from the greenhouse. Piece by piece, Hope, Pat and Adam turned the disused orangery into a winter forest-garden. The old benches were placed at intervals against the wall, a conifer and a few large tubs of winter flowers beside them. Each one looked as if the gardener had just stepped away for a moment. On the first, a garden rug, thrown across the arm with an open book and a cup and saucer beside it; the second held a trug filled with holly, a pair of garden gloves across the handle; the next a pair of black wellies, a Santa hat and a pair of gold-rimmed spectacles. All along the perimeter, between the benches, the old dresser, the greenhouse tables and wicker baskets were bursting with winter flowers in pots. And in the centre was Lily's forest, sprayed with snow and covered in tiny white lights and hung with golden apples, the floor beneath covered with white cyclamen like fallen snow.

It was going on for nine pm when they all sat in the café. Pat had warmed them each a pasty in the oven, except for Lily who was fast asleep on the office sofa.

"Now that really is a makeover," said Pat. "I can't believe we turned a pile of old junk into a display worthy of Harrods."

"I can," said Adam. "Hope has a gift, she's an artist!"

The weekend was slow and quiet at Taylor's Country Gardens. Which, though terrible for business, was a good opportunity for Hope, Pat and Adam to put the finishing touches to the rest of the garden centre. The café, in particular, was surprisingly easy to revamp since it only needed restoring to its original state. Pat's fastidious care for the red, vinyl-clad upholstery in each booth, her polishing of the chrome fittings, and her insistence on gingham table cloths, had kept the place in near perfect condition. Once the table cloths were removed to reveal the original sparkling red Formica, the Cosy Café became an authentic 'retro' diner. Impressed with Danny's transformed canary-robins, Hope placed one on each table in the café adding a tiny red succulent to each pot. By Sunday, all that was left was a final clean and tidy which Hope left to Adam and Pat. After all, she had a lot to do at home before the new week began.

While Hope was ironing school uniforms, packing school bags, signing reading records and preparing a Sunday roast, Faith planned her piece on the Applebury Christmas Tree Festival.

Chapter Five

It was Monday morning, and Danny was already standing beside the big iron shutter that secured the front door when Pat arrived to open up Taylor's Country Gardens. She smiled at the nervous young man, who had obviously grown since he last wore his 'smart' black trousers, as a fair few inches of bare ankle filled the gap between them and his trainers. He wore a white shirt, crisply ironed and slightly too big.

"You look very smart. Great to see you here so early."

"Yes, well, it's not school is it?" he said, seriously. "Its work, you've got to dress the part."

Pat realised that Danny had taken his lead from her magnificent Friday outfit, and had done his best to dress accordingly. "Come on," she said, "we'll start in the café, and then I'm sure Adam will have lots of work for you to do when he gets here." Danny was secretly thrilled to see his robins as the centre piece on each table. Pat saw the shadow of a smile on his face "Your robins were so popular we sold most of them on Saturday," she said. "Adam painted the rest himself. They're flying of the shelves!"

Danny could not help laughing at her choice of words. "I suppose they would," he laughed.

"Come on," Pat rolled her eyes, suppressing her own laughter, "we've got work to do."

Danny helped unload a delivery of goods from the local dairy, then another of bread and groceries from the farm shop, stacking it, under Pat's strict instructions, in the large storeroom, a series of marble covered shelves that formed part of the original pantry. The store room was the first in a series of rooms leading off from the narrow corridor behind the kitchen. The second led to the spacious staff cloakroom and the third to a reasonably-sized store cupboard housing all the cleaning equipment. At the back of this cupboard was another door, with an old-fashioned key in the lock.

"What's through there? "asked Danny

"It's the old scullery," Pat informed him. "A century or more ago, this was quite a fine house. This whole area was the old kitchen and that room would have been the place they prepared the vegetables, washed the clothes, dried the herbs." Pat turned the key and opened the door to reveal piles of old display cabinets, seed display stands, and other junk from the past forty years. Dust particles that had not been disturbed in probably twenty years swirled in the light from the window running the full length of the room. "I don't think this door has been opened for years," she said. "No one goes in here anymore."

They returned to the kitchen where Pat, switching on lights and equipment and preparing the café to open, explained to him the importance of hygiene, cleanliness, and safety in the kitchen. She then detailed her expectations for customer service in the café, and in the rest of Taylor's country gardens. Pat listed the many duties he might be expected to carry out. She did not want him to think this was just a matter of lolling at the cash desk chatting, as others had in the past, she warned. He must work hard, follow instructions, be on hand to help customers and carry out any and all tasks needed to keep Taylor's running smoothy and efficiently. She was particularly enthusiastic when describing the dire legal consequences should he fail to follow the correct health and safety procedures. Finally, during her alarming predictions of the impact of inaccurate stock taking, she realised that Danny's expression had moved from absorbed interest to sheer terror. "Well," she said in apology, "that's enough of that for now."

The café ready, lights on all across the centre, Pat looked Danny up and down. "You've already done a good day's work, Danny. How about a nice bacon sandwich and a cup of coffee before you get stuck in to the hard work?"

Danny had eaten nothing but cereal for the last three days and fell on the sandwich with gusto. As he ate, Pat started whipping up a batch of scones and put on a pot of coffee, explaining that it was the smell of baking and fresh coffee that was the secret of the Cosy Café's success. "We use the proper machine for the customers coffee," she said, "but this smell makes people hungry the minute they step through the door!"

Adam joined Pat and Danny in the café, impressed by Danny's punctuality. He was even more so on discovering that Danny had been working for the last hour or more. "Let me show you what we've been up to over the weekend," said Adam, proud of the transformed orangery. As they reached the arched entrance, now garlanded with tiny stringed lights and dew-covered roses, Danny whistled in astonishment.

"Wow!" he said. "It's so beautiful! Just like Christmas in the North Pole!"

Adam was touched by his childlike reaction. "It is, isn't it? Pat and my wife, Hope, worked on it over the weekend."

Danny looked at the hundreds of white plants in pots creating the forest floor, and the multi-coloured classic Christmas plants ranged across the benches. He thought of the small selection of various shrubs, roses and trees in the outdoor nursery as well as the potted and seasonal plants indoors. "Should I water the plants," he asked, "or do you do that?"

"No, Jim will not allow us to get involved in the horticulture, he's the expert."

"I haven't met Jim," said Danny, more a question than a statement.

"Jim started when my Mum and Dad first set up Taylor's. He is an authentic nurseryman."

"A nurseryman?" Danny echoed.

"Jim went to college and trained in horticulture, all about plants, where and how to grow them. He is a real expert. Before my Dad got sick and things went a bit to pot, they both used to grow most of the plants we sell. Now we buy most of our stuff in, and Jim just comes in Mondays and Thursdays to keep things ticking over."

Adam walked Danny across to the big greenhouse where all the 'bargains' had been dumped, along with all the other unwanted or unsaleable stock from the weekend tidy up.

"Well, this is your job, Danny – if it looks like it could be sold, put it on one of these tables, if not – you know where the skip is. Then just price everything at £1, at least we can get something back to pay for the lighting!"

It did not take Danny long to sort the trash from the treasure in the big greenhouse. He found some floppy, half-dead succulents and pots of desiccated soil in which were stored dusty bulbs, some with tiny green tips. He took an example of each, and finding Adam at the till, asked him what to do with them.

"Ditch them," said Adam, "I don't think they are worth wasting anyone's time on."

Looking at the plants, still fighting to live and not die, Danny determined a different fate for them. In the corner was a box of old china flower pots, sundries, and two water stained and curled books. The first, 'The New Practical Gardener, and Modern Horticulturalist,' looked far from new, or modern. But it had some beautiful pictures in it and sections on everything from the orangery to the kitchen garden. The second was a book for houseplant experts. Danny emptied everything but the books, placing the items on the saleable table. The bulbs and their pots he placed into the box, along with the several limp green plants, tucking the whole lot out of sight under a corner bench.

The café, despite its being lunchtime, had only two tables filled. Pat was serving at the front; in fact, she had wiped the tables several times and was just tidying the menus for the second time when Danny appeared carrying his box of rubbish. He asked if she needed any help, although it was fairly evident that Pat was struggling to keep herself occupied, let alone Danny. "Is it alright if I clear out all that junk in the old scullery then? Seems a shame to leave the skip half full."

"Be my guest, Danny," said Pat, sincerely impressed and slightly amused at his enthusiasm.

Danny carried his box of treasures into the scullery, placing it securely beside the old Belfast sink. The room was large, with a tall, shuttered window running the entire length of one side. All along the window an extended sill formed a shelf above the double sink and marble-topped cabinets. Along the adjoining wall, a huge built-in dresser loomed darkly behind a heavy scrubbed oak table. The tiled floor, though dirty, was intact and beautiful. Across everything lay a thick patina of grey dust. Danny pulled open the central shutters, letting in the sunlight. Behind the dented metal filing cabinets against the outer wall, Danny found a door, the key still in its lock, with a second on its attached keyring. Opening the door, he found that it opened onto a narrow path leading to the loading area and the skip. Since the scullery contents were almost entirely garbage, it took him less than an hour to empty and clean the place. Danny locked the outer door, replacing the keys. He looked at the now clean scullery with only two Lloyd loom chairs in the centre, and a collection of old framed photographs leaning against the dresser.

He stood the gardening books on a shelf. With a few spoons of compost from a split broken bag, Danny topped up each pot of bulbs, taking care not to damage the little shoots of green emerging from each pot. Turning on the tap, he watched it judder to life as a rusty gush of stored water splashed into the sink below, followed by a clear, icy stream. He dripped a few drops of water into each pot, then did the same with the other plants, topping up the compost and adding water. The window shelf became a plant hospital, as Danny added every half-dead rejected plant to the shelf. Danny hesitated as he left the room, then swiftly turned back, slipping the duplicate key for the outside door into his pocket. He swept the corridor, tidied the storeroom, then emerged into the café.

The lunchtime 'rush' had finished. Pat waved him over to where a wiry chap in khaki shorts and plaid shirt was enjoying a sausage and pickle sandwich, one of Pat's specialities.

"This is Danny Jones, the lad I was telling you about, Jim," she said. Jim nodded a greeting.

Danny, without being asked, sat at the table. "Mr Taylor, Adam, says what you don't know about plants isn't worth knowing," he said.

"Did he, now?" smiled Jim. "He's probably right, I reckon."

Danny ploughed on, single minded "I've got a question about bulbs," he said.

Jim raised his eyebrows and lowered his sandwich in surprise. "What about them?"

"Well, we've got reduced daffodil bulbs here, it says to plant them in September or early October to bloom in April, but we also have hyacinths that will be ready for Christmas. So," Danny continued with enthusiasm, "my question is, how do people get bulbs to flower for Christmas when they normally flower in spring?"

Jim was delighted, and it almost showed on his face. "Now that, Danny me boy, is a very intelligent question. That's called 'forcing' a bulb. It's just playing a trick on it to make it think the winter has been and gone, and spring is springing!"

"So, before they get to us, they've been forced?"

Jim nodded. "That's it, exactly," he said. "Normally, once they're potted up, you would leave them in a cold dark place, so they think its winter, see. Then after a month or so, they start to put out shoots…"

Danny nodded, thinking of the many bulbs he had just put on the window sill. "So, when they start to grow, they think its spring."

Jim was impressed. "That's right. And that's where people go wrong. You see, in spring, it's still cold, even when its sunny. People stick them in a hot room and wonder why they only last five minutes."

"Oh! I remember my Mum putting a big red plant in the window over the radiator."

"Bet that didn't last more than a week," said Jim.

"It didn't last long. I do remember that."

"Well, you tell your Mum, next time they need to be cold, and not too much sun!"

"Oh, it's just me and Dad now," said Danny. "She pushed off a few years ago."

"I'm sorry to hear that," said Jim, "I didn't mean to pry."

"What's done is done," sighed Danny, philosophically. "Things move on, you just have to pick yourself up and carry on, no sense in dwelling on the past." He recited a few more trite clichés that had evidently been trotted out to him by well-meaning adults.

Jim looked at him with deep concern. "It's not that simple though, is it, boy?" He took a large bite of his doorstep bread, chewing slowly.

Danny saw genuine understanding and acknowledgement of his pain. No patronising strategy to fix a wound that would never heal. It was too much. He spat out a profanity, then asked, "How long is it from the green shoots to the flower then, Jim?"

"Can be as little as a month," the gardener replied, "if you get the conditions right."

Pat approached the table with a sandwich to match Jim's, putting it down in front of Danny. "I've got to use these sausages up today, so I hope you don't mind." She looked meaningfully at Jim. "Everything alright?"

Which was a coded way of asking if he needed rescuing.

"We're alright here, aren't we mate?"

Danny nodded, his mouth filled with sausage, bread, and ketchup.

"What do you want to drink, Danny," she asked, "Coke, juice, coffee?"

Danny swallowed, ready to speak. "If it's alright, I'd like a nice cup of strong tea with two sugars."

Jim guffawed. "That's my lad! Gardeners tea!"

Pat walked to the kitchen, mildly astounded. Danny had no idea that Jim was considered a man of few words and fewer smiles. Especially since Brian had become ill. To see the two of them deep in conversation was quite remarkable. Those who didn't know Jim would call him surly, and there had even been a few complaints about him being rude and unhelpful. Jim was a reliable employee, an expert horticulturist and a loyal friend—but he most definitely preferred plants to people.

The last song died away on the radio balanced above the coffee machine. *Thank you for your calls and no doubt we will be hearing more about these 'pop-up' shops in the run up to Christmas. What do you think, a good use of empty shops, or an invitation to take the money and run? Give me a call on C2C County radio. Coming up after this, the tiny town of Applebury is hoping to make it big this year..."*

Jim and Danny carried their empties to the counter, still chatting, when Pat shushed them, pointing to the speaker overhead. "Listen! It's us!" she said. They waited for the weather forecast, cold and wet as usual, to finish, then:

"All you need is Love this Christmas, at least that's the word in Applebury this year, following its announcement of a Christmas Tree Festival leading up to a grand event on the last weekend before Christmas. I spoke with Pastor Mark Thorne of Applebury Community Church..."

Mark's pre-recorded tones explained that the village shops and businesses would be filled with Christmas trees all through December, and, on the last weekend before Christmas, all the trees would be assembled at the church for a celebration of local talent and creativity. He continued, *"...Applebury is a friendly town with a strong, close community. I came up with the idea of a Christmas Tree Festival to bring us all even closer together at Christmas time,"* he said. *"It will be a lot of fun and the theme for this first year is 'Love@Christmas.'"*

"Pastor Mark Thorne there," Faith continued, *"with a novel way to invite the whole town to church, so a carol service, a craft sale and a competition. Is that what Christmas means to you, listeners?"*

Pat raised her eyebrow. "She is twisting it all! That's not what it's like!"

"I spoke with Adam Taylor," Faith continued, *"the owner of Taylor's Country Gardens, who have donated trees to both Applebury Schools and, of course, the church."*

Adam's nerves were noticeable even through the speakers. *"Taylor's will be giving a ten percent discount on trees to any entrants of the competition. Our trees will be available from the first of December."*

"A nice gesture from Taylor's Country Gardens, who are not closed down, as I had thought, but I must

say it is the most un-Christmassy seller of Christmas trees that I have ever seen!"

Pat was incensed. Adam, listening in his office, felt depressed.

Jim just sucked his teeth with derision. "She is just stirring it up to get the listeners," he said.

"Well, she is going to ruin the whole thing before it gets started, if she carries on like that," Pat complained. "It's a chance to put Taylor's back on the map for one thing, *and* it's a chance for the whole town to have a bit of fun. A craft fair and a talent show and a whole load of Christmas trees. It will be just what the town needs! That Faith New needs to get a bit of the Christmas spirit herself!" She began to wipe the tables down with angry vigour.

Jim watched her with amusement. "A talent show, eh?" growled Jim, raising his eyebrows in Pat's direction. "Are you gonna do a turn?"

Pat looked positively fierce as she turned and pointed at him. "Jim Hargreaves, you mind your own business, and I'll mind mine, thank you."

Faith was not surprised when the first callers rang in with the usual complaints. It would be a waste of electricity, environmentally unsound, it was encouraging unhealthy competition, it would be commercialising Christmas. Objection upon objection grumbled cross the airwaves. She realised Megan and the technical assistant were filtering the callers, but her Happy Christmas feature was turning into a Grinch fest. Faith looked through the screen at them as the current caller, a 'woke' member of the County Council with his eye on a seat in the House of Commons, berated Taylor's Country Gardens, and Applebury Church, of all places, for being elitist. "If someone wants to take part, they are denied the opportunity because they can't afford a tree…"

"Councillor Waters," she reminded him, "Taylor's Country Gardens are donating three trees and giving ten percent discount for entrants to the festival."

"That's still a lot of money to spend on a tree at this time of year." Councillor Waters went on to grandstand about everything from equality and the environment, to religion and privilege, finally stating in a Churchillian manner that he, for one, would not be entering a Christmas tree, in solidarity with the poorer population of Applebury and the rest of the country, insisting that, "Having a decorated tree in order to enter the competition excludes the poorest and most deprived of our society."

Faith pointed out that the point of a Church Christmas tree festival is, well, Christmas trees and church, and gestured to the producer to rid her of the clearly self-promoting Councillor. "Stay on the line, Councillor," she said, "we have Guy Harvey, Mayor of Applebury town, and owner of Harvey's Garages, on the line."

Guy Harvey had a voice for radio, his deep, cheerful tones immediately lifting the show into the Christmas mood Faith had been aiming for. "I was feeling a bit sorry for the Councillor," he said, "in his big posh house in Golf Links Road. So I'm offering to buy him a Christmas tree and he can decorate it."

The Councillor was still on the line, and Faith asked him if he would like to take Mr Harvey up on his kind offer. Councillor Waters, not to be outdone, declined the offer but suggested Mr Harvey donate the tree to a local charity.

"Well, I'll be very glad to do so," said Mayor Harvey, "and I'm sure Councillor Waters will be happy to do the same!" Faith asked Mr Harvey who his chosen charity would be. "I would like to donate a tree to Edward Henry Court, where my Mum lives. The vicar's in and out of there like a fiddler's elbow. My old Mum loves that church."

Faith asked if Mr Harvey was connected to the church. "I'm not religious," he said, "but I do know that they do a lot for Applebury. Maybe the Councillor should pop in and have a look instead of running them down."

Megan had already lined up the next few callers "The next few will give Councillor Waters something to think about," she told Faith, as the traffic news ran. "First caller is Lee, she's a single mum"

As the song finished Faith said, "We have Lee on the line, what's your story Lee?"

"I just wanted to say I think it's a great thing the church are doing. We need a bit of Christmas joy, all of us."

"You have a story connected to the church don't you, Lee?"

Lee went on to say that she had moved into the area with her small children to escape an abusive marriage. She had taken the youngest to the church toddler group and immediately been welcomed, accepted and supported. "They have a food bank, a clothes bank, and nothing is too much trouble. It makes me so angry when the Councillor says they are not being fair." She had a catch in her voice. "I don't know where I would be without them. And I am not privileged! They treat everyone the same, without judging."

Faith asked Mayor Harvey to comment. "That's Applebury all over," was all he said.

Councillor Waters, asked to comment, insisted that, "With all due respect, Lee was only one caller and there were plenty more in need, young and old who…"

Faith interrupted him to take a call from an elderly gent who said he went to the church every week for CAMEO Club. "It stands for 'Come And Meet Each Other,'" he explained. "I'm on my own you see, since my wife passed away. I was getting so lonely," he paused and coughed away a tear. "Now I've got all my friends at CAMEO. Mark picks me up and drops me off and even gets my shopping, if I'm stuck. I feel part of a family again."

Councillor Waters, seeing an opportunity, began to pontificate on the plight of the elderly and isolated in rural England. Guy Harvey stopped his discourse with a loud guffaw. "Get off your high horse, mate, for goodness sake!" He laughed, "It's just a bit of fun, a bit of Christmas cheer!"

The next caller was the rather indignant proprietor of 'All Dolled Up,' the only hair and beauty salon in Applebury. Her teenage children had been attending after school clubs at Applebury Church from the age of four. "My kids love going there," she said, "and so do all their friends, so I don't know what the Councillor's on about."

Faith went to close the conversation, but 'All Dolled Up' was not ready to finish. "Just one more thing," she said, "I was touched by the last caller's story. Several of my most loyal customers go to CAMEO Club and they love it. 'All Dolled Up' would like to pay for a tree if the CAMEO Club would be kind enough to decorate it for us."

Her next caller, the Registered Manager of Ashleigh House Nursing Home, called in to add further praise of the Christmas Tree Festival. She said her residents were looking forward to the festival, especially the talent show, and would be decorating a tree for the competition. Her call was immediately followed by a call from Dunstan's Mobility, saying they would like to pay for the tree. There followed a wave of calls from businesses willing to sponsor a Christmas tree for the scouts, the British Legion, the dog rescue, and other voluntary groups.

Within the final half hour of the show, Councillor Waters had been soundly told off by almost every caller, and Taylor's Country Gardens had a list of orders from local traders, some to enter their own trees and some sponsoring trees for a chosen cause.

Faith rounded up the show. "It seems the season of goodwill is well and truly underway in the town of Applebury," she announced. "If you have a 'Love@Christmas' tale, we'd love to hear it." The news jingle began to play as she signed off.

Faith felt exhilarated. It seemed that the town of Applebury, with its scruffy little church and its Christmas Tree Festival, had grabbed the heart of her listeners. Maybe this was not such a bad storyline after all, all kicked off by the determination of Mayor Guy Harvey and his passion for Applebury. She asked Megan to arrange a meeting with him, today if possible, and was invited to attend that very afternoon at Edward Henry Court, a smart group of retirement apartments, just off the main street of Applebury. An unexpected venue, but then, so far nothing about this new journalistic venture had been predictable. She was to be there no later than half past four, Mr Harvey had insisted.

Chapter Six

It was late afternoon at Taylor's Country Gardens, and Adam needed a break. After carrying and stacking 10kg bags of seeds and peanuts in the wildlife department, refilling the shelves with suet balls, mealy worms, and all the delicacies needed to get the British bird through winter, he had gone to the office to re-order supplies. The message light on the phone was blinking furiously. Fifteen missed calls. All Christmas tree orders. He took the details and leaving the answer machine on, walked down to the green house, looking for Danny.

He saw with satisfaction, the two rows of tables, with the old stock displayed to advantage in neatly stacked bread trays. Cleaned and sorted, it looked so much more appealing. Danny had evidently found some *Clearance* signs which he had strategically placed, and each item was priced at £1. "Excellent!" he muttered, as he headed for the café, to find Pat clearing away some late cream teas. She saw him and returned to the counter, where she began making his favourite latte with a shot of hazelnut.

"Did you hear the radio show?" she asked. "Blooming cheek, saying she thought we were closed! Still, I reckon we got at least eight orders out of that show!" Adam looked as if he were in shock. "Sit down," she said, as she passed him his drink. "You're looking a bit shaky."

Adam lowered himself slowly onto a chair nearest the counter. "I've had orders for fifteen trees so far, and the phone keeps ringing. I've left the answering machine on."

Pat leaned back, pleasantly surprised. "And they aren't even coming in for a week," she said. "Well it's a good problem to have, I suppose."

Adam took a sip of the delicious coffee, giving himself a moment to think of other things. "Danny's done a good job on the greenhouse," he said. "Where is he?"

Pat bobbed her head in the direction of the window. "He's helping Jim outside at the moment."

Adam took his coffee and, standing at the big picture window, he saw Jim, with Danny beside him, tending the rose border. Jim lightly held the branch of a leggy bush rose in one hand while miming wind rock with the other. He indicated the area above the nascent bud and then, to Adam's great surprise, watched with approval as Danny carefully snipped off the unwanted growth using Jim's secateurs. Adam turned to Pat, eyes wide in astonishment.

"I know," she said, "I couldn't believe it, either."

Adam smiled. "I didn't really want to take Danny on," he said guiltily, "even for two weeks, and he's already proving me wrong."

"Me too," agreed Pat.

Adam watched as the two finished their work and began to walk back towards him. "If things pick up here because of the Christmas Tree Festival, we might be able to offer him a job, you never know," Adam mused. "He and Jim seem to have hit it off, anyway."

"Talk of the devil," said Pat, as the two rose pruners appeared. Jim waved a greeting. "Come on, you two," Pat said, thumping a tray piled with leftovers down on the table beside Adam. "I've got some bits and pieces here that won't keep until tomorrow. Sit down and we'll have a cup of tea before we close the place up."

"You've done a great job in the greenhouse, Danny," said Adam. "I'm impressed."

Eyeing up the thick slices of cake, savoury pies and sausage rolls, Danny sat down immediately. Jim put his hand on Danny's shoulder, looking at Adam. "This lad's a find. You want to hang on to him, he's quick to learn and don't mind hard work." Jim took his seat, picked up his steaming mug of tea and tapped the edge of Danny's mug. "Cheers," he said, "well done, Danny."

Adam caught them all up on the rush of Christmas Tree orders, warning them that things might get busy. "Let's hope they do," said Pat, "it's been pretty dreadful so far this year." She picked up the remains of the feast on the table, wrapping them tightly in a brown paper bag. "Here you are Danny," she said, "can you take these off my hands?"

"You'll need more than a paper bag," Jim said, "it's pouring out there." Pat snatched up a plastic carrier from behind the counter and handed it to Danny with an impatient glare at Jim.

"Can I drop you home, Danny?" asked Adam, looking at the skinny lad with his lightweight jacket. "I've got to drive past your estate to get home, so it's on my way." Danny hesitated, torn between the need to maintain his privacy and the need to get home without getting soaked.

"Go on you two," Pat interjected, settling the matter. "If you get going, me and Jim can lock up." She watched as they left, Danny waving a final goodbye with his bag of goodies, by way of thanks.

"Bless the boy!" she said with a smile. "Looks like his first day has been a real success"

Jim gave her a concerned look. "Are you getting soft in your old age?" he asked.

"Speak for yourself, Jim Hargreaves," she retorted, flicking him with the tea towel. "And less of the old, thank you *very* much!"

****

As Adam and Danny left Taylor's, Faith was walking into the reception area of Edward Henry Court. A lady wearing a lanyard and badge labelled 'Mrs Lori Hazell – Manager' came to the desk. She explained the retirement development of thirty or so flats, maisonettes and bungalows, all centred on this shared hub. In the distance, Faith could hear a round of light applause followed by a piano playing and, by the sounds of it, the tenants singing along.

"It's Monday Melodies today, as you can tell. Do come in." Mrs Hazell smiled. "We are so pleased to have you visit us." She led Faith to a comfortably laid out seating area. Indeed, this shared space looked a great deal like a luxury hotel.

"Mr Harvey said he would meet me here," Faith said, looking at her watch.

"Oh, he's running a bit late, but he should be along soon," Mrs Hazell explained, with a meaningful smile. "Maybe I can help until he is ready?"

"I wanted to get a sense of the community here in Applebury," Faith began. "To be honest, I was quite surprised at the response to our piece on the festival. There seems to be a real feeling of…." she struggled for words, "loyalty, or maybe kinship?"

"Spot on," Mrs Hazell said, "we're just a small town, not quaint enough to be a village, but not big enough to have our own railway station or cinema." She described the bare bones of the town. "There are a couple of pubs, one spit and sawdust, one gastro; one doctor, one vet, lots of indie shops amongst the chains, and the usual supermarket, travel agent, and three charity shops."

Faith smiled at what seemed a very accurate description of many small towns edging the English countryside. They spoke about Edward Henry Court and the residents' contribution to the Christmas Tree Festival. Applebury Community Church, it seemed, meant far more to Edward Henry Court than the expected funerals and monthly 'in-house' church service. Far from ticking the 'elderly duties' box, then moving on, Pastor Mark and his wife Debbie valued the skills of the older people in the community, and encouraged them to contribute. Thus, it was that many premature babies left the county hospital in tiny hats and cardigans from 'Knit and Natter,' many a newly-widowed person found sympathy at the CAMEO club, and the church youth groups were never short of volunteers.

"It's a happy place, this," said Mrs Hazell. Faith listened and took notes as Mrs Hazell listed proudly the accomplishments of each of her 'ladies and gentlemen' as she called them.

She enthused on the Edward Henry Court entry to the Christmas Tree Festival, which would be hung with crochet angels, and, instead of tinsel, mini bunting. Edward Henry Court were teaming up with the church's CAMEO club to create the bunting, each triangle would have the name of a favourite song and its special meaning. A distant burst of applause and laughter was hard to ignore as Faith admired the first of many bunting triangles passed to her. Carefully handwritten, beneath the silhouette of a jiving couple, were the words "Rock Around the Clock, Peter and Gloria, our first dance," then a gold triangle saying, "Be My Love, Allan and Mary, 1950." Faith admired several more, depicting melodies from the Forties to the present day. Her compliments were drowned in a further, louder, burst of applause and even some cheering.

Snatching the pile of pre-bunting triangles from Faith's lap, Mrs Hazell jumped to her feet. "You'll want to hear this," she said. "Come and meet Mr Guy Harvey."

Faith, puzzled, neatly slipped her iPad into her leather carry-case, and followed Mrs Hazell down the corridor to the 'community lounge,' as the big, unexpectedly cosy room was called. Faith stopped short as she entered the room, to see four men in knitted fair isle tank tops over striped shirts, singing 'Bye, Bye, Love' in perfect harmony, to the delight of the audience. As they segued smoothly into 'Elvira,' the bass singer, a striking man with a look reminiscent of a Fifties crooner, caught her eye and nodded a smile in her direction.

Faith looked at Mrs Hazell in amazement. "That's…?"

"Guy Harvey, yes!" she confirmed, with an expressive smile. "Not what you expected?"

"I had a jovial, rotund old chap in mechanics overalls in mind," she giggled.

They turned to watch the singers, not one of them rotund or elderly. The group continued with a further selection of mid-20th century hits. After about an hour, the lead singer stepped forward. "Our final song, in honour of our guest," he announced, "a little bit of Queen!" Everyone turned to look at Faith as, inevitably, the band sang the first few lines of 'Radio Gaga.' Faith realised that her visions of old dears singing wartime refrains were off, way off, when the chorus began, and almost the entire room thrust their arms in the air. After several encores and a standing ovation, supported by walkers and walking sticks, 'The Four Pops' left the makeshift stage and joined Faith at a table at the back of the room.

Guy introduced himself, then his brother, uncle, and son, who all left soon afterwards, leaving Guy to his 'paparazzi moment.' He was describing his role of mayor and suggesting some possible journalistic angles, when a rather glamorous, though frail-looking fan approached, and tapped Guy on the shoulder. Guy immediately put his arm round the lady, "Sis!" he cried, hugging her close. "Have a seat. This is the famous Faith New," he said, "and this is my mother."

Guy's mother seated herself in the chair beside Faith, as her son began to launch into his hopes for the 'Applebury's Got Talent' competition, dominating the conversation and quite overwhelming Faith with his familiar enthusiasm. The older lady, noticing Faith's predicament, began to stand, leaning heavily and rather theatrically on her walking stick. Guy immediately stood, "Hey, back in your seat, Sis," he said. "What do you need that I can't get for you?"

"Guy, dear, would you get me a cup of tea," she asked, "I'm so parched after all that singing." Guy set off and immediately his mother leaned over confidentially towards Faith. "He was always very passionate about his music," she said.

"So he wasn't always a mechanic and businessman, then?"

"Oh yes, dear, of course he's always been a mechanic," she said, with an air of offence. "It's the family business." As if Faith had somehow missed the point, she clarified, "There's been a Harvey's Motors in Applebury since 1923, when my own Grandfather set it up!"

"But Guy..?" ventured Faith.

"Guy and the boys have always liked to sing when they work, and they did a few very successful gigs for a few years, but…" Faith was hoping for a newsworthy tale of family conflict or corruption, but the old lady froze into silence the minute her son reappeared.

"They're really very good," Faith remarked. "I mean *very* good. I imagine they will win the talent contest hands down."

"Oh, it's not a competition," said Guy, as he unloaded three mugs of tea from his tray, followed by a plate of French fancies to share, which he alone proceeded to devour. "It's just a chance to show off," he laughed. "There's a lot of talent in Applebury. You'd be surprised, eh, Sis?" he said, looking at his mother.

"'Sis,' is that short for Cicely?" asked Faith, politely. With no answer except a sudden silence, Faith felt she had put her foot in it somehow, but was not sure exactly what she had stepped in. "I'm sorry," she said, "maybe I shouldn't have asked."

"Oh no, dear," said Sis, "My name is Maria, Maria Goode. You see, Guy calls me Sis because that's what I was for the first twenty-odd years of his life."

Guy took up the story. "I needed my birth certificate to get a passport. My Mum and Dad kept saying they had lost it, so I said I would just apply for a copy. That's when they sat me down and said my sister here was really my Mum." Guy's tone was cheerful, light hearted even.

Faith, internally, sank into a deep, deep well. *My sister was really my Mum!* It would have been that simple. It was only a second or two, but Maria saw it.

As Guy opened his mouth to embellish the story further, his mother-sister cut across him. "It was a long time ago, water under the bridge," she said, waving the topic away with a jewel covered hand, an indication that the topic was closed. Beneath the table, she put her hand on Faith's clenched fist. Looking into her eyes, she said "Those were different times. We all did what we hoped was best for everyone." Faith nodded as Maria continued, "It is an interesting story, if you would like to hear it one day, just pop in and see me."

Faith faked her way through the next twenty minutes, then, her professional mask intact, made her escape. She cried all the way home.

****

For the first time in a very long time, Danny went home smiling. With a paper bag stuffed with scones and butter pats in foil packs, Danny pushed the door open. He could smell toast cooking and something crackled in the frying pan. His dad leaned out of the kitchen door to welcome him. "Alright son," he smiled, "tea's nearly ready."

They never discussed Dad's 'moments.' Danny and Kit had a silent agreement that what happened yesterday was gone. Today was a new day, and Kit seemed like his Dad again, for now.

"How was college," Kit said, "been baking?"

"I was at work experience, Dad, remember?"

Kit nodded, although of course he had no idea where Danny had been that day, or the preceding four days which had been a blur of booze and misery.

Danny plumped the fat scones on the table with the butter. "Lady in the café gave me these, we can have them for pudding."

His dad smiled. "And how was it, your first day, then?" Danny told him enthusiastically about the garden, old Jim, and the work he had done. "Good man," his father said. "Proud of you. Now come on, grab the plates, I made your favourite." Sure enough, Kit scraped two fried eggs, and thick slices of fried corned beef onto the plate. The microwave pinged and Kit poured a generous helping of baked beans on the toast. The two of them sat at the kitchen table, chatting, rebuilding.

Later that night, Danny slid the key to the scullery into the 'treasure' box he had kept on his bookshelf since childhood. These days it contained mostly a few photos of his mother, the gold cross and chain she had left behind when she went, and a photo of the three of them together before she left.

Chapter Seven

On Tuesday morning, Faith was at her desk early again. The phone-in had caught the imagination of every town across the region it seemed, and she had Guy Harvey to thank for that. She opened her computer whilst looking at the emails on her iPad.

There was a light tap on the door and Hope walked in. Faith was surprised, but not displeased to see the woman's smiling face.

"I just wanted to thank you," she said. "My in-laws own the Garden Centre, and you interviewed my husband, Adam."

"I did," said Faith, mentally putting the nervous young man of Friday afternoon with this feisty young woman. The only thing they had in common, she felt, was their look of total exhaustion and determination.

"We've had fifteen tree orders, just yesterday alone! Thank you!"

"I'm glad it's helped," said Faith. "I'd like to know more about the garden centre and the church. Maybe you can help, if you've time?"

Hope looked at the clock. "I'm really sorry," she said, "time is always tight in the morning, but you should pop in to Taylor's again. We've made a few alterations since you last came in."

"I may well do that," said Faith.

Hope smiled and left. She had promised the morning to Agnes who needed to go into town, and the afternoon to the garden centre, which meant she had about 30 minutes after the school drop-off to put some washing in at home. At some point, she should ring

Adam and let him know there may be an unscheduled visit from the radio journalist who had inspired the big makeover at Taylor's Country Gardens.

Had Pat realised this was the case she may have been considerably less joyful as she arrived to open up the Garden Centre. The day was gorgeously sunny. Hanging baskets and tubs filled with bright cyclamen edged the smartly swept entrance. The place looked welcoming, so much more like its old self. Danny was at the front of the garden Centre, a pile of newly pulled weeds at his feet as he wiped the rather weather-worn 'Taylor's Country Gardens' sign with his sleeve.

"You'll ruin your coat, young man," she called, taking a box full of her homemade cakes from the back of the car.

He turned and saw her. "Just tidying up," he said.

"It makes a huge difference," Pat smiled, passing him the box of baked goodies. "Here, take this while I open up. You can come back and finish that later."

Once in the café, Pat got a good look at Danny, the bottom of his sleeves and the front of his coat looked wet. "Did it rain before I arrived?" she asked, perplexed.

Self-consciously, Danny told her he had washed the sign off using the outside hose and given himself a soaking in the process. Removing the coat, Pat saw he was wearing yesterday's shirt, newly washed and ironed but no jumper.

He saw her looking. "I've only got hoodies," he said, "I didn't think they would be suitable for work. So this is my Dad's shirt."

"That's kind of your Dad." Pat said.

"Yeah, well, he doesn't know, but he never wears it, so…"

"I've had a thought," said Pat. "When we *had* staff, we had a staff uniform of sorts. I'm pretty sure we've got some stashed away somewhere."

Adam walked in as she was speaking and remembered that there used to be a time when all staff wore the red shirt with the cream and gold Taylor's Country Gardens logo. "But that's all gone west now," he laughed, "I've no idea where they are, or why anyone would want to wear them."

Pat looked deflated, and slightly annoyed at Adam who had never been good at reading the unspoken agenda in any situation. Unseen by Danny, she rolled her eyes expressively in his direction. Adam, none the wiser, looked Danny up and down.

Unexpectedly, Danny offered his own view of staff uniform. "Corporate identity," said Danny. They both looked at him in confused admiration. "We did it at college," he continued, "customers know who works at the place, and staff feel proud to be part of the company." Adam raised his eyebrows. Danny went on, "Like a nurse or a postman, or if you go into a McDonalds, you know straight away who works there."

Adam saw the boy's wet coat and finally caught on. "That's a good point. Maybe we should revive the Taylor's staff uniform. I think there might be a box of them in the office, under the table. I'll have a look." He strode off. "I'll be right back!" And sure enough, by the time Pat had made two coffees and a tea, Adam was back with a dusty box clutched to his chest. Inside were assorted polo shirts, some still in their cellophane wrapping and a couple of long-sleeved fleece jackets, which had obviously been washed and returned by departing staff.

"Do you know, I think I've still got my uniform somewhere," Adam mused. "Maybe I should dig it out."

"It would make sense," advised Danny authoritatively, "because we are going to get very busy up to Christmas."

"I admire your optimism," Adam chuckled, "help yourself to whatever fits."

Danny's warning turned out to be more accurate and more immediate than anyone had expected. Yesterday's short piece on Radio C2C had piqued the interest of former customers, who 'came to see the old place' as several of them said. To Adam's disappointment, a fair few visitors, whilst chatting at the till, had said they thought Taylor's had closed. Calls continued to come in from local organisations wanting to sponsor a tree, having realised that this was an opportunity for advertising as much as anything. So much so, that Adam had to ask Danny to sit in the office and take orders, while Adam manned the till.

At Applebury Church, Mark was having the same interesting 'problem,' taking requests for entry in to the festival, with the hallooing and crying of babies and toddlers and the buzz of the 'Who Let the Dads Out' group in the background. Debbie joined him in the office, bringing a mid-morning cuppa.

"It's wonderful," he said, "but," he held up his notebook, "we've got twenty-three entrants so far, and it's still November."

Hope was giving the same news to Brian as they both looked out across the lawn to a little robin, singing his heart out on a branch of the apple tree.

"Robins always make me think of Christmas," he said.

"Let's hope this Festival helps transform things for us all." Hope told him the tale of Danny's creative canary transformation. His face clouded over, reminded of yet another of his unwise buying decisions. "It will take more than a few novelty flower pots to dig us out of debt," he scowled.

It took all of Hope's compassion and self-possession to rein in the 'and who's fault is that' remark, that jumped to her lips. It was a source of constant bitterness to her, that Brian's pride and insistence on doing things his way had resulted in the collapse of both his business and his health, leaving the rest of the family to pick up the pieces. Much as her head knew that Brian was a good man who had made foolish decisions, her heart resented the time and energy devoted by them all to save the business and keep Brian from seeing the cost to the rest of them.

"This Christmas is off to a very good start," she said, going on to explain about Faith's programme and the impact it was having on sales. What Hope did not understand was that Brian, looking at her lovely, tired, and determinedly optimistic face, knew very well that his son and daughter-in-law were bearing the brunt of his downfall.

He took her hand. "I'm so sorry, love, and I'm very grateful to you all."

Hope was taken aback at the expression of raw misery in his eyes. She looked away, sorry for her own thoughts. "It's alright, Dad," she whispered, looking back at him. "It's alright."

Agnes swept noisily into the kitchen. "I'm back!" she called.

"Right on time!" smiled Brian, through his tear-filled eyes. He squeezed Hope's hand. She smiled back.

"I've brought some tea-cakes. Hope, can you stop for a quick bite?"

"I would love to," said Hope. "I'm at the Garden Centre this afternoon."

"It's that busy?" asked Brian, brightening up.

"Only Adam on the tills so we've had to put the work experience boy into the office to man the phones, and its only his second day. I said I'd get there asap."

"Can't Pat do it?" asked Agnes.

"Not easily. The café is quite busy anyway, and we are thinking it will get busier after the radio show."

"What about the weekend?"

"I'll be there all day, both days, I suppose," Hope forced a smile.

"There is an alternative," Agnes suggested. "We always used to have Saturday girls and boys, as you know!"

Hope laughed, remembering how she had taken a Saturday job and ended up marrying the boss' son. "I would, but all the interviewing will take a while, and we need someone now," she sighed.

"Would Rosa do it?" asked Agnes "We know she is sensible and she knows her way around the store. It will give you time to look for someone more permanent."

Brian, with a sad smile, said, "Then you can be at home one day at least!"

Hope finished off her tea-cake and got ready to leave. She kissed both her in-laws on the tops of their heads. "That's certainly worth thinking about," she said, "I'll ask her." She put her coat on and grabbed her bag. "If you put C2C on now, you might catch a bit about the festival at the end of the Faith New show," she said. "See you Thursday!"

Agnes tuned in to hear Pastor Mark's familiar voice, "…We've already had to recruit another volunteer just to take bookings," he enthused. "We are looking at how to organise things on a much bigger scale for the trees, and of course for 'Applebury's Got Talent,' on Saturday night."

"Debbie, my researchers tell me that you will now be charging for tickets to the talent show, and for entry to the Christmas tree competition," Faith said. "Some may say you are cashing in on its unexpected success."

"That's most definitely true," agreed Debbie, to Faith's surprise. "We think a tin a ticket is a good way to help out the food bank. With the trees as well, we could get a hundred tins or more – it's so exciting!"

Mark took up the story. They had planned that Applebury shops would display their trees in windows all along the high street, but now many other parts of town had developed the festival theme. The dance school, whose theme was inevitably the Nutcracker, in addition to their tree for the church festival, would be decorating the big pine tree growing outside their studio, and Mark also had it on good authority that the British Legion, the doctor's surgery, and the supermarket would all be doing the same.

Faith talked of the lovely people she met at Edward Henry Court, and the story of their tree decorations. Listeners called in with their own stories, and one said that their whole street, which was naturally lined with trees, would be lit up. Offices and factories across Applebury called in, and soon listeners from across the county were calling to talk about their 'Love@Christmas' plans.

Calls were beginning to become a bit 'samey,' when Faith caught Megan and the production team looking through the glass and laughing, as they put the next caller through. She looked at them suspiciously, "Our next caller is…? There was no prompt on the monitor in front of her.

"It's Guy Harvey here," boomed the now familiar voice. "I'm at work," he said, "working on Tom Dean's van, best butcher in Applebury I might add, but wanted to remind you about 'Applebury's Got Talent' on the last Saturday before Christmas, at Applebury Church. There will be free mince pies and hot chocolate in the interval!"

"Oh yes, thank you, Mr Harvey, and I'm sure Tom Dean is very grateful for your mention! And can you give us an example of the kind of talent that will be there?" She shook a playful fist at the still giggling Megan, already feeling the show slipping out of control. "If Mr Harvey's quartet is any example of the standard, it will certainly be a show worth seeing."

"And hearing," added Guy. "Well, as it happens, we've hit a quiet spot so…" He made a theatrical pretence of calling his team from their labours, "Oy! Eddie, Andy, Dave, come on and get yer groove on!" With much clanging of spanners and heaving of sighs, the group gathered for an impromptu performance. Faith was well aware that she had been set up, as the hearty tones of The Four Pops swelled in a beautiful chorus of 'Pretty Woman.' The phones, texts and emails went wild, firstly in praise of The Four Pops, then with announcements of other acts featuring in the talent show. Faith closed the show with The Four Pops singing, "It's beginning to look a lot like Christmas!"

Hope, at Taylor's Country Gardens, hummed along with them as she worked at the cash desk. The place was most definitely busier, meaning that for the first time in a long time both cash desks were open. With Adam at one and Hope at the other, they rang up several sales during the unexpected afternoon rush. Adam was efficient, but not overly comfortable with the repetitive chit-chat required. He marvelled at Hope's ability to respond to each "nice weather for ducks," or "soon be Christmas," as if it was her first time of hearing. Hope had an easy assurance about her and was more often than not able to tempt her customers into an extra purchase at the till. Hope offered to stay on the cash desk to deal with the last few customers, which gave Adam the opportunity to get back to managing the accounts, ordering extra trees, and answering the phone to all the orders that were coming in.

Later, when it got quieter, Hope proposed the idea of Rosa working on Saturdays. "Actually, it was your Mum and Dad's suggestion," she continued, "what do you think?"

I think it's a brilliant idea," he said. "I'm all for it. Let's hope Rosa feels the same!"

****

"Another successful show, Faith," exclaimed Miles, as they shared a 'catch-up' coffee. "We're getting a lot of response to the phone-ins, and listening figures are up." He passed her a print-out of the listening figures and online activity. Faith smiled, sceptically. "What's up, Faith, not happy?"

The number of calls to the show during the Christmas Tree Festival segment were double those of the earlier topics. The feel-good sense of community had charmed her listeners. This Christmas season, Faith had dug into a rich seam of goodwill, comfort and joy. The story was almost writing itself with characters at once new yet familiar, to each of her radio audience. Yet her journalistic gut told her there was a far deeper, richer treasure beneath all this Yuletide glitter.

"Oh, I'm happy it's going over well," she said, "but I feel there's another story somewhere that I haven't found. As if I'm missing the point, somehow. It's all a bit shallow, a bit too 'wholesome.'"

"Faith, I'm sure if anyone can find depth, discord, or doom, in a story about a Christmas tree festival in a little English town, I'm sure you can!"

"You make me sound so cynical," answered Faith, "I just want to find the story behind the story. It doesn't have to be sad, or bad, but it needs to have substance."

"Well, go ahead, but do not entirely extinguish the spirit of Christmas from Applebury's 'Love@Christmas' Festival," he begged, "please!"

The spirit of Christmas. The phrase stayed with Faith all the way home. *The spirit of Christmas*, she thought, *what is that?* Once home, she researched the 'spirit of Christmas,' but mostly it came up with commercialised spins on giving, which essentially meant buying expensive gifts. Christmas cheer was mostly alcohol, and goodwill a once-yearly virtual-signalling by people who generally gave more help to animal charities than their fellow human beings. *Was* she missing the point? Remembering Miles' 'doom and gloom' remark, was she simply looking for depth where there was none?

Faith read back what she had written "Ye gods!" she exclaimed. "I *am* doom and gloom!" She bashed out an email to Pastor Mark, poured herself a large glass of wine, and flopped on the sofa while her 'meal for one' heated in the microwave.

The following morning, Wednesday, Faith went into the office even earlier than usual to review her interviews and notes of the last few days. She checked her emails – no response from Pastor Mark, but then, she had emailed rather late last night. She checked the show's social media pages, alive with comments on The Four Pops, and left a message for her assistant to contact Guy Harvey to invite them on the show for Thursday.

The door crashed open, making Faith start. It was Hope, cleaning tools in one hand and the vacuum cleaner hose in the other. "Oh! I'm so sorry," Hope said, with a tinge of irritation. She was on a schedule after all.

Faith smiled up at her. "This place is already ship shape," she said, "I wouldn't bother."

"I'll just give it a dust and empty the bin, then."

"How's the Garden Centre doing now?" Faith asked, "with this festival being so popular?"

"We've had so many orders for trees. Your show has really made people think about Christmas. 'Every tree tells a story,'" she air quoted the phrase. "That's something you might put in your show, the story behind the tree."

Faith gave a sardonic smile "Free advertising for local shops and businesses—they'd all be ringing in to complain I was giving publicity to their rivals."

"Oh no," Hope was quick to respond, appalled that Faith would think she was fishing for more publicity for Taylor's Country Gardens. "Not just the commercial ones. There's Edward Henry Court and then the nursing home, the donkey sanctuary out at

Applebury fields, they're doing one covered in donkeys. Then the schools, of course, and the farm museum are doing a Victorian tree."

Faith turned to note down those places on her PC. Hope, seeing Faith turn away, felt she had said quite enough. She took the bin and emptied its meagre contents into the half-full black sack she had left at the door.

"Thank you," said Faith, thinking that her investigation into the 'truth' behind all this festive cheer may as well start there. Taking that as a dismissal, Hope went to leave. "Hold on, er, Hope?" Faith checked she had remembered the name correctly, as Hope nodded, "If it's not the free advertising that is attracting people, what is it, do you think?"

Hope gave the idea a few moments thought. "I suppose the festival is just like the church, it's about people, real people. Just like this festival, 'Love@Christmas,' it brings out the best in everyone. I'm not a great one for radio, but I tune in every day now, and I hear a lot of the school mums talking about it."

Faith smiled, "But why is that?" she asked, "it's not glamorous, or scandalous, or escapist. Honestly, I'm glad Applebury's 'Love@Christmas' Festival is so successful, but I have no idea why!"

Hope laughed. "Well, don't tell anyone that!"

They both laughed. Hope was enjoying this; it was rare to have someone interested in her opinion. She took out her duster and began to wipe down the various surfaces. "I suppose Pastor Mark would say that Christmas is a time for giving *and* forgiving," she said. "Your program is helping people to remember that."

"Do you go to the church?" asked Faith, to Hope's surprise.

She hesitated, *better be honest*, she thought. "I used to go regularly when I was young, but I just don't have the time now," she confessed, "and Applebury Church is, in a roundabout way, the reason Adam and I met." Faith looked at her to continue her story. "When Dad retired, we moved here. The first thing my parents did was to find a church. They found Applebury Church, where they met Brian and Agnes who own Taylor's Country Gardens. It was a really busy place back then, I was nearly sixteen and didn't know anyone, so between them they decided a Saturday job would be a good idea for me. Adam was working there at weekends to help his Mum and Dad. We met; we fell in love. So, it turned out to be a *very* good idea indeed. We've been married seventeen years and have four children!"

"Your parents must be pleased," said Faith politely, since the area of marriage and children was always a bit dodgy for her. She waited for the inevitable 'how many children do *you* have.' However, Hope's next sentence was not what she expected.

"They *were* very pleased. They both passed away some years ago now."

"I'm sorry to hear that," said Faith, "they must have been young."

"No, they were in their forties when they adopted me. I'm just glad they got to see Rosa and Briony, but neither of them met the little ones, sadly." Hope sniffed away a tear. "I've got to get on." She flung her duster into the carry all, grabbed the bin bag, and flew out of the door with an awkward wave.

Faith sat paralysed in her chair. Could it be....?

She shook herself into reality. Hope, her thick mane of deepest black curly hair, athletic build and olive skin bore no resemblance whatsoever to the tiny blonde self, reflected in her blank computer screen.

Faith murmured, *Where ever you are, may you be happy, may you be loved, may you be safe, my Angel.*

****

Agnes and Brian were wrapping shoe boxes in Christmas paper, ready to be filled with gifts. Already active in the usual 'shoebox' scheme, bringing gifts to children in war zones far away, Applebury church had adopted the scheme for themselves. Christmas boxes went to anyone the church knew of who lived alone.

"Don't tire yourself out, love," worried Agnes.

"I've only just started," he said, irritated by her anxiety. "I'll stop if I feel tired."

"The doctor did say not to do too much, love," Agnes cautioned.

Brian set his face to concentrate on the job in hand, ignoring her.

She chatted a little about the church, the grandchildren, each sentence ending with little concerned comments. "Are you sure you are okay?" "Should you be stretching like that?" "Let me do that."

Brian was fit to bust as he expertly sliced, trimmed and taped the paper to each shoe box. Placing the last neatly covered box on the stack beside him, Brian stood and reached for a new roll of paper.

"Oh, do be careful!" exclaimed Agnes, gesturing to steady him.

"For goodness, sake," he hissed, "I think I can cut wrapping paper without dropping dead!"

The minute he said the words, he wished them back. Agnes went pale, looked into her lap at her folded hands, snatched back from that involuntary gesture of panic. He could see her using every muscle to contain her emotion.

"Agnes, it's time we talked about this. We can't go on pretending that everything is okay." Agnes looked up at him, her eyes brimming with tears. "I let you all down, I admit it," he said. "I don't blame you for being angry."

"Angry?" exclaimed Agnes. "Is that what you've been thinking? We're in this together, Brian, always have been. I am angry in some ways, but not at you, never at you." She collected her thoughts and considered whether to share them with her husband or not, then resolving that honesty is always the best policy. "I'm angry with myself for not doing more to help, for not seeing how hard you were working to get things back on track, for being so wrapped up in the family that I wasn't even there when you nearly *died*!" She shouted the last word and grabbed him tightly. "I can't do without you Brian, I can't!"

He wrapped his arms around her. "Agnes," he whispered, "I couldn't leave you; you know that."

Chapter Eight

Faith struggled to keep to the agenda as the station was overwhelmed with calls relating to the Applebury Festival. The show had opened with Faith promising a visit from The Four Pops in the last quarter of the show, which had been assigned to the Christmas Tree Festival.

Even when the item on the agenda was some national issue, or serious local concern, contributors would invariably finish off with a 'Can I just say,' 'I must just thank,' or 'A Merry Christmas to…' It seemed the news of Applebury Christmas Tree Festival and its message of love continued to sweep the county, indeed the whole of Middle England. Other villages and towns were calling in with the history of their own traditions and some had simply followed Applebury's lead and were holding their own 'Love@Christmas' event.

Halfway through the show, The Four Pops arrived, bringing jovial pandemonium to the studio. They had promised their Christmas Classics selection, which included such sacred tunes as 'Rockin' Around the Christmas Tree' and 'Let it Snow.' Guy's roguish banter threatened to take over the show. and Listeners were somewhat astonished to hear the normally detached, unflappable, and deadly serious Faith laugh as she tried – with little success – to steer the program through the hour of Four Pops mayhem. The show closed with a beautiful performance of 'White Christmas.'

The news and weather forecast gave Faith a few minutes to thank them, off air. Impulsively she asked Guy if he thought his mother would be up for a visit, to follow up her story. He was sure she would, he said, and then asked for her phone number so he could let her know. He smiled as he said it. Faith was in a hurry to get back as the weather jingle had just played, giving her less than a minute to get back to the microphone. The three other 'Pops' were smirking in the doorway as she quickly scribbled her personal number on the back of his business card, shook his hand once more and returned to her seat as the weather forecast finished.

Faith had planned to cover the serious topic of car parking charges during late night shopping on tomorrow's show. But things had taken an unexpected turn, and her instincts told her to carry on down that path. "I have it from a reliable source at Taylor's Country Gardens," she said, "that every tree tells a story. If you have a tree in the festival with a particular story behind it, we'd like to hear it. Give us a call tomorrow on…"

Within minutes, Megan, possibly the most efficient producer ever, had lined up the first three Christmas tree tales for the next day.

****

Thursday was Hope's day at Trevone Manor, assisting Casper, the events designer.

"Those brights look amazing in the cloakrooms, Hope," said Casper, "that's the sort of touch that makes all the difference."

This Thursday, the UK's leading modern design company (as it said in their brochure) had arranged a "traditional twist" Christmas weekend for their most important suppliers and clients. Casper's was the job Hope had trained and longed for. However, the closest she could get was her weekly assists in creating the perfect Christmas backdrop for successive customers' specific requirements. A job she loved.

Today they were removing all the red and gold 'vintage' ornaments from the natural holly, ivy and pine arrangements and replacing them with fuchsia pink, electric blue and acid yellow dyed, eco-friendly, hemp baubles.

Hope smiled at Casper. "'Christmas trad' to 'Christmas trendy' in one crazy afternoon," she joked. They stood back and surveyed their work. "It looks fabulous, Casper." She pointed at the tree, decked only in tiny pink, yellow and blue lights. "And that really is stunning!"

She folded the lid on the box of last week's festive decorations. "I'll put these in the store room," she said.

"Actually," Casper said, "they might as well go in the attic, we've got red white and blue after this, then rainbows and ribbons, then winter whites all over Christmas. We won't be using those again this year, if ever, since every year we buy new."

Hope and the two assistants trudged up the narrow stairs to the enormous attic at least one third full of boxes. Festoons, wreaths and swags of garlands hung over the beamed rafters in every shade of Christmas. She recognised elements of the woodland Christmas she had brought Rosa and Briony to see when they were just toddlers. Festive deer, owls, angels, and snowmen jostled for space amongst the many Yulctide figures stacked and standing higgledy-piggledy on every available flat surface. An idea was brewing in her head as she joined Casper in the now-transformed ballroom.

"The attic is stuffed full of redundant Christmas decorations," she said. "Do you think the owners would sell any? They would look great at Taylor's."

"I doubt the owners know or care about their old decs. It's a shame, really," Caspar replied, "but there it sits, ten years or more of Christmas past, gathering dust!"

"How much would you charge to take it off your hands? I would like to use it at the garden centre, if you want it gone…" she said, hopefully.

"I'd have to ask," said Caspar, doubtfully. Then, seeing Hope's disappointment, "Of course, it's a terrible fire risk…"

Hope smiled her agreement. "Dreadful," she said, "all those old plastic models and paper garlands…"

"Not to mention all those straw animals and light-up snowmen. You'd almost be doing Trevone Manor a favour," Caspar declared, "if only they knew it!"

Hope did a little dance of joy. "Thanks Caspar," she said, joyfully.

"You've got to take the lot, mind, no picking through and leaving me with the junk."

"I get it, all or nothing. I'll call Adam and we'll collect it today."

She rang Adam, who arrived with his van. Several trips later, the last ten or more years of Trevone's Christmas decorations were piled in one of Taylor's store rooms, which led off the café and opened on to the 'new' industrial greenhouse, which his parents had added to the main building in the early Eighties.

Faith drove to pick the children up from school, the back of the old Zafira still stacked with the last few bits of Trevone's Christmas clear-out. She dropped

Callum and Briony off at home, saying that Callum would be bored at the centre...

"I won't be, Mum, I will be reeeeaaaaaally good," he promised.

"Look," said Hope. "I've just got to help Daddy and then I will be back."

"I'm taking Lily because you will fight if I leave you both here, plus Lily can amuse herself."

Callum looked at her. "I don't want to help Daddy, anyway, so goodbye." He stamped off to the house and was a thorough nuisance to the older girls for the rest of the evening.

At Taylor's, Hope settled Lily in the office with a DVD then her homework, then hurried to the store room at the end of the big greenhouse. Danny and Jim were busy pulling some big piece of equipment away from the wall. "What *are* you two doing?" she asked.

Jim appeared theatrically blowing cobwebs from his face. "This is all the old Christmas Grotto stuff, Hope. More like Christmas Grotty now, though..." he said swatting dusty polystyrene 'snow' from his jumper. "I haven't seen it in years. Danny remembers coming here, and he remembered a sleigh, so we had a look, and we've found it!"

Hope screamed with delight. "I remember being an elf!" she said, helping them pull at the sleigh, clearing away the boxes and detritus of Christmas past. Jim reached behind the sleigh and pushed open the double doors to the greenhouse behind, filling the store room with light.

"I wish we had Santa's Grotto here," said Danny, wistfully, then, remembering that he was seventeen and an adult, he swiftly added in a lower voice, "for the kids." Danny started to speak again, but Hope held her hand up to stop him.

"Just a minute," she said, "I have an idea." Her eyes sparkled. "We have a chance to Christmasify the whole place," she said, "it will be fabulous! And, like Danny says, we must start with Father Christmas." Hope continued, "Suppose we do to this greenhouse what we've done to the orangery, but make it into the North Pole – in other words, the 'gifts and toys' department?" She hurried into the store room and pushed open the double doors at the back. The others followed her as she hurried through the doors.

"So," she said, "we throw open both sets of doors and this," she indicated the store room, "becomes Santa's Workshop!"

"And it's right beside the café," said Jim, "so you can't miss it!"

"You walk through Santa's Workshop straight into the North pole!" Danny exclaimed, "it will be amazing!"

Jim looked at Danny's excited face. "I think we can do most of the hard work today. Then I'll come in tomorrow as well."

For the rest of the day, they set to work, clearing the place of the remnants of the bargain basement and, following Hope's instructions, creating a positively Whovillesque scenario in the greenhouse. Meanwhile, Hope inspected the contents of each of Trevone's boxes. Dividing Taylor's Country Gardens into zones, she had the relevant boxes moved into place ready for the next day. Snowmen, polar bears and penguins for the north pole; elves, gnomes and fairies for the garden section; a huge selection of light-up candy canes and gift boxes were to adorn the homes and hardware section; and, of course, the woodland animals for the wildlife area. The rest, an assortment of lights and sparkles and garlands were to form a festive backdrop throughout Taylor's. The store room looked much bigger once it was cleared. But the sleigh took up a lot of space.

"With this in here, there's no room for anything else," complained Hope.

"It looks so good though," Jim said, "now it's cleaned up."

Hope had to admit, the old red, green and gold sleigh looked very authentic.

"I have an idea," said Danny, "but it's probably rubbish..."

"Go on, Danny," encouraged Hope.

"Well, on the American movies they always have photos with Santa, but people have cameras on their phones nowadays. Could we put the sleigh in the café for photos? Free photos?

Jim caught the festive mood. "It will look like Father Christmas just parked his sleigh outside his workshop, ready for loading up after a bit of shopping at Taylor's."

"That's a brilliant idea," Hope said, "maybe we can find an old Taylor's sign and put it up behind the sleigh."

"I know!" shouted Danny, "I know! Hold on!" He ran off through the café, disappearing into the corridor behind. Jim and Hope looked at each other.

"Don't look at me," Jim said, "I'm as mystified as you are!"

Danny reappeared, carrying a pile of old framed photos and a box of rolled posters balanced on a huge, oval tray. "Look at this lot," Danny said, kneeling as he placed his load on the floor.

"Oh, my days," said Jim, unrolling an old, but pristine poster for 'Taylor's Country Gardens Christmas 1994.' Where ever did you find this lot?"

"They were in the scullery, or the skip," Danny replied. "They looked too important to me to throw away."

"They are," agreed Hope, "very important. Look at this, Jim," she said, passing him one of the framed photos. It was a large colour photo of Agnes and Brian at the opening of 'Taylors Country Gardens.' Agnes, smiling broadly, held the infant Adam in her arms. "And this, is this you, Jim?" The second was a photo of the full staff, with Agnes, Brian and Jim at the centre.

Danny looked over his shoulder and laughed. "What?" Jim asked, as though the sight of his shoulder-length mullet and thick moustache was unremarkable.

"Freddie Mercury," Danny said, "cool!"

Jim rolled his eyes and smiled. "I was going for Magnum P.I., actually."

They dusted off a succession of framed photos, from various important moments in the life of Taylor's. "These will look great in the café," said Hope, "along with the posters, if we frame them. Well done Danny, what a find!"

"And this might do for behind the sleigh," Danny said, standing the wooden oval on its edge. A few chips in the paint and years of dust only added to the charm of the original hand-painted sign that Danny held up for their approval.

"Taylor's Country Gardens" it read, in glorious red, cream and gold.

114

Hope couldn't help but hug the boy. "Perfect," she said. "Perfect!"

****

While Taylor's Country Gardens was undergoing its second Christmas transformation, Faith was paying a second visit to Applebury Church. During her first visit, Faith had been given a potted history of the place, and an impressive summary of the many helps and activities on offer. This time she was looking for the reason this modest Christmas event in an insignificant small town was causing such a stir.

"I think we are going to have to stop at 100 trees at the church," Mark said, equally excited at the turn events had taken, but not as mystified as to the cause. "It's Christmas!" he exclaimed. "You can feel it every year!" A cynical smile fixed itself to Faith's face.

"You don't believe?" Mark asked.

"I've never really enjoyed Christmas," Faith acknowledged to herself as much as to Mark and Debbie. "It's just a time when people eat too much, drink too much, and spend too much. It's all fake bonhomie and commercial greed."

"I can see that you would think that," said Debbie, "especially since your career has been spent in debunking pretence and revealing the truth."

Fake nodded agreement. "It doesn't take much research to discover that 'Christmas' is a marketing campaign, 'Santa' is really a Coca-Cola icon, and Jesus was born in April. I just can't abide deception," she said simply.

Debbie saw there was more to this than intellectual cynicism. "I have to agree with you," she said, to Mark's bewilderment. "It's the most profitable time of year for retailers, and we know many people here who go into dangerous debt to buy gifts they can't afford. It's a time when people who are lonely feel lonelier still, and people who are bereaved remember their loved ones with a deeper sense of loss.

Faith met her eyes. "How depressingly realistic," she said. "What happened to 'tidings of comfort and joy?'"

"I have that all year round, Christmas or not," said Debbie, "but I think you know that."

Faith smiled. "They do say it brings out the best in people," she observed.

"It does bring out the best in us all," said Mark, "people are thankful, more generous, more kind, more forgiving. I always say Christmas is…"

"A time for giving *and* forgiving," Faith finished his sentence, to his surprise. "One of your 'flock' told me you'd say that," Faith said.

"And they were right," said Mark.

As she drove out of the spacious carpark, Faith glanced in her rear-view mirror to see Mark and Debbie waving goodbye from the church door. She realised that she had enjoyed meeting the pair, in their ramshackle place of work and worship, which, the pastor confided, was held together with string, 'no more nails,' and prayer. She believed they were amongst the few 'believers' she had come across who genuinely tried to live out the faith they professed. Nevertheless, she could not extinguish the nagging sense that there was more to this story. Something lost and something hidden – and she was determined to find it.

Faith pulled into her drive and was just unlocking her door when her mobile rang. She was surprised to hear Guy Harvey on the phone, then remembered she had unwittingly given him her personal number. "Mother says you can visit her tomorrow if you want. Only get there before four pm, because that's when the entertainment starts."

Faith smiled, walking into her lounge and kneeling to light the wood burner. "Does that include The Four Pops?" She laughed.

"No laughing matter, young lady, it's a serious business entertaining that lot. They're a pretty hard crowd to please."

"Because they've heard it all before?"

"No, because they're mostly half deaf!" he laughed, "but no, the band are not playing this time. Twice in one week would be a touch excessive, too much of a good thing."

"You've got to leave your audience wanting more, so it is said," Faith joked, pulling a 'ready to eat' salad from the fridge.

"You're welcome to hang around afterwards if you like, unless you've had a better offer. They have the singalong, then a fish and chip supper."

She looked at the unappetising bowl of leaves in her hand. Fish and chips and a singalong was actually a very appealing prospect.

"I'll need to check my diary," she said, "but I will try to stay, for a few minutes at least."

Faith forbore to tell him that her Friday nights usually involved a microwave meal for one, a glass of wine, and a disaster movie.

****

On Friday morning, Hope, to her surprise, felt a dash of disappointment that Faith was not in her office. She had enjoyed her chat with the big 'star' who turned out to be quite ordinary after all. Hope cleaned the desk, looking forward to putting the finishing touches to 'Taylor's Country Christmas' once she had dropped the children at school. It was a shame Faith New had visited when she did, Hope thought to herself. Although it had been Faith's dreary pre-makeover impression of the place that had inspired the transformation, Hope wished that Faith could see Taylor's Country Gardens today, fairly bursting with holiday cheer.

As she lifted the keyboard to wipe underneath, she knocked a pad of yellow post-it notes to the floor. As she picked the pad up, returning to the desk, she had a daring thought. *Why not?* she told herself, and grabbing a pen she wrote a short note, which she stuck to the monitor.

Not long afterwards, at Taylor's Country Gardens, Pat opened up as usual, and Danny raced through each area, switching on lights and checking everything was in order. When Adam arrived, Danny was putting out the last of the outdoor stock and Pat had the first batch of scones baking.

Adam, eyes locked on his iPad, literally bumped into the sleigh. "What's that doing here?" he asked, rubbing his bruised knees.

"Adam, you need to take a look around you," said Pat. "Danny, Jim and Hope worked hard yesterday, really hard."

"We did indeed," said Jim, walking through the main doors with a trolley of potted firs and pines in different sizes. "Here Danny, give me a hand with these."

The two of them placed the trees around the sleigh, Danny closely mirroring Jim's layout on his side of the sleigh.

"What are *you* doing here, Jim?" Adam cried, doubly confused.

Jim shook his head. "I reckon you and your wife need to work on your communication," he replied tersely. "Come on, Dan, let's get Rudolph and the gang." The two headed for the big greenhouse. Jim turned to look back at Adam. "Well, are you coming or not?" Adam hurried after them, as Pat tutted with amusement.

They returned, Jim with a light-up snowman under each arm, Adam with a bale of fabric 'snow' under one arm, and a light-up birch tree under the other, and Danny with a near life-size model of a deer, proudly carried in both arms. By the time Hope arrived at Taylor's, the scene was set. Red-nosed Rudolph stood proudly on a snowy woodland, surrounded by sparkling ice-covered trees. The sleigh, dusted with frost, stood at the entrance to 'Santa's Workshop' ready to be loaded with all the toys Taylor's had to offer.

The four of them, Hope, Jim, Pat, and Adam, looked proudly at their newest department.

"Excuse me!" called an irritated voice behind them. "There's no one at the cash desk!"

Hope raced off to the till, apologising as she caught up with the owner of the unhappy voice.

"Look at all the customers!" Danny said.

Adam looked about him. People were already walking through the doors and admiring every newly ornamented department. Jim, looking at Adam, but nodding towards Danny, observed, "We're going to need more than one extra pair of hands tomorrow."

"I could come in, if you want me to," Danny said.

"I would be grateful if you would," said Adam, "we'll pay you."

"And for every Saturday up to Christmas," Pat added, "won't we, Adam?"

So, it was agreed. Danny was to be part of the new Saturday team, along with Rosa.

Jim agreed to come in Sunday. "Just for Christmas," he said, gruffly.

****

Faith saw the note on her screen as she walked through her office door, refillable coffee cup in hand.

Taylor's Country Gardens at Christmas is well worth another look, she read. A smiley face punctuated the sentence.

"Maybe I will," she said to herself.

Faith, inspired by Hope's suggestion, had invited studio guests that Friday to give the story of their own Festival tree.

Care4Canines dog rescue, whose tree would be a tribute to all the successful 'dogdoptions' over the years, was followed by the Applebury Arts Collective, raising funds for the RSPB with their tree full of felted robins. More 'tree-tales' followed, each one representing a history, a tribute, or a charity. Then, following the scheduled guests, there was a wave of callers wanting to tell of their connection with Applebury and the tale of their tree.

Many were still waiting to tell their own tale when the program ended and Faith, as she signed off, promised to continue with the subject next week. As planned, Faith headed for Edward Henry Court almost immediately after her programme ended, to keep her appointment with Marie. On impulse, she stopped off at a supermarket and picked up a 'Christmas Florals' bouquet, the leaves having been sprayed with some sort of glittery substance.

Maria was delighted with the gift, arranging the flowers in a crystal vase as she and Faith talked. "It's a lovely place you have here," Faith said. The tiny, open-plan flat, like Maria, settled on the tasteful side of gaudy. Bright colours, rich textures, her home was more like an artist's retreat than a retirement apartment.

"I am happy here." Maria responded. "After my husband passed away, I just couldn't settle in our home. Too many memories, everywhere I looked. I kept expecting him to walk through the door, and I would forget to lock the doors because that was always 'his job.' It just got too much for me," she said. Placing the vase on a little side table, Maria signalled to Faith to sit on the teal velvet armchair. "So, Guy and his brother found this place for me." She herself sat on the matching chair, opposite Faith's. "It's close to the family, full of my friends, and Lori is always here if there's an emergency. You can't keep calling people five or six times a day at work every time something goes wrong."

Faith suspected that she was speaking from experience and imagined Guy's patient exasperation. They chatted some more, Faith losing her sense of resolve, until Maria, passing her a cup of tea in a decent china cup, said, "Now that's not the real reason you are here, is it?"

Faith raised her eyebrows and smiled a 'you've got me' smile. "No." She took a deep breath. "*Here goes,*" she thought. "I was interested in your own story. You said that Guy thought he was your brother."

Maria hesitated, put down her pretty Derby tea cup on its matching saucer.

Faith saw she was struggling to begin. "I'm sorry," Faith said, 'I have upset you; I shouldn't have brought it up." As she said the words, Faith realised that every journalistic bone in her body would normally have given no regard to the feelings of her subject. She told herself to switch off the empathy and put her reporter's brain in gear.

Maria said quietly, "You haven't upset me, dear, not at all. Guy would say…"

Faith immediately realised that the 'child' in this story, albeit now a man in his fifties, was equally a part of this story. "Would he be annoyed that I am looking into this?"

Maria laughed out loud "Good heavens, no," she said. "Guy tells everyone about it. He says he's proud of me! Can you imagine that?"

Looking at this neat, sparkling little lady, Faith could well imagine her son's pride.

"You see," Maria continued, "it was no different back then to how it is now. Young people met and fell in love, or lust even, yes, even in the tight-laced Fifties and Sixties, and sometimes things went a bit further than they should have. The difference between then and now is the way unmarried girls were seen if they got into trouble."

"That's an old-fashioned expression," said Faith.

"It certainly is," said Maria, "but that's exactly what happened to me. It may sound a little naïve, but I hadn't actually realised that what John and I were doing could actually result in a baby! We were all taught that you had to be married to get 'in the family way,' so I didn't make the connection!"

Maria paused and offered a biscuit, which Faith waved away.

"Anyway, I was probably about half way through my pregnancy when I couldn't hide it anymore. My parents went mad, called me all the names under the sun. Then everything happened so fast, it was like I was in a horrible dream, watching myself. I had to go away, I was seventeen, you see, the oldest of five, and there was no way my little sisters and brother could know. It all had to be a secret..." Maria breathed in sharply, remembering the feelings of that time. "It was the shame, most of all," she said. "The way they looked at me, so disappointed and disgusted. I felt...forsaken."

Faith pretended to make notes, unsure if she could hold herself together.

Maria gave a scornful laugh. "Even so, I remember thinking what hypocrites they were. If me and John had been married, it would have been celebrations all round."

"He would have married you?" Faith asked.

"Without a doubt, but they wouldn't give permission. He was called up for National Service and they said he would never come back, once he'd finished, so it was decided I should go away to have the baby, then come back home as if nothing had happened, leaving the baby to be adopted."

"And yet you didn't, in the end. What happened?" asked Faith.

"It was a very 'hole in the wall' affair. I stayed in hiding at home for a few weeks, then my Mum came with me to the mother and baby home, I cried all the way there, saying I wanted to keep the baby."

Faith understood, really understood. She winced at her own memory.

"Are you alright, dear?" Maria asked, noticing.

"I'm fine," Faith smiled, "please go on."

"She left me there, but as she was leaving, there was a girl at the top of the stairs crying, they hurried her out but we could still hear her screaming and crying for her baby." Maria sat back in her chair; her eyes closed. "Where is my baby, where did you take my baby!" Maria clasped her hands to her stomach, opened her eyes and leaned towards Faith, her eyes filled with tears. "I've never heard a cry like that in my life since, and I hope I never do again. It was like a wounded animal."

She paused to wipe her eyes. Faith went to speak, to apologise, to stop the woman speaking at least, but Maria could not be stopped. "Anyway," she went on, "they showed me to my room and I had barely unpacked when my Mum came back for me. She just couldn't do it."

Faith smiled, Maria topped up her own tea cup and Faith's and continued. "Mum took me to stay with my auntie in the New Forest. I had Guy a few weeks later. When we went home, Mum and Dad just made out he was theirs. Our Stephen was only four at the time and mum was thirty-seven, so it wasn't impossible. In fact, she had Ruthie a year later." She laughed, "So Guy is older than his Auntie Ruth!"

Faith wanted to get back to the point, "So, what happened to John?" she asked.

"He came home from National Service, we got married and had two more sons."

"And Guy…?"

"Guy was nearly four years old when we got married and no one knew, or if they did, they pretended not to. So, it was better to leave things as they were."

"He was none the wiser, I suppose?" Faith suggested.

"He wasn't, bless him. I kept thinking he would realise, but he never did. We had to tell him in the end, he was nearly twenty-one!"

"How did he react when he found out?"

"He was shocked, of course, to find out, at that age, that I was his Mum and not his sister, but he understood."

Maria mistook Faith's silence for disagreement; she tried to explain further: "You have to realise that even in the enlightened 1980's, in a small town like this, to be an unmarried mother was still a disgrace. So, Guy understood completely why we did what we did."

"I *do* realise that," Faith said quietly. Maria looked closely at her, but let the moment slip by.

"So," Faith asked, "Guy sees you as his sister or his Mum?"

"There was always a much closer bond to Guy than to my brothers and sisters. I nursed him from the minute he came home, you see, that creates a bond."

"It's a beautiful story," Faith said. Maria's hands flew to her face in horror. Faith suddenly realised the implication of her words. "Oh no! I didn't mean…I won't be sharing your story," she said.

Maria looked through her fingers, "You won't?"

"No," Faith reassured Maria. "It's just research into a topic that may or may not come to something."
The chorus of 'Country Roads' carried up the stairs from the shared lounge below.

"Come on, dear" said Maria, almost snatching away Faith's tea cup. "They've started!"

Downstairs, a banjo and accordion duo singing in close harmony led the singing. Faith had intended to make excuses and leave, but the sight of thirty or more older folk belting out 'Achy Breaky Heart' was irresistible. She and Maria found a table and it wasn't long before Faith was singing along to 'Stand By Your Man' with the rest of the audience.

After forty-five minutes there was short interval.

Maria stood. "Sorry dear," she said," two cups of tea at my age…I'll be back in a minute."

Faith quickly checked her phone for e-mails.

"That's the trouble with young people these days," a familiar voice said, "never off their phones." She looked up; Guy was standing beside the table, wearing a distinctly 'country and western' inspired outfit.

"Don't tell me you're performing here again?" she asked, watching Maria weaving her way between the tables towards them both.

"I'm afraid they just can't get enough of me!" he replied. Maria by now had made her way to their table and was standing beside him.

"Don't be daft!" She laughed and elbowed him in the ribs. She explained that their second act had cancelled at the very last minute, and Guy had stepped in. There was a round of applause, and no small amount of heckling, as Guy stepped up to the microphone, settling a guitar onto his shoulder.

"Of course, he plays the guitar as well," Faith thought to herself, "of course he does."

His repertoire of good old country favourites soon had the audience tapping their feet and clapping along. Guy caught Faith's eye and winked. Maria, noticing the wink, watched Faith's engaged expression and, like any meddling mother, could not resist 'helping things along a bit.' As the whole room cheered the final song, Faith smiled at Maria, who, overcome with motherly zeal, mouthed, "He's single, by the way!"

Faith's smile fell from her face as quickly as her hands reached for her bag and coat. "Well, I must be going," she said. "Thank you for your hospitality and the entertainment was *very* good. "I really must be going," she repeated, throwing her coat on as she hurried out of the nearest exit.

"But I thought…" Maria protested.

"I really have to go, sorry," Faith muttered.

Chapter Nine

It was just after nine am Saturday morning, and Agnes was washing up the breakfast things when there was furious hammering on the kitchen door, which then flew open. Hope barged through, pulling Callum, none too gently, behind her. Brian, already seated in the lounge with his newspaper, heard the commotion and heard his wife exclaim "Well, here's a lovely surprise!"

Callum, eyes rimmed with spiky wet lashes, face red with silent fury, appeared and leaned on the door frame to the lounge, looking at the floor. Hope's words followed him. "I'm sorry to dump him on you, Agnes, but I can't leave him at home and I have to go to work." It had obviously already been a chaotic morning, and Callum, who's only antidote to chaos was to become furiously chaotic himself, had finally found his mother's breaking point.

"He's making a massive fuss because I'm taking Rosa and Lily to work with me, because I can't leave Briony in charge of both the little ones if he is going to fight and argue." Callum looked at Brian, eyes filled with anger and hurt as his mother's fury echoed down the hallway. "He's been fighting with Lily, terrorising Briony. I'm so tired, I just don't have time for another one of his stupid tantrums and all his jealous nonsense, and now he's made me late. It's just the last…" Her voice faded as Agnes evidently shut the door, hoping to prevent Callum hearing the rest of his exhausted mothers' tirade.

"Let's walk back to the car," said Agnes, steering her daughter-in-law out of the back door and along the driveway.

Brian looked at the little boy, shaking with his determination to hold his eight-year-old dignity in one piece. Callum waited for another 'telling off.' Instead his grandfather beckoned him into the room with a comic expression of horror.

"Phew, your Mum's in a right old state!" he said. A little smile crept to Callum's lips. "Sometimes people say things they don't mean when they are tired and cross," Brian said.

Callum, still in the doorway, heaved a long-repressed sob. "It's true though, Grandad, isn't it?" Brian looked on as the child recited a litany of every name that had been hurled at him through his short life. "I *am* jealous, and I *am* odd, and I *am* cross, and I *am* a nuisance *on purpose*. I *am* a pain, I *am* a pest, and I *am* clumsy, and I'm scruffy, and I don't listen and I'm *rubbish* at football, and I *am* difficult, and..." he searched for the sum of all those things, "*I am a liability*!"

Brian opened his arms and pulled the sobbing child onto his lap, hugging him close and saying into his ear. "I know lad, I know." Tears fell from his own eyes as he whispered, "I know how it feels to be a *liability*."

Agnes walked Hope back to her car where Rosa looked troubled and Lily sat looking extra 'good.' Agnes, having consoled Hope with a hug, and reminded her that she was a good Mum in a difficult situation, waved her and her daughters off to Taylor's Country Gardens.

She walked slowly back to the house, stopping for a few tears of her own. Then, at the door took a deep sniff, squared her shoulders and opened the door expecting to face the angry fallout from both Brian and Callum. Instead, she found the sleeping boy, exhausted from crying, curled up on his Grandad's lap, as Brian wept silently.

****

Taylor's Country Gardens was busy. "Proper Christmas busy," as Pat put it. The little team worked hard to keep up with the demands of an unusually high number of customers. Yet as the rest of the team felt that exhilaration of industrious flurry, Hope had a horrible weight of guilt tugging at her all day. As soon as they arrived, Lily had run to Pat, who had said, "Three times in a week, Lily? You'll be on the payroll soon!"

Hope re-lived her outburst that morning over and over again, seeing Callum's confused little face as she 'dumped' him with Brian and Agnes. *Had she really used that word?* She felt a cringe of self-recrimination. The monotony of working the checkout and later restocking shelves gave her time to think. Callum, like his father, was most content when life was orderly and reasonably predictable. The year following Brian's illness had lurched from habitual calm to frantic disarray, with the occasional spike of panic.

With every report of Callum's difficult behaviour at school, backed up by stubborn, bad tempered sulks at home, Hope now realised she saw him as her as her 'challenging' child. She recognised this morning's surge of angry despair as her own helpless reaction to far bigger problems than a fractious little boy. As the crowds of shoppers dwindled towards the end of the afternoon, Hope found Adam and Lily restocking the

'Vintage Christmas' display beside the café, as Pat cleared the last of the cream teas from the café tables.

"Lily," she said, "can you stay here with Auntie Pat, while I speak to Daddy for a few minutes?"

"Time for a hot chocolate?" Pat suggested, as Lily opened her mouth to object. A day of being mostly tucked away in the office watching Disney films, with the occasional opportunity to 'help' had not been as thrilling as Lily had imagined. Lily shoved the poinsettia she was holding into her father's hands, and scampered to the nearest café table.

In the quiet safety of the office, Hope explained, tearfully, the events of the morning. "I just want to go and give him a great big hug," she said, "and tell him I love him, and I'm sorry." Within minutes, Hope was on her way, as Adam phoned his parents.

Adam Taylor, a gentle, quiet man, closed the door to his office and clenched his teeth together. Swallowing back dry sobs that, he knew, must not be allowed to escape. Not for any old-fashioned belief that 'real men don't cry,' but simply because he feared that if he began to weep, he may never stop. They had been so 'solid' he and Hope, not so long ago. Established in his own business, based on his reputation for accuracy and efficiency, and Hope with her part-time design job, gave her time to be the wonderful mother she was to their four children. Now, he was working at least twelve hours a day, seven days a week, to keep both his own and his father's business running. Hope was working three jobs, supporting his parents and caring for the family. They had promised each other that their children would always come first. Now, he hardly saw them, and Hope was so busy 'spinning plates' as she put it, there was no time to be a mother to any of them. He knew it was his fault. His love for his parents and his foolish pride. Thinking that he could apply logic and hard work to fix the problem. To see his beloved wife almost broken was more than he could bear. He pushed invisible tears from his eye sockets as the door burst open.

"Dad, we're running out of carrier bags!" It was Rosa. "Dad," she said gently, "what's wrong?"

"All okay here," he lied.

"You can't fool me, Dad," said Rosa. She pulled up a chair beside him and shut the door. "What's up?"

"I am just tired," he lied again. "That's all."

"Dad," Rosa said, "I know you, remember, I'm your favourite!" Adam laughed. It was a little family joke, that every child was Adam's favourite. "And," she continued, "I'm old enough to understand what's going on. You and mum are doing your best to keep things normal, but I can see the strain you are both under."

Adam looked down at the floor avoiding her gaze. "I'm so proud of you, Rosa," he said. "I'm sorry I've let you all down."

Rosa was silent for a moment, her face a picture of confusion. "Let us down?" she said, "you are so wrong, Dad."

Adam raised his head, surprised at her words. "The little ones don't understand, but Briony and I know how difficult things are for you and Mum right now. We've learned a lot, Dad, we've learned a lot about integrity and loyalty and...love."

"Love?" Adam repeated.

"It's hard to explain," she said, "but I see it, whenever I am with you, Dad." She thought for a moment, unable to put her thoughts into words. "Hold on," she said. Taking her locker key from her pocket, she retrieved her purse and took a small laminated card from one of the pockets. "Grandma gave me this," she said. "This is *you*, Dad, this is what you do every day. Read it." She passed it to him, then left the room, closing the door behind her.

Adam read: *Love is patient, love is kind. It does not envy, it does not boast, it is not proud. It does not dishonour others, it is not self-seeking, it is not easily angered, it keeps no record of wrongs. Love does not delight in evil but rejoices with the truth. It always protects, always trusts, always hopes, always perseveres. Love never fails.*

****

Hope was crying as she arrived, to find Agnes already at the gate to greet her. Agnes took her hand. "Come and see this," she said. The sound of laughter greeted her as she walked through the kitchen door. Brian and Callum were both seated at the kitchen table playing tiddlywinks. Seeing her, Callum hesitated. Hope ran to his chair and, kneeling, she took his face in her hands.

"I'm so sorry my darling boy," she said, and kissed him. "I didn't mean to leave you out, I wasn't thinking. I love you and I'm so sorry for the way things have been." She hugged him tightly.

"It's all right, Mummy," he said, his head buried in her shoulder. "I found Grandad, instead!"

Brian smiled up at his wife. "You certainly did, Callum."

Putting his arm around his grandfather's shoulders, he said to his mother, "I think I had better come back tomorrow. We didn't finish our game."

"Callum, I don't think…" Hope began.

"I would love that, Callum," cut in Brian, "we will leave the game exactly as it is."

Agnes' delight at this turn of events shone from her face. "I could make pancakes, if you come for breakfast," she offered.

"Come on, sunshine," Hope said as she stood to hug Agnes and Brian, "let's go home and I'll drop you off here tomorrow morning." They stopped off on the way home at the drive-through and bought an ice cream.

"What about the others, Mummy?" Callum asked, as they sat together on the sofa.

"This is just for us," Faith said.

"Just for us!" repeated Callum, with a contented smile.

****

At Taylor's Country Gardens, Rosa and Danny worked to cash and wrap as quickly and courteously as possible, without holding up the rest of the queue. Danny noticed with awe Rosa's knack of making each customer feel like a friend for the few minutes of shared interaction. For him, unless the customer simply wanted to pay and go, each transaction was torture.

"How do you do that?" he called across to her in a lull between customers. She looked at him enquiringly. "Keep having the same conversation over and over again, the weather, Christmas plans, the price of tinsel, it's like we're on replay."

Rosa thought about it for a second. "It might be the fiftieth time *we've* talked about the rain, but it's the first time for them. Besides, I just like talking to people."

A customer appeared and Rosa smiled broadly. "It's getting dark out there," the lady said, as she unloaded her basket onto the cash desk. "Christmas is coming," Rosa agreed.

As the short friendly dialogue ended and the lady left with her big bag of Christmas shopping and a happy smile, Danny said, "And that's how it's done, Ladies and Gentlemen!"

They both laughed, then stopped instantly as they spotted Adam walking towards them.

"Look busy!" hissed Rosa, giggling.

"Look busy?" Danny exclaimed, "I *am* busy!"

A gentleman approached, holding a large white poinsettia in one hand and a Christmas cherry in the other, he headed straight for Danny.

"Which one of these is easiest to care for and lasts longest?" he asked.

Adam hurried to help, then stopped in his tracks as Danny answered. "This one," he said, touching the winter cherry, "likes a bright sunny windowsill, and this one," pointing to the poinsettia, "prefers lots of light but not too bright – so if you have a north facing room, that would be perfect for the winter cherry. Best to avoid the radiator, though." Adam and Rosa looked on in stunned admiration as Danny continued, "Whichever one you choose, only water them when the compost is dry, and keep them away from draughts or sudden changes in temperature."

The customer, obviously impressed with Danny's knowledge, went on, "My wife is home from hospital tomorrow," he confided, "she loves to garden but won't be able to get out there. I want something she can 'tend' if you know what I mean."

"Then, I would go for the poinsettia," Danny advised. "If you get her some plant food and a spray to mist the leaves, she can keep it going well after Christmas."

Adam was dumbfounded at this new, talkative Danny, who continued to discuss the benefits of different winter plants with this customer.

"Do you have a few minutes, sir?" Danny asked. "Only, I think we could make up a little indoor garden for your wife, if you don't mind waiting."

The man's eyes shone. "An indoor garden would be perfect."

"It'll take me about twenty minutes to set up," advised Danny. "Time for a coffee while you wait."

Adam stepped forward, nodding his approval. "I'll staff the cash desk, Danny," he said, "while you make up the gentleman's order."

As Danny walked away, Adam gave his daughter a hug, despite the waiting customers. "Thanks, love," he whispered.

Not long afterwards, Danny carried his 'indoor garden' to the café. A container set in a wicker basket and filled with winter plants, all in white. He talked through each plant, "There's your Christmas tree," he said, pointing to a miniature conifer, hung with a spiral of tiny silver stars, "and then white rose and cyclamen." He pointed to a little circle of green shoots. "And these are paperwhite narcissus. She will be able to watch these grow every day, and with any luck, they'll be out for Christmas."

The old gentleman's eyes filled with tears. "My wife will love it," he said. "I can't thank you enough."

"I'll leave it here and carry it to your car when you are ready."

"No time like the present," said his happy customer, as he swallowed the last of his coffee. Danny carried the planter out to the car park, as the gentleman paid for his 'custom made garden' as he called it. Danny returned to the store, smiling.

Adam returned his smile. "Well, if we had an award for customer service, Danny, you'd be getting it today, well done!"

"You were amazing," said Rosa.

Danny blushed, "Well, he knew what he wanted, and I knew what we had in stock," he said.

"Except the paperwhites," said Adam. "I didn't order any this year. Where did you find them?"

"Erm, they're in the scullery" Danny confessed. "I, well, I rescued them, and all the other ones you wanted chucked in the skip. They're all doing well as it happens."

"In the scullery?" said Adam, "that old junk room?"

Reluctantly, Danny invited Adam to take a look at his collection of 'hidden treasures.'

Adam followed Danny to the back of the café, through the store cupboard and into the old scullery. Now brushed and scrubbed clean, the room was filled with thirty or more containers of various types and sizes, each sprouting a very healthy-looking plant.

"Good Lord!" Adam exclaimed. "How did you manage all this?"

"Mostly those old books," Danny replied, pointing to the two battered volumes on the table, "and I can ask Jim."

"So, Jim helped you with this lot?" asked Adam, assuming Danny had simply been following the instruction of an expert. He was dumbfounded when

Danny admitted that Jim knew nothing about the plants in the scullery.

Suddenly aware that he had a room full of 'stolen' stock, Danny was worried. "Am I in trouble?" he asked.

"Most definitely not!" responded Adam, "this is marvellous!"

****

At home, Hope and Callum prepared the evening meal. Callum, standing on a kitchen chair, peeled potatoes, as Hope fried onions and minced beef in a pan.

"...and it's Dad's favourite, too," he continued, "but he's not keen on peas in it."

"I didn't think shepherd's pie had peas," grimaced Hope.

"Grandma used to put all sorts in when Dad was growing up." he replied, knowingly. "It was disgusting, actually."

The chatter continued as the two of them prepared Callum's favourite meal. Hope felt a little stab of affection when, offered a 'treat' for tea, Callum chose Shepherd's pie over any takeaway. There was also a large tub of newly bought vanilla ice cream in the freezer, at his request.

As Hope spent some much-needed time with her child, Faith thought of the child she had given up for adoption. Guy Harvey's mother/sister story had awakened an unwanted response in her mind. The carefully constructed armour she had built over that deep, deep, pain had been breached. Faith had always thought the term 'given up' to be a bald-faced lie, at least in her case. "Snatched away, stolen, taken," she muttered, pouring a glass of wine, "not 'given away.'"

She looked out across the city through the big floor to ceiling windows of her kitchen. It was a clear evening and the stars and moon seemed close. Somewhere, she thought, her daughter may be looking at the same sky.

"Here's to you!" she said, holding her glass up to the moon in a toast. *May you be safe, may you be happy, may you be loved, my Angel.*

****

At Taylor's Country Gardens, they were all gathered in the café, lights out, doors locked, shelves restocked, and planning the next day's staffing. Pat cleaned and sorted the café counter as Lily carefully placed a menu on each table, ready for the morning. Danny was disappointed that Adam had turned down his offer to work the next day.

"I really wish you could, Danny," he said, "but you've been here all week on work experience. I'm pretty sure it's not legal to have you work seven days a week. We'll see you Monday. Jim has agreed to work tomorrow, so we will be fine."

"Jim's in tomorrow?" said Danny hopefully, "I might just come in to see him, not to work."

Adam smiled "You must show him your plant hospital when you are next in, Danny, he'll be so impressed."

Lily looked up from her work. "A plant hospital?" she cried, "where?"

Pat looked equally curious, "What's all this?" she asked.

"Can we show them?" asked Adam. Danny nodded, part proud and part self-conscious.

Adam reminded them all of the 'big clear out' as it had been named. "I told Danny to take a quantity of dried-up bulbs and half-dead old plants and chuck them in the skip." Adam paused for effect, and indicated that everyone should follow him. He continued as they walked towards the scullery. "Instead," he said, "Danny ignored me and ..." He pushed the door open, moonlight flooded through the window, throwing a violet sheen across the rows of newly budding blooms and spiky bulbs. Danny flicked the light switch, and the room filled with golden light from the old filament bulb.

Plump, jade-leaved Christmas cacti bloomed in luminous pink, alongside bright red kalanchoe and a rainbow of cyclamen. A few pots of slender paperwhite narcissus, already in bloom, adorned the oak dresser, and the marbled surface under the window was spread with neat rows of bulb-filled clay pots.

Pat and Rosa gasped in wonder, Lily jumped up and down in delight. "It's magic!" she cried. "All the flowers are magic!"

Chapter Ten

Danny walked home that evening, cold though it was, with a growing sense of joy. It was a long, long time since Danny had felt enthusiasm for anything at all, and to be wanted, even respected, was so unfamiliar as to border on scary.

Adam had paid him in cash for his day's work, and offered him a regular Saturday and holiday job. Pat had given him a couple of 'left over' pasties, neatly wrapped, which he hugged to his chest. Danny felt proud and happy. He looked forward to surprising his Dad with a free supper and news of his success. At the corner shop near his house, he stopped and put a tenner on his phone – which had been 'emergency and incoming calls only' for several weeks – then headed for home.

"Dad, I'm back!" he shouted, walking into the kitchen and putting the pasties, still wrapped, onto the table. "Dad?" The two rooms downstairs were empty, he ran up the stairs, the old feeling of dread growing in his stomach. Kit was in his room, combing his hair. The place smelled strongly of aftershave.

"Hello, son," he greeted Danny. "Your old man's got a date. How do I look?" he asked, spinning round.

"You look great, Dad," and he did, which did not make Danny feel any less worried. "Where are you going?"

"I'm going out. On a date. With a woman. Alright with you?"

"Dad, don't be like that. I worry about you."

"I don't think I have to ask your permission, do I, you little...?" His dad swore at him, and informed him that he would go where he wanted, when he wanted, and with whom he wanted.

A few pointless minutes of accusation and retaliation, then Danny watched the door slam as his father left. Alone in the kitchen, he ate one of the pasties, put the other in the fridge and made himself a cup of tea, thankful that there was milk in the fridge. He ran upstairs, stashing his days' pay in the treasure box he hid behind his mum's photograph. Carefully folding his staff uniform, he spent the evening half-watching TV, as he waited for his father to return. Kit did not return that night. Danny had finally fallen asleep in the chair at three am, had woken at six am, freezing cold, then climbed into bed.

He slept until ten am, had a quick, pointless search for his father, then set off for the garden centre, eating last night's leftover pasty on the way.

****

While Danny was shutting the door on his empty house that Sunday morning, Agnes was opening her door to welcome Callum and Hope. The house was filled with the scent of fresh coffee and sweet pancakes. Callum ran straight past Agnes to find Brian and finish the game they started yesterday.

"Bye then, son!" laughed Hope as she hugged Agnes goodbye.

"He's only got time for Grandad, now." Agnes smiled. "I think we are both surplus to requirements."

"Thanks for this," said Hope, "and thanks for yesterday." She hugged Agnes one more time, then left.

Agnes' heart was singing as she watched Callum lead Brian to the breakfast table. "I won, Grandma," he said, matter of factly, "so now it's time for pancakes."

Brian caught her eye and winked; Agnes knew at last her husband was on his way back. Brian knew that the day Callum came weeping to his Grandad was the first day of his own healing. The utter, helpless despair of the little boy reflected his own misery. With another little soul to nurture, Brian seemed to grow stronger each day, both physically and spiritually.

Agnes stacked the dishwasher as Brian helped the sugar-coated Callum to wipe his face.

"I'll wash that pan when I get back," she said, putting her jacket on.

Callum turned in his seat. "Where are you going, Grandma?"

"Church," she responded, "as usual."

Callum looked at her in puzzlement, and then at his Grandad, in a 'she's lost her mind' expression. "Leaving me and Grandad behind?" he asked. "That's not very kind, is it, Grandma?"

"Well…" Agnes looked at Brian, "Grandad usually…"

"Grandad usually takes too long to get ready," interrupted Brian, "but not this time, Grandma." He laughed. "Come on, Callum, let's get our coats on."

Callum chose not to go in to Sunday school with the other children. The friendly clamour around Brian as they arrived, coupled with the prospect of spending an hour with 'the noisy kids' as he later put it, had convinced the boy that he would be much better off at his grandparents' side. This was a singing church. The music team, with Grace on piano and Doug on guitar, joyfully bashed out each tune with gusto, leading the congregation in a series of heartfelt professions of praise and glory.

Callum watched them closely, particularly fascinated by the syncopated rise and fall of Grace's hands, as they flew across the keyboard. His delight was infectious, filling both Agnes and Brian with fresh zeal. But more moving still, was the tender little squeeze Callum gave to his Grandad's hand when Pastor Mark asked them all to "Pray for those who are sick."

Agnes and Brian were intrigued by Callum's reaction to Mark's sermon. He did not fidget, or ask to go out, or even fall asleep. Instead, he listened with rapt attention to every word.

Preceded by the well-known 'no room at the inn' Bible reading, Mark numbered the many prophecies fulfilled at the birth of Jesus. "The Messiah everyone was longing for had arrived," Mark concluded, "but there was no room for him." Mark looked across the congregation, "The person they *said* they wanted was right in front of them, but time after time they pushed him away…"

"So, this Christmas," Mark said, summing up, "in the words of the old hymn:

> *Joy to the world, the Lord is come,*
> *Let earth receive her King;*
> *Let **every** heart prepare Him room.*

****

At home after the service, Callum had persuaded Agnes that he was 'really excellent at peeling.' Consequently, he and Brian were on KP duties, while

Agnes carried on with the one hundred and one other preparations that go in to making a simple Sunday roast.

Scraping away silently at an enormous potato, Callum had been deep in thought for some time. Then, stopping, he announced, "I'm like Jesus, aren't I, Grandad?"

Amused, Brian and Agnes stopped what they were doing to look at Callum.

"Everybody likes the idea of me, but no one wants me in real life."

After a moment's shocked silence, Callum found himself smothered in hugs and kisses and reassured that he was always loved and always wanted.

They set back to their jobs; Brian looked across Callum's head at his loyal wife. "Grown-ups are just silly sometimes, they get so wrapped up in their own lives, they don't see the good things right in front of them."

****

Faith parked up outside Taylor's Country Gardens and was impressed before she even stepped inside. Hanging baskets and terracotta pots overflowing with bright Christmas blooms edged the building and two tall fir trees, covered in tiny white lights, stood either side of the main entrance. With her scarf wrapped around her face and her hat pulled down low, Faith hoped to explore the much-changed building without being recognised.

An hour had passed quickly as Faith strolled through each charmingly set out area. From the exquisitely designed greenhouses and Santa's Workshop to the more practical garden tools and products sections, the whole place was transformed from the depressing remains of a once prosperous business to a festive, popular and very much alive family enterprise. As she reached the café, Faith removed her hat and scarf. At that moment, Hope, who was returning a dustpan and broom to the cleaning cupboard, recognised her.

"Hello, Faith," she greeted her, "I'm so happy you came to see us again. What do you think?" She indicated the entire garden centre with a wave of the dustpan.

"It's absolutely beautiful," said Faith, "it doesn't look like the same place."

"I'm just about to have a coffee break, would you care to join me?" Faith said she would love to. "You find us a seat, and I'll get our coffees," Hope said.

Faith found a table and 'people-watched' the café. An elderly couple of ladies brushed past her, struggling with shopping and walking frames. Faith saw Pat signal the pair to sit down, carrying a tray of tea and scones straight to their table. One of them reached for her purse and Faith watched as Pat signalled that no payment was required.

Hope returned and they began to talk about the changes at Taylor's Country Gardens. A few minutes later, as Hope was explaining the serendipitous 'purchase' from Trevone Manor, Faith was distracted by a similar event. Again, the customer was seated at a table, and a generous latte and large portion of cake was placed in front of him, this time by the young café assistant, accepting nothing but a smile in payment. Hope was speaking, but Faith had not heard a word, concerned she had uncovered some sort of scam.

"I'm sorry, Hope," she said, "I wasn't listening, um... I've been watching and I'm fairly sure your aunt and her assistant are giving away freebies."

Hope laughed. "Oh, that assistant is my eldest daughter, and you are absolutely right, those freebies are PIFFs."

"PIFFs?"

"Yes, it stands for "Pay It Forward, Friend," she explained. "Taylor's have done PIFFs as long as I can remember. Especially at Christmas. Customers come in, have one coffee, but they pay for two, then Pat can pass that kindness on." Hope looked across at Pat, hard at work behind the counter. "Although I think more recently, she has secretly been the main donor."

"That's genuine goodwill," said Faith.

"That's Applebury," said Hope, "people look out for each other."

Faith watched Hope's daughter clear tables, chatting easily with customers.

"Your daughter looks like you," she said. Rosa looked over and waved.

"She does," Hope replied. "Lily, my youngest, was here yesterday; I have no idea who she looks like." Hope stood, "I'm sorry," she said, "but I really have to go and give Jim a break from the till."

"Not at all," Faith reassured her. "I'm going now, too, just going to pay for this, she held up a little fused glass decoration. "I have a weakness for angels," she confessed.

As Faith left, Danny appeared at the tills where Jim was handing over the 'hot seat' as he called it, to Hope. "Whatever are you doing here on your day off?" asked Jim.

"Nothing better to do, really," joked Danny.

"Well, you've turned up just at the right time, as it happens." Jim smiled. "I hear you've got some sort of a plant recovery unit going on. I'd like to take a look at that." They walked through the café and into the scullery. Danny stood nervously awaiting Jim's verdict on his work. Jim walked between the pots, touching the compost, inspecting leaves.

"And these?" Jim said, pointing to the big wooden shutters.

"I keep them closed at night," Danny said. "Keeps the warmth in and the sunlight out."

Jim nodded. "And where'd these paperwhites come from then," he said, picking up a little pot with a cluster of elegant thin necked narcissi.

"They came out early," said Danny, "the rest are in here." He opened the long sliding doors under the sink, where at least thirty pots of bulbs were beginning to sprout. "I'm forcing them, like you taught me."

"Well, knock me down with a feather!" cried Jim, clapping his hands together in approval, "I reckon they're right on target for Christmas!"

"Do you think they're good enough to sell?" Danny asked, nervously, "only it was a shame to chuck them out."

"I should say so," Jim chuckled. "Looking at this lot, I reckon we can put most of them out for sale right now." Danny was uncertain until Jim, not given to displays of emotion, clapped him on the shoulder. "You've done well, Danny, very well."

****

That night, after the evening service, Mark and Debbie were setting up the church hall ready for toddler group the next day. Mark had been gluing down the curled edges of a line of cheap carpet tiles. The hall bore all the marks of a hurried '90s renovation which was now, literally, falling apart at the seams. The latest addition to Mark's long list of grumbles against the trustees.

"I just don't understand their logic," he grumbled. "On the one hand they are thanking God for sending all these people to church, but on the other, they are refusing money to keep the place in good order."

Debbie said nothing. Given space for a 'good old moan' as he put it, Mark usually argued himself back into a position of resigned forbearance. Although, she had to admit, the building seemed to be falling apart around them.

"All this talk of 'priorities,'" Mark continued, "as if I don't always put the needs of the people before repairs. But there comes a point when you have to look with the eyes of our *congregation*. They deserve a decent place to worship in, don't they?"

Debbie went to speak, then thought better of it as Mark went on. "And don't tell me we need to sell up and move." He spoke in a high-pitched whiney voice, intended to mimic the absent leadership team. *"But Mark, the church is on prime building land." "But Mark, the church has a huge car park." "But Mark, don't you see..."* Mark stood, hand on hips. "No, I don't see. As a matter of fact, I don't see at all!"

Mark sighed deeply and looked at Debbie's concerned face. "I love our church family," he said, "but just lately, I think they've lost sight of what all this," he swung his arms wide, indicating the whole building, "is really about."

"They are all good people," Debbie reminded him, "good, prayerful people."

Mark looked sceptical, "Well, something's not right," said Mark. "As it says in the Good Book, 'You do not have, because you do not ask,' James 4:2."

Debbie smiled, "Maybe we have all been asking for the wrong thing."

"Meaning?" Mark demanded.

"Thy will be done?" she said quietly.

"Well, I doubt very much His will is for us all to stand in a draughty old ruin that lets the rain in."

"Exactly, and that's why they want to sell the place," Debbie reasoned, "to finance a newly built, purpose-built church, not too far from here. It makes sense, really."

"Not to me, it doesn't," said Mark. "We are right in the centre of town. Why should we move off this site?"

Debbie opened her mouth to give her opinion, but was cut off by her enraged husband. "Twenty-five years or more of my life I've put into this place. Twenty-five years of sermons and visits and clubs and holiday camps and old folks and baptisms and funerals. Twenty-five years of hard work, with no help from anyone."

Debbie smarted at this. "You have always had a very supportive team around you, Mark," she said, "including me!"

"Oh, of course I know you support me, love," he said, blind to her hurt. "I didn't mean that. But you'd think they would trust me to know the will of God for the church that I have pastored for all these years. It's so…frustrating."

"They just see an opportunity to build a new church at little expense to the congregation."

"You know how I feel about that, Debbie," Mark persevered, "a church is not about the best business decisions, profit and loss with an eye on the prize." Mark looked and sounded angry, but inside, his heart was breaking. "I have built this place up from next to nothing and I have no intention of de-camping to some trendy place on the outskirts of town. Until I get a direct and clear message from the Lord Almighty Himself, this is where Applebury Church stands, and this is where it shall stay!"

Chapter Eleven

This Monday, a week until Christmas eve, was usually the busiest of the year. Pat could have done with Danny's help setting up for the first rush of customers, but Danny was not waiting at his normal spot by the door. Pat pulled her coat tighter around her against the rain and wind as she unlocked the big iron shutter and walked to the café, turning on the lights as she went. He hurried in, just a few minutes later, and Hope arrived to find Pat taking the chairs off the café tables in a very dramatic fashion, and giving him an 'it's not good enough!' scolding. She noticed the young man was shaking with cold. "I think Danny gets the point Auntie Pat, and he can't be that late, I've only just got here."

"Well, I'm just used to him being here *on time*, that's all."

"You mean early, don't you?" Hope said, her eyebrows raised in exasperation.

Pat stood in front of Danny, who looked miserable. "I'm sorry," she said, reaching to touch his shoulder. Danny flinched away, but not before she felt the dampness of his shirt. "Oh heavens, boy, you're soaking wet! Go get one of those dry shirts from the office. I'll make you a hot drink."

"Missed the bus," mumbled Danny by way of explanation, and headed for the office.

The truth was that his father had returned at about eight that morning, a rambling, angry drunk. Danny had tried his best, but everything he said, everything he did, only served to throw fuel on the fire of his father's rage. Finally, afraid for his own safety, coatless and without bus fare, Danny ran out of the house and to the only place he felt safe. Throughout the day, Danny phoned his father at every opportunity, but the electronic response was that his number was not available. Between calls, he threw himself into his work 'like a lad possessed,' as Jim remarked.

In the lull just before lunchtime, Jim watched Danny through the café window. He was taping bubble wrap and sacking around the outdoor taps. Pat joined him, bringing Jim's usual mug of tea, and a coffee for herself. "There's supposed to be a frost tonight," she said, handing over his mug. "Good job you've got him insulating the taps."

"That's the thing," said Jim, "I didn't tell him to, he just knew it needed doing. That kid's got a future, if he wants it. He's a hard worker, and he understands plants."

"He's not great with people, though," said Pat.

Jim, still looking through the window, grinned. "As I said, he's a good kid!" He clinked his mug against hers. "I've had an idea," he said, and headed for Adam in the office.

Danny looked up and smiled at Pat, giving her a wave. She waved back and then beckoned him in, pointing at her mug. Danny gave her the thumbs up, and within a few minutes was seated in the café with a bowl of hot home-made soup, and a couple of crispy bread rolls.

"Now get yourself on the outside of that lot," Pat said, "you've got to look after yourself, young as you are!"

Danny began to thank her, but was unceremoniously shushed, as Pat held her hand to her ear. "It's us!" she said, running behind the counter to turn the radio volume up.

"I took a second visit to Taylor's Country Gardens yesterday," Faith was saying, *"and I swear I have been sprinkled with Christmas from my head to my toes."*

She went on to talk about the PIFF scheme, well known at Taylor's, then asked listeners to call in with stories of their own local hero, or good neighbour. Pat was both flattered and flustered when the first few calls were from longstanding customers, thanking Pat for all her kindness to them, both inside and outside of Taylor's Country Gardens.

This inspired other listeners to call in with thanks for good deeds done by neighbours, friends and even strangers.

"In a world when every hour brings news updates full of the very worst examples of human behaviour," Faith said, wrapping up the show, *"Today has been a reminder of all that is good about people. Thank you for listening, this is Faith New, and that was the GOOD News!"*

****

At around three pm, Grace appeared, as expected, to check that the work experience placement had gone well. She was walking towards Danny, who gave her a nod of acknowledgment, but she was intercepted by Adam who, with a quick glance at Danny, ushered her into the office.

Jim signalled to him from the Christmas tree lot just outside the front door, the place was getting busier with after-school families arriving to choose their tree. "What's with the long face?" asked Jim.

"Grace is checking up on me today, and Adam just took her in the office."

"And what's your problem with that?"

"I was late this morning, and the plants I took…"

"You didn't take them, they were being thrown out, and you've brought them back to life," Jim reassured the nervous young man. "No, I reckon they're talking about something completely different. Now give me a hand netting this ten-footer," he said, lifting a huge pine tree to be netted.

They had been working for nearly an hour when Grace appeared and asked if they could both go to the café for 'a conversation.' Danny threw Jim an 'I've had it' gesture as he followed her into the café. Adam was already seated at the table as they sat with him,

Danny sat head bowed with his arms folded, hardly daring to look as Grace drew out a folder with his name on the front. He did look and was surprised to see her broad smile

"You certainly have made an impression on this place in such a short time, Danny," she said. "Let me list some of the words used to describe you," she held up a page from her file. "Punctual, efficient, responsible, creative, uses his initiative, works hard."

Danny half laughed. "Are you sure that's me you're talking about?"

Adam took a deep breath. "The thing is, Danny, we have been really impressed, all of us."

Adam found himself getting flustered, Grace interposed. "It's not every student of mine that is offered employment in his first week, then offered a full-time job in his second."

Danny took a second or two to register. "A full-time job?"

Jim kept bobbing his excited face round the door between customers, which Danny found a little alarming. It was as if everyone had a big secret, that they were about to share with him. He looked across at Pat, also smiling.

"I think Jim had better tell you," said Adam, "or he's actually going to burst." He beckoned Jim over, and Jim seemed to cross the twenty feet from the doorway to the café in two massive steps.

"Well, lad, what's your answer?" he asked. Danny looked at him in confusion.

"We haven't got round to that yet, Jim," explained Adam.

Jim rolled his eyes. He looked directly at Danny. "When these two have finished dillydallying around with their reports and suchlike, they were working their way up to offering you the job as my apprentice."

"What, for real?" Danny almost yelled, "I can work here every day?"

Grace explained the agreement they had come to. "You'll be employed here four days a week, and then one day a week at college, doing your Practical Horticulture Certificate."

For a second, they mistook Danny's shocked silence for reluctance.

"It's a two-year commitment," said Grace, "so you'll need time to think it over, no doubt."

"Oh, no I won't," said Danny with purpose. "I don't need time. Yes!" he said. "Yes, of course, yes please!"

"I will gladly set the wheels in motion right away," Grace said with enthusiasm.

"Right," said Jim, "off you go, lad, and take care of that Christmas tree queue."

Danny leapt up and hurried outside. Adam rebuked Jim. "You could have let him have a few more minutes, Jim," he sighed.

Jim shook his head. "Poor lad was close to tears, Adam. He needs a few minutes to sort himself out."

Sure enough, when Jim followed Danny outside, he found him, red eyed, but smiling at the edge of the Christmas tree area.

"Thanks Jim, I thought I was going to lose it in there," he said.

"All part of the service, old chap!" said Jim, with a playful bow.

The rest of Danny's afternoon was a joyful blur. At the end of the day, walking home with a bag of Pat's 'leftover' goodies in his hand, he dreamed of a future he had never imagined. He had refused an early lift home from Grace, insisting he needed to complete his days' work at Taylor's. In truth, he did not want to risk Grace seeing his father if he was having 'one of those days.'

Closer to home, the cares of his current life began to overshadow his dreams of the future, and he braced himself for whatever he might find at home. He needn't have worried; the house was empty and in darkness. Danny flicked on the light, but no light came. In the kitchen the kettle still felt slightly warm. *He's gone to top up the key card for the meter*, Danny thought, relieved that his father would soon be safely home.

"This house is freezing," he said out loud, as he walked upstairs to change out of his work clothes. The only light was from the torch on his phone, but he saw immediately the empty treasure box laying on his bed, the contents scattered, his money gone. He did not need to explore further, a cursory glance through each room in the house showed him that anything that could be carried away and sold had gone.

Back in his own room, curtains open to let in the glow of the streetlight, He switched the phone torch off to conserve his battery. Carefully he regathered his photos and other mementos and neatly set them back in the box. The gold of the lamplight caused a spark of reflection on his bed cover. It was the key to the scullery. Danny turned it over in his hand, framing a bold idea. It was so cold; he could see his breath. He got into bed, opened the bag of café leftovers and began to eat the sausage roll Pat had packed away for him.

Since his Mum had left, Danny had watched his father fall apart, leaning more and more on drinking to help him cope. His Dad was not a bad man, nor a bad father, and Danny knew that. In fact, he often wondered if he was responsible in some way for his father's decline. Could he have done more, said less, needed less? For the past six or more years, Danny had colluded with his father in pretending his 'problem' was not a problem at all. Through a series of lost jobs, driving convictions, relationship breakdowns, bailiffs and benefits applications, the secret remained a secret.

School had put the change in Danny's behaviour down to his transition to senior school and adolescence. There were no responses to letters, or calls from school, and no one turned up at parents' evenings. He was just another underachieving boy from one of 'those' families. In reality, all of this sullen, underachieving child's energy and effort had gone into surviving the sudden desertion of his mother, and watching the progressive self-destruction of his only remaining parent.

These days, Danny reflected, were just a cycle of relapse and reform. His Dad would be back, they would pretend nothing had happened, and life would go back to 'normal' for a few months. Danny swore, brushing away the unwanted thoughts and memories with the flaky pastry crumbs that had fallen on his bed. He curled up in bed and tried to talk himself out of what seemed a very reasonable – if risky – answer to his current problem.

The next morning, Danny woke early. Despite the dark outside and the cold inside, he was resolved to stick to his plan as quickly as possible, mainly so there was no opportunity to really think about what he was about to do. Danny checked his father's room, then looked downstairs in the futile hope that he had returned. Cold water and a dried-out scone were not the best breakfast he had ever had. But definitely not the worst, and better than nothing at all. After his meagre breakfast, Danny ran upstairs, pulled out his old school rucksack from the bottom of his wardrobe and carefully crammed it with as many of his belongings as possible. Rolling a sleeping bag tightly into a plastic bag, he secured it to his rucksack. Finally, he added the scullery key to his keyring, put on his coat, and walked to Taylor's Country Gardens. Arriving before anyone else, Danny quietly unlocked the side door to the scullery, stepped in and hid his stuff under one of the big old tables.

When Pat appeared to open up for the day, Danny was waiting as usual.

That night, Danny said his usual goodbyes, hid out of sight around the back of the building and simply crept in through the scullery door, once he had counted everyone out. Danny did not dare to venture into the café or the rest of the building for fear of the alarm going off. But this little section of the centre, being locked away from the rest and containing nothing of value, had never been added to the network. For Danny, though, there was a warm radiator, electricity to charge his phone, hot and cold running water in the staff toilet right next door and of course the growing bulbs to keep him company.

Sitting on one old Lloyd loom chair, with his feet up on the other, Danny looked about him at his new refuge with satisfaction. He noticed his salvaged gardening books on the windowsill and, taking the biggest back to the table, he wrapped himself in his sleeping bag and began to read. Over the next few days, Danny's evenings were spent reading James Anderson's horticultural handbook, the 1874 edition of "*The new practical gardener and modern horticulturalist: With guidance on landscape gardening, soil, preparing seed beds, fruit trees, propagating, grafting, pruning, and more.*"

Chapter Twelve

Faith was at her desk when Hope entered her office on Wednesday morning, dragging the vacuum cleaner behind her as usual.

Faith apologised, "I'll get out of your way," she said. "I'll just pop down to the canteen and get a coffee."

Hope nodded her thanks and started her cleaning routine. She had just about finished, and was unplugging the vacuum cleaner, when Faith returned with two cups in her hand.

"Flat white, no sugar, wasn't it?" Faith said, placing the two cups down on the desk. Hope looked surprised. "Go on," Faith smiled, "I know I'm your last office and the place looks immaculate. Have you got a few spare minutes?" She gestured for Hope to sit.

Hope shrugged. "I suppose I do, now!" She laughed, picking up the coffee cup and sitting on the edge of the chair.

"I just wanted to thank you again for the tip-off about Taylor's, Faith began, "Pat's PIFFs has really inspired people. I'm going to feature a 'good neighbour' slot in every program until Christmas."

"Really, it's me who should be thankful, Faith," said Hope. "Your program has certainly put Taylor's on the map. We are actually taking on staff to cope. I'm sure every shop, showroom and office in Applebury has an entry in the festival!"

"We're doing an outside broadcast this Friday, and I'm ashamed to say I have never actually seen Applebury properly," Faith confessed.

"Oh, you should," Hope urged her. "Park at the top by the church and walk through the high street to the square. It's not the most picturesque town, but at this time of year with all the lights and trees, Applebury is really quite magical!"

"I'll go today, after the programme finishes," Faith promised, "then I can cover it on the show tomorrow."

"The church will be overflowing with trees with all this publicity!" Hope laughed as she gathered up her cleaning tools. "Thanks for the coffee," she said, standing. "I've got to go, I'm afraid it's the…"

"School run," Faith finished her sentence. "I remember."

****

Hope's throwaway joke that the church would be overflowing with Christmas trees was far more accurate than she realised. Looking at his list of deliveries and pre-orders, Adam thought it wise to phone and warn Pastor Mark. It was Debbie who answered the phone. Sounding concerned but thrilled, she asked Adam what they should do.

"Maybe put a limit on the number of entrants?" Suggested Adam, "have a look and see how many trees you can put inside the church and hall. Maybe put the big church tree outside?"

"Now that's a really good idea," agreed Debbie, as she said goodbye. "Now I've just got to tell Mark!"

"Tell me what?" asked Mark, who had walked in as she put the phone down. Debbie explained about the 'wonderful problem' as she put it, of the boom in entrants for the competition.

"I'm sure there's no need to panic," Mark said, "we have a sensible plan and we will stick to it."

They had listened to Faith's show daily since she started to cover the festival. It was clear that the Christmas Tree Festival was a success, and that there would be far more entrants and visitors than they had ever imagined. As today's show finished with Faith's now customary, "Thank you for listening, this is Faith New, and that was the *GOOD* news!"

Mark looked at Debbie. "On second thoughts, Debs," he said, trying to sound more composed than he actually felt, "we are definitely going to have to replan the sensible plan!"

****

After the show, Faith had driven to Applebury, and was following Hope's suggested route through the high street to the square. She had wanted to see the effect of the festival on the town itself, and decided to take a stroll through the town, shopping for a few bits and bobs as she went. Faith was enchanted as she strolled the length of Applebury High Street. Almost every window displayed a poster for the festival, and many displayed their festival tree.

The travel agent, Hart's Holidays, had a tree covered in hearts and toy aeroplanes, while just a little further along the road the bookshop had created a tree from a spiralling stack of books. Tim's Trims, the barber with moustachioed and bearded baubles, particularly caught her eye. Shop after shop revealed the character and creativity of the people of Applebury. She took photos for the station's social media pages and typed notes as she went, ideas for the broadcast on Friday. Reaching the town square at last, Faith realised her 'bits and bobs' had become three carrier bags. A beautiful hand knitted jumper for Megan, several gift boxes of retro sweets for the office staff, and a box of artisan chocolates for herself—which probably would not make it to Christmas.

She stopped to look at the huge fir tree, festooned in lights, which stood at the centre. This pedestrianised area was populated by banks, a chemist, and a number of small independent shops, each window decorated in some way with seasonal cheer. In the window of the bakery was a large tray of Christmas tree gingerbreads. Next door, not to be outdone, the Tasty Tea Room's window displayed their 'Festival Menu.' This included Christmas Pasties, Santa Sandwiches, and 'Elfy Snacks.' Faith turned, laughing, from the window to see Guy Harvey leaving the bank and walking towards her. She looked about her, but there was no escape. He was dressed in his garage overalls, under a scruffy padded jacket. A far cry from the dashing cowboy she had last seen.

"Hello there!" he said, "excuse my appearance, I had to get to the bank before closing."

Despite her attempts to appear indifferent, Faith's unease at this encounter must have shown on her face. Guy pulled his jacket closer as a gust of icy wind blew the last of the autumn leaves along the pavement. "This is awkward," he said, with an expression of mock anxiety.

"Awkward?" she echoed.

"Mother confessed," he said. "She feels dreadful and promised not to stick her oar in anymore." A smile crept to Faith's lips. "You'd think at my age," he continued, "that it would be impossible to be embarrassed by your own mother, but it seems not!" He looked into her eyes. "I really am sorry," he said, "I don't know what she was thinking."

Faith laughed. "Well, I think we both know what she was thinking."

"Yes, well, of course, I do know what she was thinking, but she had no business saying it. Ridiculous notion. Well, when I say, I don't mean, er…"

He was tying himself in knots. Faith took pity on him. "It's really okay," she said. "It's me who should apologise for running away."

"Not at all," said Guy, "I think I would have run a mile too!" Guy fell silent and appeared to be deeply interested in the star on top of the town Christmas tree. Then he turned to look directly into her eyes. "Faith," he said, "I can honestly assure you that I am a confirmed bachelor with no intention, even if it were possible, of stealing your heart away."

And at that moment, Guy meant every word he said. After his wife died, leaving him with two young children, he had given up his hopes of a music career and thrown himself into being a dad and running the garage with his father and brothers. Now his son was grown, with children of his own, Guy filled his empty hours with public service and a few local gigs with The Four Pops. He really had no time or inclination towards romance.

He noticed she was beginning to shiver with the cold. "Shall we?" he said, gesturing towards the café. The golden glow of the windows and the smell of fresh coffee was tempting, and her resolve began to weaken. "What's that?" he said in an official tone, "you wish to interview me in my capacity of Mayor of Applebury?"

He looked at his watch. "Well, if you insist, but it'll have to be quick, fifteen minutes and no more."

"That's very good of you, Mr Mayor," replied Faith, in mock ceremony, and walked through the door as Guy held it open for her.

They did indeed begin with Guy, as Mayor, proudly telling her about the events which made Applebury unique. As he spoke, Faith was aware that Applebury was typical of every small town, irreplaceably unique, yet endlessly replicated. Maybe that was why the Applebury Festival was becoming the most popular item on C2C's menu. Formalities over, they chatted easily until Faith realised the staff were rather pointedly sweeping the floor around them.

Guy looked up. "You'll be switching the lights of on us in a minute, Bridie," he called to the lady cashing up behind the counter.

"Oh no, Guy, you take your time," she said, with a slightly sarcastic tone, "really."

Guy grinned an apology, "That's very good of you Bridie, my love, but we must be going."

He helped Faith into her coat and walked her back to the car park. Faith watched him walk away as she started the car. Then recognised within herself a long-stifled sensation. "Oh no!" she told herself, "definitely no! *NO! NO! NO!*"

****

Wednesday evening presented a problem for Danny. Adam insisted he have the next day off, although Danny begged him to let him work. "Everyone needs a break," Adam said. "Besides, I'm sure it's not legal to have someone work with no day off, ever!"

"Well, *you* do," said Danny, trying to argue his case. "Sadly, I have no choice, but I can assure you I could really do with a break," Adam replied. "In fact,

I have to leave early today for the littl'uns parents' evening, so I'm really glad you're here. And we need you in Friday, for sure."

"I do need to be in Friday," Danny smiled, "because we're putting out the paperwhites for Christmas." He was referring to the fifty or more little pots of delicate narcissi that he had nurtured back to life. He and Jim had decided that this weekend would be prime time to put them out. Danny had placed each plastic pot inside a smooth terracotta pot decorated, at Hope's suggestion, with a simple red hessian ribbon.

"We have to look after our staff, especially staff as good as you," Adam went on, "so, have tomorrow off and we will see you Friday, bright and early."

Not long after this conversation, Adam and Hope, having dropped their two youngest children at home with their big sisters, were at the Junior School Parents' Evening. Lily's teacher had been all smiles and praise for their little dynamo daughter, but the serious expression of Miss James, Callum's teacher, prepared them for a very different report.

Miss James complained of their son choosing to stand in his tightly zipped coat at the edge of the playground, rather than join with the other children; distracting others during rehearsals for the nativity play; not listening to instructions; messing around when he should be sitting still; and generally, a totally different child from the one described in his report from last year. His teacher had couched her words in 'teacher speak' sentences, but Hope could easily translate the underlying meaning. Callum had become, according to his teacher, attention seeking, defiant, lazy, withdrawn.

Finally, with a well-practised, confidential, sneering smile, Miss James leaned in towards Hope and Adam. "We wondered," she whispered, desperate for some staff room gossip, "is everything alright at home?"

Adam stepped in, feeling Hope rear up beside him. A mother lion about to rescue her cub. "Since you are asking *now*, Miss James, yes, there have been some complications at home," he said.

"Children do often pick up on tensions," she condescended, digging for scandal, "between parents…"

Adam began to make some polite noises, but shut his mouth as Hope squeezed his hand. "Here she goes," he thought, with joyful dread.

"So, these changes in Callum's behaviour have been evident since the beginning of September?" asked Hope, mildly.

"I'm afraid so," Miss James nodded with a condescending smirk.

"And you've only thought to point it out to us now, nearly three months later?"

"Well." Miss James, somewhat taken aback by Hope's response, tried to retrieve her lost ground with a textbook response. "The 'behaviours' have become more marked over time," she confirmed, "but I have to say that at this point, Callum's work has deteriorated and his conduct has become challenging to the point of concern. I was hoping we could work together to get Callum back on track."

Hope drew in a deep breath, which Miss James, foolishly, took for defeated acquiescence. "From September to December my eight-year-old son has had a total personality change, his work has deteriorated and his behaviour has become challenging and unmanageable?"

"Well, not unmanageable," Miss James responded, rather less sure of herself, "but unusual for Callum."

"Unusual for Callum," Hope stated coldly. "Unusual for Callum from September to December. Unusual for Callum, and you never thought to call me?"

"I believe you both work," Miss James said, blindly ploughing the same dangerous furrow.

"Yes, Miss James, I do work," Hope said. "Yet despite my three jobs which start at five every morning, and Adam having to run his own business at night and his father's during the day, supporting Adam's parents, especially my sick father-in-law since his heart attack, running a home and bringing up four children, *one* of us is at the school gate *every day*!" Hope's voice began to rise again, "And the only time you came out to speak with me was to scrounge a ruddy free Christmas tree!"

Other parents began to look through the door, hoping for some entertainment. Miss James reddened, "I'm sorry," she said, "I was unaware that…"

"Callum's life has been turned upside down over the last year, everything that was 'normal' is changed." By now Hope was talking to herself as much as to the shaken Miss James. Hope looked at Adam, "He must have been so confused, so worried."

Miss James, by now, felt equally remorseful. "I'm truly sorry, Mr and Mrs Taylor," she said, "with all the bustle of the Christmas term, I broke one of my cardinal rules. I saw only the behaviour and not the boy."

Hope looked at the young teacher, who's eyes were brimmed with tears, remembering her own actions only the previous weekend.

"Maybe we all did, Miss James," she said softly.

****

Worried at what she might see, Danny turned down a lift home from Pat, and walked home. For once, there was no bag of broken cakes or unsold savouries to take the edge off his hunger. As he approached his home, Danny could see the lights were still out, but let himself in, hoping that he would just find his father sitting in the dark. The stale air hitting him as he opened the door was enough to let Danny know that his father simply had not been home. He checked his phone, no answer to his four or five texts. He dialled his father's number, and unexpectedly the call was answered.

"Danny boy!" his father shouted. There was noise in the background, laughter and music.

"Dad, are you okay, Dad?"

"Yea, mate, I'm fine!"

Danny seriously doubted that. "Where are you Dad?"

"I'm with some friends…" he was distracted, joining with the laughter of the 'friends' Danny could not see.

"Are you coming home tonight?"

"Hell, Danny, what's with the third degree. I'm just out with my mates, alright?" he seemed to fade out of the conversation.

"Dad! Dad, the electric's off."

"You can look after yourself, son, you'll be alright, you'll be alright!" There was a surge in the sound, a roar of laughter, "What? Got to go mate, seeya!" And the phone went dead.

With the prospect of a cold night ahead, Danny switched on his phone torch and hunted the kitchen cupboards for something to eat. The fridge, completely empty, was also stinking after three days without power. Apart from salt, pepper and vinegar, the cupboards really were bare. It had begun to rain heavily outside. He just piled into bed to keep warm and was soon asleep.

****

"Morning, Hope!" Faith called, as she hurried past the open door of an adjoining office. Hope returned a 'good morning,' as she wiped scattered biscuit crumbs from a desk.

Yesterday's parents evening had shaken her. She had taken this early morning job to keep things 'normal' for her family while she and Adam tried to rescue the family firm from bankruptcy. Last night, she and Adam had talked, really talked, something they had not done for a long time. Failure to communicate, often the first symptom signs of dying marriage, was, in this case, a sign of their mutual love and respect. Neither wanted to burden the other with their 'selfish' sorrows, they had both chosen to keep quiet and carry on until things got better. With no one to talk to, least of all each other, life had become a dreary, endless grind. Worst of all, their children, the innocent parties in all this adult folly, were suffering the most. They had made some decisions last night and Hope saw a happier family life ahead.

She pushed open Faith's door – the 'star' was already at work, outlining her show for the day, and adding snaps from yesterday's Applebury evening to her social media accounts. She looked round as Hope entered the room. "Sorry," she said," I'm messing up your schedule."

"I can start in this office from now on," Hope suggested, "then I'll be well clear by seven-thirty."

"That's kind of you," Faith said, but in truth, she enjoyed her early morning chats with Hope, and was reluctant to let them go. Although, of course, the girl had a job to do. "Maybe after Christmas, if I keep doing these early starts, but for now I'm happy to keep things as they are," she said, "if it's okay with you?"

Hope was surprised that her 'okay' was even part of the equation, but it was a nice thought, if unnecessary, following last night's conversation. "Thank you," she smiled, "but I have just given notice here. I won't be back after Christmas."

"Oh, I'm sorry to hear that," Faith said, "have you found another job?"

Hope explained her dilemma, that working extra hours to keep the family afloat had actually had the opposite effect. "Adam and I were so focussed on his father's illness, and the troubles around that, we couldn't see how the fallout was affecting the children," she said.

Faith saw her distress. "Sometimes life makes choices for us, decisions are taken out of our hands," she said, "but it seems to me you've taken back control."

"I have, haven't I?" Hope agreed. "Thank you!"

Hope was still smiling as she drove home. "I have the power!" she shouted, punching the air, collecting looks of alarm from surrounding traffic.

****

Danny dressed quickly and ran for the free college bus. College was warm, at least.

The class tutor was surprised, but pleased to see him. The other students were piling in, a boisterous bundle of adolescents hyped up by Christmas fever and energy drinks. Greeting each other and the long-missed Danny, things began to get out of hand. The teacher looked at Grace, silently appealing for her to fix the escalating class wobble.

Grace called the class to order. "It's great to see you Danny, thank you for coming in." Danny looked confused, but since being in class had given him the opportunity to charge his phone, he simply smiled. "As you know, Danny has been so successful on his work experience," Grace announced, finally securing the attention of the group, "that he has been offered a full-time job"

Cries of 'yes, mate!' 'get in!' and similar congratulatory phrases rang around the class room. Grace carried on. "And he is going to talk to us about what he has learned about the world of work, then Danny will answer any questions you may have."

Danny looked horrified, but after a fairly painless thirty minutes, he had given them a brief outline of his employer, his job and his hope for the future. Just before break time, Grace thanked him and steered him out of the class. "I understood you were at the Garden Centre from now until you start the apprenticeship," she stated, with some irritation.

Danny bluffed an explanation. "I've got the day off, so I thought I'd just come and check there's nothing I should be doing, forms to fill, or anything."

"It's great to see you here, Danny," she lied, her mind racing as she heard the noise behind the door she had just shut.

Danny heard it too. "Blimey, Miss, was I like that?" he said, shaking his head.

Grace smiled, he had only been working at the Taylor' s for a couple of weeks and he had the weary attitude of a worldly-wise old workhorse. "You were always a bit more grown up than most of them, Danny, I guess."

He smiled. "Is there anything for me to do?" he asked.

"Not really Danny, unless you've got personal items to pick up, you're done with us until you start in the main college next term."

"I've really got to go back into the classroom," she said. "If you hang on until break time, I'll bring you out your phone and charger and anything else that belongs to you. You could check lost property while you're waiting."

Grace, having found nothing of Danny's in the classroom, put his unanticipated appearance down as another example of teenage boredom and thought no more of it. Danny knew very well that there was nothing of his in the classroom, but having been given his now fully charged phone, he went to the office to trawl through the lost property box as Grace had suggested. He claimed a dusty pair of ski gloves, a woolly hat and a fairly decent pair of smart black trousers, none of which had ever belonged to him. He thanked the school secretary, who seeing how much he had to carry, suggested he help himself to one of the many sports bags which had been in the box for months. Danny thanked her politely, hung around the warm college until lunchtime, scrounged a few leftovers from his mates, then used his college bus pass to get back to Applebury. Home, as he had expected, was dark and empty. He packed his work uniform in the sports bag and, after waiting a couple of hours, walked back into Applebury and the warmth of Taylor's Country Gardens. There was a wooded area opposite the garden centre where Danny could wait unseen, as, one by one, his workmates left. Once Pat had locked the big iron grille and at last driven away, he made his way unseen into the grounds and finally, the scullery.

****

"Thanks so much for your calls, and remember to post your PIFFs on our social media page." The news jingle began to play. "Until tomorrow, this is Faith New and that was the *GOOD* News!"

Faith got a thumbs up from Megan, and behind her, Miles Carter was clapping. "We need to talk," he said, as they walked towards his office.

"That sounds ominous," she grimaced.

"Not at all," he reassured her. "Applebury Festival has become a bit of a phenomenon since you started the programme. The network has picked up the idea across all the other county radio stations, but ours has been the most successful." He looked both exultant and relieved.

"Our gamble paid off, thank goodness!" Faith said.

"It certainly did," Miles agreed. "Pat's PIFFs have gone viral, and apparently there's even a meme of Boromir saying, 'One does not simply decorate a Christmas tree!'"

Faith laughed. "Outside broadcast tomorrow had better go well, then."

Miles nodded. "That's the thing – local TV news wants to interview you. They're going to come and film you at work during the OB tomorrow, then, Monday morning, they've asked if you will be on their breakfast show."

For the first time in a long time, Faith was excited, and, honestly, a bit overwhelmed.

"They're coming along at noon tomorrow, so pick your interviewee well," he said. "They are going to the garden centre and the church for some side shots, but the main focus will be on the town square."

She knew exactly who she wanted to be interviewing when the TV crew arrived. Back in her office, she gave Guy a call.

Chapter Thirteen

As with any 'spontaneous' media event, this outside broadcast had been meticulously planned. Scheduled 'key player' interviews, balancing information, humour and sentiment were to be interspersed with unrehearsed and unpredictable contributions from members of the crowd. By the time Faith arrived, with the crew and equipment already in place, the town was thronged with people. The square was lined with stalls for the customary Friday Christmas Market and the C2C broadcast truck sat neatly at the back. Pushing through the waiting crowd, Faith realised that her daily invitations to their town centre transmission had been spectacularly effective.

By midday, when they arrived in Applebury Town Square, the TV crew had already filmed at the church and garden centre. They stayed for a while after her interview, recording the event, but Faith, immersed in the controlled frenzy of the show, had hardly noticed when they left. Later that evening, as she watched the regional news, she delighted in the skills of those who had distilled hours of footage into three minutes, which absolutely captured the essence of Applebury and its Christmas Tree Festival.

Almost immediately the piece finished, Miles called. "This will really raise your profile, Faith," he congratulated her, continuing in a dramatic 'radio announcer' voice, "no longer a faceless radio star, Faith New, star of stage and screen!"

She remained silent, for just a moment too long.

"Faith?"

"It's not a path I have ever chosen to take," said Faith. In fact, she had always protected her privacy. Rarely appearing on TV, except when called to comment on the consequences of one of her exposés, Faith had avoided discussion panels, comedy quiz shows, and any other kind of public exposure outside of her own field. Particularly since her decision to move to regional radio, Faith had assiduously played down her 'celebrity' status.

Miles pushed on. "Never say never!" he joked, "this could be the start of something big."

Faith thanked him, realising that this was not the time to explain further, and brought the conversation to a friendly close. Almost immediately, the phone buzzed again. It was Guy. "Business in the town is booming, thanks to you," he said. "I think the Applebury Festival is here to stay."

"The Four Pops did well," Faith remarked. The group had featured briefly at the very beginning of the piece and of course, Guy as Mayor, along with Mark, Debbie, and Adam, had all featured in one way or another.

"I think we all did," Guy agreed. "The gang at Edward Henry Court send their congratulations. They were all buzzing about it!" Faith asked if he had been performing there again, since it was Friday. "Nothing quite so interesting," he said. "Mother's Christmas tree lights went. I had to go and sort them out. Why she won't get a nice set of LEDs I don't know."

"I remember those old-style lights!" Faith laughed. "You have to test every one!"

"Yep, I reckon they're in a union," Guy laughed, "one out, all out!"

"Ah, that's one advantage of not having a tree," Faith said, "no fussing about with lights."

Guy was horrified. "You don't have a tree?"

"I have to own up," Faith said. "I haven't bothered for ages, with only myself to see it there doesn't seem much point."

"So, you're telling me that Miss Applebury Christmas Tree Festival doesn't actually have a Christmas tree of her own?" he said. "I'm appalled!"

Faith laughed at his comic, though genuine, horror. "I've got some angels. I usually hang them from the weeping fig," she said pathetically, then held the phone away from her ear as he guffawed.

"That really won't do at all," he said, once he had recovered. "Tell you what, I'll meet you at Taylor's Country Gardens tomorrow at ten. I'll buy you a coffee by way of thanks for all you've done for our little town, and then," he paused for effect, "I will not let you leave without buying a Christmas tree."

"How can I resist?" she laughed.

****

Adam had returned from his 'five minutes of fame' in the Applebury broadcast to find Jim and Danny putting the finishes to a new display immediately inside the main entrance. A pyramid of pallets, carefully disguised with horticultural fleece 'snow' was laden with pot after pot of Danny's plant rescues. At the centre a potted fir, covered in candy canes, mirrored the mainly red and white blooms beneath.

"It's magnificent!" Adam said. "Looks great, but most of all, the plants are in top condition, all credit to you Danny!"

"I reckon they'll all be gone before Monday," Jim said, by way of agreement. "Time we started growing our own again."

Friday flew by for Danny, who alternated between the cash desk and the café for the rest of the day.

****

After the broadcast, there had been many calls to book tickets and, even at this late stage, requests to put a tree in the festival. Mark and Debbie had realised that they needed more than goodwill and a godly prayer to prevent the whole festival descending into chaos. They hurriedly devised a plan to cope with the huge success of the event. All four inside walls of the church could be lined with trees, as could the foyer and much of the adjoining hall. They had, indeed, stopped at 100 trees, but Debbie had allowed a few extras to stand outside. They had been forced to abandon their original 'come one, come all' approach to Applebury's Got Talent, for the sake of time and quality. Nevertheless, there were a few surprises in store for the audience. By Saturday morning, rehearsals had begun, Grace and Doug were practising their accompaniments, and three hundred mince pies had been ordered from the bakery.

Saturday morning at Taylor's Country Gardens was busy – so busy that Adam could only manage a cursory wave at Guy and Faith in the café, as he rushed to help Rosa at the cash desk, already backed up with a queue of impatient shoppers. "It's going to be unmanageable, Mum," he was saying into his mobile phone as he helped, beckoning Danny over to pack, speeding things along a bit. "I'm sorry to ask, but I don't know what else to do."

Agnes gladly agreed to care for Callum and Lily so that Hope and Briony could join Adam at Taylor's. Hope quickly dressed her two youngest children who had been lolling in their pyjamas, while Briony sulkily applied a thick layer of makeup because, God forbid, "Someone I know might see me!"

"Grandma, we're here!" shouted Lily, as Agnes welcomed her with a hug, then in a joyful squeak, "What will we get up to, Grandma?"

Agnes, who wanted to protect Brian from the extra strain of having two excited children in the house, had a plan. "Well, I've got a bit of shopping to do in town," said Agnes, "you can both come with me."

"Can we get unicorn stuff?" demanded Lily.

Callum's eyes widened in horror. He looked at his Grandfather with that age old look of a man in need of rescue. "Callum," Brian said, "I could do with a hand sorting out my shed, if you don't mind missing the shopping trip."

Callum turned to his Grandma as he removed his hat, coat, and gloves at speed. "I'm afraid I can't go shopping, Grandad needs me."

Agnes looked at the two conspirators, then at Lily. "Well, it's just you and me then, Lily. Let's go and find some unicorns!"

Faith and Guy had found a small, potted tree that could easily fit into the footwell in the back her car. His attempts to persuade her into a floor-to-ceiling Scots pine had been unsuccessful.

"This is quite enough for me," she said. "My house has never seen a Christmas tree, so I don't want to overdo it!" She had bought a few white lights and a star for the top, which she threw onto the passenger seat, closing the door just as Guy closed the door on the safely stowed tree. Both froze, aware of how uncomfortably close they stood, and how inconveniently pleasant that closeness felt. Faith stepped back, hurrying round to the other side of the car.

"Thank you, Guy," she said, looking far calmer than she felt. "I have enjoyed this morning."

"Likewise," Guy responded, giving her a thumbs up. "Until next time."

He hurried to his car, jumped into his seat and, out of sight of Faith, bowed his head onto the steering wheel. "A thumbs up?" he growled in embarrassment. "A thumbs up?" he cringed, imagining how his awkward gesture must have looked to Faith. Raising his head, he looked in the rear-view mirror. "Guy Harvey," he told his reflection, "you sure are a smooth operator."

****

Hope saw her phone buzzing later in the afternoon. It was Agnes. "What's happened?" she asked, imagining all sorts of trouble.

"Nothing at all," Agnes assured her. "We are having a lovely time. "The reason I'm ringing is Callum has asked if he can go to church with us tomorrow, and now Lily wants to go too…"

"As long as you're sure," Hope interrupted.

"Oh, that's not all, Agnes continued, "we wondered if they could stay here tonight, then we'll drop them with you afterwards. Is that okay?"

Hope imagined her morning, with no early start, no squabbles. She had no difficulty agreeing to the plan and was overjoyed to hear the huge whoop of delight from Callum in the back ground when she said yes.

So for the second Sunday in a row, Brian found himself in church, his new 'best pal' beside him. As they walked to their seats, Grace was sorting her sheet music onto the piano.

"Are you playing the piano again?" Callum asked, running up to her.

"I am," Grace responded, charmed by the little fellow's interest. "Do you like the piano?"

"I like that this one," pointing to her left hand, "dances one tune, and this one," he said, taking her right hand, "dances another tune, and together they make a whole song."

Grace looked at Brian, then back at Callum. "That is the best description of piano that I have ever heard," she beamed.

"We'd better sit where we can see your dancing hands then, Grace," Brian said, guiding Callum into the front row. Callum found the service full of music and joy, just as fascinating as last week. When his sister trotted off to Sunday school, Callum stayed close to his Grandfather, and in the final hymn he joined the singing with gusto. Agnes and Brian chatted with friends who were delighted to see Brian looking so much better. Grace caught Callum's eye as he watched her packing away her music. She beckoned him over.

He traced the notes on the sheet music. "Is this how you know what to play?" he said. Grace nodded, showing him how the dots and lines were a special language. She pointed to each note as she played the corresponding key. "I really liked the songs we sang today," he said.

Grace asked if he had a favourite. Calum thought for a second. "I can't remember all the words he said but, it started…" He began to sing, exactly at the pitch the song had originally been sung, "O holy night, the stars are brightly shining…" His beautifully clear treble rose and Brian, picking up Greg's guitar, strummed the accompaniment. Grace, finding the song in her hymnal, began to accompany them. He read the words beneath her music, focused only on the fusion of his melody with her accompaniment. One by one, the scattered conversations across the church fell silent as the purity of the child's singing filled the church.

> *"Oh, night when Christ was born,*
> *Oh, night divine, O, night divine…"*

A hush followed for just a few seconds, then a round of gentle clapping. Brian, moved to tears, knelt and hugged his grandson. "Did you like that Grandad?" Callum smiled. Brian nodded, unable to speak.

Grace, her hand on Callum's shoulder, looked up at Agnes. "Callum has a natural gift for music, I mean, far greater than most."

Callum spun round. "Will you teach me piano?"

"I would love to, until something can be set up with a qualified music teacher," Grace offered.

"Aren't you qualified?" Callum asked.

"I can play, certainly, but I think you will need a proper teacher," she said, more for Agnes' information than Callum's.

Callum looked at Grace, his mouth twisted in thought. "I think you'll do to start with," he declared, to the amusement of them all.

Lily ran up clutching a glue covered toilet-roll donkey. "Look what I made!" she yelled, pulling them all back down to earth.

Brian took a moment, before the opportunity was lost, to hug Callum close. "I'm proud of you," he whispered.

As they climbed into the car, ready to take the children home, Callum said, "Grandad, can we go and see Santa's Workshop?"

"Oh yes, it's amazing," boasted Lily. "And the Winter Wonderland is beautiful, too. I have seen it *all*!"

Brian realised they were talking about Taylor's Country Gardens. He had left the place eighteen months ago in an ambulance, and he was reluctant to go back, even now.

"Callum," Agnes asked gently, "haven't you seen Santa's Workshop, like Lily?"

Lily, triumphant, boasted, "Callum is not allowed, because Callum is naughty, only *I* am allowed" She smirked smugly at her older brother.

Brian turned in his seat to see Callum's hopeful expression give way to defeat. "That's it," Brian said firmly. "Taylor's Country Gardens here we come. Step on it, Grandma!"

A nearly full car park, freshly planted tubs and baskets, garlanded pillars and a queue to buy Christmas trees gave Brian an inkling of the transformation of Taylor's Country Gardens. Walking in, the display of Danny's plants was only the first in a series of remarkable innovations. He stopped for a moment, enjoying the beauty of the cheerful blooms and emergent narcissi. Brian could almost feel the health returning to his body and soul as he toured the old place. The Winter Wonderland, the North Pole, and each neatly themed zone in its festive splendour convinced Brian that Taylor's Country Gardens, like its owner, may still have some life ahead.

As they emerged, smiling, from Santa's Workshop, the old sleigh sparkled with the reflected tree lights. "Well, I never!" Brian gasped, "after all these years!" He stood to take a photo, as Agnes and the children sat in the sleigh, when a hand reached over to take the camera.

"Jump in, Dad, and I'll get one of you all."

"Daddy, we came to see you!" called Lily.

"What a lovely surprise," Adam said looking at his father, grabbing him in a hug. "It's good to have you back."

Brian could see Pat, waving from behind the busy counter. She blew him a kiss.

He waved back. "Who's the new waiter?" he asked, spotting Danny.

Adam shared Danny's unusual history at Taylors. "In fact, he's responsible for the display at the entrance," smiled Adam, "every single pot was nurtured by him."

"In the plant hospital," Lily interjected. She waved at Danny who, looking up, had seen them all looking at him. He nodded self-consciously, then scurried off to the kitchen with his tray of cleared crockery. He soon reappeared, minus his apron.

"Pat says I should introduce myself, Mr and Mrs Taylor," he said, nervously, "and that maybe you could stay for lunch here, once you've had a look round."

"That *is* a great idea," said Brian. "If you've got a minute, Danny, I'd like you to tell me about the display at the entrance." They walked together towards the show of glorious colour. "So, these are from the plant hospital?" Brian asked.

"They were going to be thrown out, Danny replied. "It seemed a shame." Brian nodded agreement as

Danny continued, "So I used deep pots because of the large root structure, one third grit and the rest compost. I kept them in the scullery where it's cold, then when they started to shoot…"

"I see you've met my apprentice, old pal!" boomed a voice behind them.

Brian turned to see Jim. "What are you doing here on a Sunday?" he asked.

"I work here," quipped Jim, "remember?"

The three of them did a 'horticultural' tour. Danny enthusiastically pointing out the hanging baskets that he and Rosa had made up. "We can charge twice as much for a planted pot or basket as for individual plants, so it's worth doing," he observed.

"A head for business, too," said Brian, impressed. "I can see a future for you here."

"I think I'd better get back, Mr Taylor," Danny said, in a failed attempt to hide his pleasure at Brian's remark. "Café's getting busy for lunch." He strode off, beaming.

Agnes, meanwhile, had phoned Hope to tell her the change of plan and seated herself, Lily and Callum in the café. Brian walked to join them, Jim having returned to the cash desk. Just as he arrived at the café, he was hailed. "Mr Taylor, can you help us?" An older couple stood before him, evidently Christmas regulars who had no idea that this was Brian's first and only visit in a long time. "We've bought our tree here, a big Scots pine, for twenty years. But we've just downsized."

"I see your problem," Brian said. For the next ten minutes, he advised them on the relative benefits of Nordmann firs versus Fraser firs, helped them pick a tree and walked them to the cash desk. Agnes could hardly contain her amazement and joy, as her husband joined her in the café.

"Well," he beamed, "shall we start with ice cream?"

At home, Hope received a second call immediately after she had spoken to Agnes. It was Grace. "I'm just ringing about what happened with Callum this morning."

Hope's heart fell. "What *did* happen?" she asked, imagining some catastrophe.

"His singing," Grace said, "haven't they told you yet?"

Hope was bemused and intrigued. "Callum and Lily are still with their Grandma and Grandad," she said. "I'm afraid I haven't heard about Callum's singing."

Grace went on to tell her about the Callum's unexpected solo and her belief that he should build on his natural potential. "Really, Hope," she said, "it would be a pleasure to get him started on that path, but actually, there's another reason for my call. I've had an idea."

After a brief discussion, Hope agreed to talk to Callum as soon as he got home. Not too long afterwards, Callum and Lily piled in, full of ice-cream, chips and joy. She looked over their heads at Brian and Agnes. "Thank you both so much," she said.

"We've had a wonderful time," Brian said, "so thank *you*," he said, looking at the grandchildren.

"Grace rang me," Hope said, with a look of confusion, "she was very impressed with Callum's singing."

Callum, who had been concentrating on pulling his gloves the right way out again, heard his name mentioned. "I did sing, didn't I, Grandad?" he asked. "Everyone clapped, didn't they?"

Hope looked at Agnes for confirmation. "It's true," she said, "he was exceptionally good."

Hope kneeled beside Callum. "Grace has asked if you would sing at the talent concert," she said, "but you don't have to, only if you want to."

Without hesitation, Callum said, "Of course I'll sing. Will you be there, Grandad, like today?"

"I will," smiled Brian.

Chapter Fourteen

There was something both new and nostalgic in the story of a small English town and its Christmas Festival. Faith's early morning TV appearance had been re-played as the 'Applebury Phenomenon' featured in successive regional newscasts. 'Love@Christmas' had been embraced across the social media sphere, and a clip of The Four Pops had become a viral meme.

"I am thrilled our gamble has paid off," Faith remarked to Miles, "but I still have this nagging feeling I'm missing the point, somehow." They were catching up after her Monday show.

"Maybe, just this once, Faith," he replied, "it's just an honest story, with no scandal, corruption, or dirty dealings."

She smiled as she opened the door to leave, "I know," she said, "old habits die hard!"

"Things will be back to their gloomy normal in January," Miles sighed, "just enjoy this while it lasts."

Faith nodded, 'gloomy normal' was less than a fortnight away. "I guess I can bear all this comfort and joy for another week or two," she laughed.

She grabbed her coat and bag from her office and left the building, only to see Hope walking into the car park toward an old silver Zafira. Faith waved and walked across to Hope who was, by now, loading several extra-large carriers into the back of the car.

"Christmas shopping in town," Hope explained. "The grandparents are picking Callum and Lily up, so I've got the whole afternoon!"

"It's a bit of a walk from here to Supertoys," Faith remarked, seeing the carriers in the back were all from that bargain superstore.

"Cheeky free parking, though," Hope said. "I've saved a fortune!" She closed the boot and locked the car.

"Have you got much more to do?" Faith asked.

"Not much," Hope replied. "I'm on the home stretch now. I was heading for the shopping centre for something for the in-laws, and of course Rosa and Briony."

"Ah yes, teenagers," Faith laughed. "The smaller the present the bigger the price tag, so they tell me."

"Who ever said that is absolutely spot on," Hope giggled. She had a sudden impulse. "I was just going to treat myself to a cup of tea and a cake at Bella's, before starting on the next round. Would you like to join me?"

"I'd love to," Faith replied, delighted to be asked.

They walked across to Bella's and spent a very pleasant hour together. Afterwards, as Hope walked on towards Sparchester town centre, and Faith returned to her car, each reflected on the serendipity of their meeting and the friendship that was growing from it.

Wednesday morning, Faith was putting the final touches to her Christmas Eve broadcast plan, the first after the festival, and the big finish to her Applebury Christmas series. She had phone-in slots scheduled for the usual key figures, three for the talent contest stars and winners of the tree competition. The rest, she hoped, would be listeners calling in with their own Christmas Eve stories.

Faith had just pressed 'send' on the last email, when there was a tap on the door, and Hope appeared with a coffee in each hand. "A bit cheeky, I know," she grinned, "but I don't think I'm going to see you at work again. I finish on Christmas Eve."

"Thank you," Faith said, gesturing Hope to take a seat, "and it's not cheeky, perfect timing, actually. This festival is taking up a lot more of my time than I had expected, and of course I need to find something to follow the big success of Applebury after Christmas."

"Oh, yes, my mum-in-law said you are guest of honour at the talent show," Hope giggled, "and at the Sunday Service. You really know how to have a good time!"

Faith shared her amusement, but surprised Hope with her response. "Honestly, I'm looking forward to it. Are you shocked?"

"I suppose I imagined you living a far more glamorous lifestyle, rubbing shoulders with the rich and famous."

"It all loses its shine after a while." Faith shrugged. "I am actually looking forward to this weekend, sad as it seems!"

"My son is singing," Hope said, "and his Grandad is his accompanist."

"You must be very proud of him," Faith said. "What is the song?"

"It's all a big secret," Hope said. "I take him to practice, but I have to leave so I don't spoil the 'big reveal' on Saturday."

Faith saw the immense love and pride behind Hope's humour. "What a lovely thought," she said. "Grandfather and grandson singing together. Are your other children performing?"

Hope shook her head and counted her other children off on her fingers. "Rosa, too busy studying. Briony, 'too cool.' Lily, simply not interested."

Faith laughed. "Too cool!"

Hope laughed with her. "I know, I've never been cool in my life!" She paused for a moment, "It'll be the start of Christmas for us."

"That must be a noisy affair," Faith observed, "with the four of them…"

"And Adam's parents," Hope added. "Yes, it is chaotic, and I love it, even though It's the complete opposite to all my peaceful childhood Christmases. Just me, Mum and Dad."

"I do apologise," Faith said, as Hope's eyes misted with nostalgia. "I'm making you sad."

"Not at all, they are very happy memories. I had the best childhood. How Mum and Dad made me feel like the centre of their universe without turning me into a spoiled brat, I don't know!"

"You said you were adopted," Faith asked, more casually than she felt. "Were you ever curious about…" she paused, afraid to say the word.

"About my birth mother?" Hope finished the question. "I was and I wasn't," she said. "It never occurred to me that I belonged anywhere else, I just felt very blessed to have such great parents."

"They sound like wonderful people," Faith said.

Hope nodded. "Mum and Dad told me anything I wanted to know, and encouraged me to look for her when I turned eighteen, if I wanted to, but I didn't. Does that sound heartless?"

"Not at all," said Faith, "I imagine it was exactly what your mother would have wanted."

"My birth mother," corrected Hope. "I wondered in 2002 whether she would try to find me, as it was legal then, but she never has." Hope, thrown a little off balance by the turn in their conversation, asked, "Is an adoption feature one of your plans for January?"

"It's a possibility," Faith said, although she had never considered it until now. "Did you ever try to find out more about her?"

"I never felt more than curiosity really, until I had my own children, and realised how hard it would be to give a child away. Then after my parents passed away within two years of each other I wanted to find out more, so I applied to look at my adoption file." Faith nodded to her to continue. "It turns out mine was a private adoption. There was hardly anything in the file, and nothing in there that I didn't already know."

Faith, so personally interested, tried to appear indifferent. "So, you don't blame your," Faith was careful to say it this time, "birth mother for what she did?"

"Like a lot of adoptees," Hope said, "I have always been grateful to her for the life I have had, but lately," she thought for a moment, struggling for the right word, "lately, I have felt enormous compassion for her."

Faith's questions, of course, had nothing to do with a proposed feature on adoption and everything to do with her own 'lost' daughter. Hope's words had been comforting. Not that she had doubted that an adopted child could feel just as loved, safe and wanted as any other, but that the child would bear no grudge against the one who had 'given' them away.

"Compassion?" Faith asked, as Hope explained further.

"From what I know, she was a bit of a wild child and I was the result. My oldest girls are around her age now. I can't see either of them being able to cope with the birth, let alone being a Mum. Poor girl."

Faith, struggling to appear unmoved, feigned a sudden interest in her emails. Hope took that as her cue to leave.

"I had better be going," she said, "you must be so busy."

Faith turned back to her, "I'm sorry, I didn't mean to be rude." She smiled, wiping a tear from her cheek. "I'm touched by what you have said. You bear no bitterness or feelings of rejection, just compassion. That's very forgiving."

Hope stood to go. "There is nothing to forgive. A very young girl in a horrible situation had to make a tough decision. She gave me to a couple who had given up all hope of having a child, hence my name."

"They must have been overjoyed," Faith said, by way of goodbye, as Hope opened the door to leave.

"Oh, they were," Hope smiled, "delivered to their door on Christmas Eve, Mum said I was the only Christmas present they ever needed." With a smile, Hope left.

Faith stared at the closed door. Christmas Eve. For a foolish minute or two she fantasized that Hope would turn out to be her own, but with a shake of the head she dismissed the idea.

"Preposterous idea, Faith!" she admonished herself and got on with her work.

Hope gave a passing thought to Faith's plans for a feature on adoption, but it was soon lost in the pre-school scurry to find Christmas cards, gloves and Callum's lost shoe.

Tuesday's show, with its theme of family traditions, was nothing short of hilarious, with warm tales of Christmas past, time-honoured recipes, and tipsy grandmas. The only controversy being whether presents should be opened first thing in the morning, or after the Queen's Speech. The program seemed to be over far too quickly. Faith signed off with a promise to continue in the same vein the next day. As she packed up her things to leave, she was pleased to see an email confirming her meeting at Applebury church on Friday. A last check to finalise arrangements for the weekend. She was putting her phone in her bag when it buzzed a call.

It was Guy. He spoke before she could say 'hello.' "My grandson tells me I'm a gif, thanks to you."

Faith laughed. "It could be worse, you could be a 'meme.'"

"No doubt that'll be next," Guy said in theatrical resignation.

"My boss tells me The Four Pops are trending on social media. You're very popular."

"I don't mind a bit of fame and fortune, if I must."

Faith had an idea. "We've had a great show today, all about the family…"

"It was a great show, we had it on in the workshop."

Faith thanked him, then put her idea to him. "I know it's a bit late notice," she said, "but since you're a family group, could you spare an hour to come in and give us a song or two?"

Guy, a showman to his core, agreed immediately, saying he could 'shuffle things around a bit' at the garage. The Four Pops were to open the show on Wednesday morning.

"Well, if that's it," Faith was about to close the conversation, but Guy spoke.

"There is something…" he said, suddenly serious. He lost his nerve. "How's your Christmas tree doing?"

"Um…it's flourishing," Faith replied, realising that she had no idea why he had called her in the first place. "Why?"

There was a pause, then Guy spoke very quickly. "I was going to ask if you'd like to go out to dinner tonight." Faith took a moment to respond; he took her silence as a refusal. "Don't worry," he said, backtracking, "it was just a thought, we seemed to get on…"

"Yes," said Faith. "Yes, I would love to go out tonight." She smiled as Guy let out an audible sigh of relief. They made arrangements to meet at a restaurant close to Faith's home that evening.

****

"You look stunning," Guy said, as she walked up to meet him at the bar. A smart waiter showed them to their table.

"This is perfect," said Faith. They were in a secluded corner hidden from most of the other diners.

"Yes, well I don't want to be recognised," Guy said seriously, "you can't be too careful!"

She smiled, wryly. "Sorry I was a bit late," she said, "it's so long since I've been on a date. I didn't know what to wear, I must have changed five times!"

"I'm just glad you didn't stand me up," Guy said. "And I'm also glad you think this is a date."

"Oh, isn't it?" She blushed like a teenager. "I just assumed…"

"It is a date," said Guy, "but I wasn't sure I'd made that clear."

They laughed and fell awkwardly silent as the waiter brought their menus, recited the specials, then left them to decide. The self-conscious small talk as they scanned their menus convinced Guy that he had made a huge blunder. After the waiter had taken their order, he decided to come clean.

"I don't know about you, Faith," he admitted, "but I find all this…one on one stuff, a bit hard to navigate, best behaviour and all that. I'm not sure it's going to be a good idea after all."

"I was thinking the same thing," Faith admitted, "been all around the merry go round before. At my age I can't be faffed with all the hard work of a romance."

She looked so weary and so deadly serious, he laughed out loud. She could not help but join in.

"How long have you been…on your own," Guy asked, trying to be tactful.

Faith sighed, irritated at Guy's lack of directness. "To save time," Faith said, "and to avoid confusion, we should be straight right from the start." Guy bowed his head in agreement. "So, to answer your question," Faith continued, "I've always been single, I've only had two serious relationships, and neither of them lasted more than a couple of years." Seeing his eyebrows raise, she said, "And no, I'm not into 'free love' either. People say I'm married to my career, and I suppose they are right in a way. I'm just too…independent to rely on other people."

She waited. "Your turn," she prompted.

"I married nearly thirty years ago," he said. "Carol was my childhood sweetheart. We had David, then Emma a couple of years later. When Emma was about six months old, we found out that Carol was very sick. She died of cancer almost exactly a year after her diagnosis."

Faith said nothing, but laid her hand on his. He appreciated her silence, free of platitudes and useless sympathy.

"Well, I had two kids and a mortgage," he said, "so I had to grow up pretty fast. I knocked the part-time music career on the head, and threw myself heart and soul into running Dad's business. So, when you say you are married to your work, I completely understand."

"Maria told me you are responsible for Harvey's Motors' expansion and success. You must be proud of that. She said you saved the business."

"Dad was very happy with doing repairs from his inspection pit and selling a few second-hand cars," Guy said. "The business was doing fine, but I think he knew I needed to be busy, so he just let me get on with it. After Carol died, I was completely lost, so the truth is I didn't save Harvey's motors, Harvey's Motors saved me."

Faith looked at Guy with a new understanding, his determined optimism and big-hearted character were borne out of tragedy. He caught her eye. "Well, that's enough of that!" he declared. "Now we can just get on with enjoying each other's company. Do you fancy sharing a pudding after this?"

The waiter had already set their drinks on the table, Faith lifted her glass. "I'll drink to that," she said.

Guy clinked her glass with his, "Here's to a friendship with no faff!"

****

Pat, meanwhile, was in a heated telephone discussion with Adam. "Absolutely not," she said, "I won't have it."

"But, Auntie Pat, a lot of companies do it now, and it encourages people to stay and buy more."

"That's the problem, isn't it?" Pat insisted, "encouraging people to drink, maybe even drink and drive."

"It's just a bit of mulled wine, Auntie Pat, not enough to make anyone over the limit."

"I'll make a cinnamon fruit punch," she said, "you can warm that up and serve it."

"Seriously, Auntie Pat, I know you are teetotal, but that's no reason to stop other people having a bit of Christmas Cheer, and it's good for business."

"Taylor's has done fine up to now without plying their customers with drink, young man!"

"Auntie Pat, I'm the manager and I'm telling you that we will be greeting our customers with complimentary mulled wine and mince pies this weekend."

"And I am telling you, Adam, that if you do, I will not be coming in to work."

She hung up on him, furious. Then rang her brother, but the phone was already engaged. Adam, of course, had immediately rung his father, hoping for some back up for his brilliant idea. Instead, his father was entirely in agreement with Pat.

"It's exasperating!" he complained to Hope, as they stood in the kitchen. "Neither of them will see sense. It's just a few mince pies and some mulled wine, for goodness sake. I can't see why they are so set against it."

Hope looked at him enquiringly. "Can you not?" she said.

"Why are you looking at me like that?" Adam said, baffled.

"Adam, when has Auntie Pat ever had a drink, that you can remember?"

"Oh, never. She's a teetotal. Wouldn't even touch it at our wedding, if you remember."

Hope had her own theory on Pat's unshakeable determination to steer clear of any event offering, or even food containing alcohol.

"It's ridiculous," Adam continued, "her one-woman mission to save the world from the demon drink."

"It seems a shame to fall out with the family over it, though," Hope said, as she stirred drinking chocolate into a small jug of milk and put it in the microwave to warm. "Auntie Pat has worked for practically nothing for the last couple of years." Taking a sherry glass from the cupboard, she said, "There must be some way to compromise?"

"After all the changes in the last few weeks," Adam said, fuming, "why has she chosen to dig her heels in over this?"

The microwave pinged. Hope poured a quantity of creamy hot chocolate into the sherry glass, adding a whirl of squirty cream on top. Adam was still pacing the kitchen. "It's just a bit of festive cheer. After all, what could be more festive than a glass of mulled wine and a mince pie?"

Hope sprinkled sugar crystals onto the whipped cream, popped a candy cane into the glass and handed it to Adam. "What indeed?" she smiled.

Adam held the glass in front of his eyes. "Except maybe this delightful Christmassy concoction."

"And it's a whole lot cheaper to make than wine, and a lot less messy than mince pies," Hope added. "So everybody's happy."

Adam handed her his phone. "Here, take a photo," he said, holding up the 'Christmassy concoction.' I'll send it to Auntie Pat with an apology."

A few moments later, Pat heard her phone peep a message alert. She found a photo message from Adam. "Who needs mulled wine when you can have this?" it said. "What do you think?"

She smiled. Relieved. She did not want to fall out with Adam, but rules were rules. She stabbed out a reply. *It looks perfect. Christmas in a cup. See you tomorrow, xxxx.*

****

"I'd better order a taxi," Faith said, as they finished their second coffee. They had talked like old friends and neither wanted the evening to end.

"A taxi? You didn't drive here?"

"When I said this place was just around the corner, I wasn't exaggerating. It took me about 15 minutes to walk here through the park."

Guy looked at her ultra-high heels. "Really, you walked here?"

"These shoes are purely for sitting in," laughed Faith. "These," she pulled a pair of trainers from her bag, "are for walking."

"I could drop you home," Guy suggested.

Faith hesitated. She rarely shared her address, and certainly had no intention of inviting Guy into her home.

"Strictly friends," Guy reassured her, "and what sort of friend is it, who invites a lady out to dinner and then lets her make her own way home?"

She accepted the lift and directed him to her home. As she had said, the journey was barely ten minutes by car. He pulled into the drive and stopped right outside the front door.

"I nearly forgot," he said, slapping his hand to his forehead. "If you open the glove compartment, there's something in there for you."

"This is for me?" Faith said, holding up the little tissue wrapped gift she had found.

"It's from Mum," he said. "Her 'Knit and Natter' gang are making Applebury Angels for the craft stall on Saturday."

"Oh, I love angels," Faith cried, hastily pulling off the wrapping. She held it up as Guy switched on the interior light. A little crocheted Angel with a golden halo, pale hair and a tiny microphone in her hand.

"It's me!" she said. "Oh, I'd rather have this than the most expensive bauble angel in Harrods!" Her sheer, honest delight enchanted him.

"The best gifts are the ones money can't buy," he said tenderly.

"Tell Maria thank you," she said, still looking at the angel, then unexpectedly she reached across and kissed his cheek. "And thank *you*, Guy, for a lovely evening."

With that, she leapt out of the car and into her house, shutting the door behind her before Guy had time to speak.

"Friendship with no faff," he said out loud as he drove home. "I think not!"

Chapter Fifteen

"A very wise man told me," Faith said, as she opened Thursday's show, "that the best Christmas gifts are the ones money can't buy. I have a Christmas card here that has been specially made for me."

She looked at the tissue and glitter covered card that Hope had left on her desk that morning. A very red-faced angel, with excessively long eyelashes and googly eyes, stared back at her. Inside it read, "Happy Christmas, Faith New, from the Taylor family," surrounded by hundreds of x's. She closed the card and re-read the label at the back. "Hand Made by Callum and Lily."

"I can honestly say, in all my years of broadcasting, I have never had a more valuable, or a more beautiful, Christmas card. Thank you, Callum and Lily."

"How about you," she asked her listeners, "what is the most precious gift you have received that money can't buy?"

Heart-warming tales of triumph over hardship, health restored, romance, friendship, love and family filled the show. At almost the end of the program, after a show filled with a happy mix of opinion, humour and sentiment, Megan waved from the producer's box. "I believe we have one last caller," Faith announced, seeing Megan's enthusiastic smile. She wondered what could be so exciting about this very last-minute call.

Then a voice she had not heard in decades stuttered, "Hello, Sarah-Faith."

It was like being hit by a train. The breath went out of her. She was transported back nearly forty years, to the day this man stood still and silent as his wife tore Faith's life apart.

"Sarah-Faith Browne," he repeated, "It is you, isn't it? I saw you on TV."

Long before Faith had cut herself from her parent's lives, her father had distanced himself. Slowly disappearing, figuratively if not actually, into a shadow of the father she had loved before everything changed. "Won't you meet up with me, Sarah-Faith?" he whimpered. "Your mother's gone. It's just me, now."

"My mother is dead?" she repeated, flatly. She thought it would not hurt, but it did. Faith could not speak. She held the desk as if it were the edge of a bottomless chasm.

The smile fell from Megan's face, her well-meaning prank had somehow thrown the station's star performer into a state of paralysis.

"Come on, love, won't you speak to your old dad, you loved me once?…"

Faith actually thought she would vomit, or faint. She told herself to get a grip, but her body would not move and her brain had stopped processing anything but the sound of that unwanted voice. There was dead air, while she pulled herself back from the dark hole of memory she had been thrust into. She looked up through the glass at Megan's horrified face and slowly moved her head from side to side. The producer clicked on the next tune, then rushed in offering water. Faith, trembling and drained of colour, hung on to the arms of her chair as if she were about to fall.

"What's happened, Faith?" Megan asked, near to tears. "He said he was your dad, he wanted to surprise you."

Faith nodded, she simply could not speak, she took her bag and left the building, feeling that her legs could hardly carry her. The show finished with another two songs, back-to-back. Faith drove home on autopilot and sat in darkness. She did not cry, she did nothing at all. It was as if everything inside her had shut down. There was no room in her head for reasoning or recrimination, or even revenge. She only knew that if she relaxed the tight, tight thread that was holding her soul together at this point, she would break for ever.

The phone began to ring of course, then the doorbell. The press were outside already. She switched off both her phones, and went upstairs where she sat on her bed and looked out at the night sky for hours.

****

Hope had been sitting in the hairdressers, a Christmas treat which she owed to the recent surge in profit at the Garden centre. Faith's 'good news' program had become essential listening at the salon, as with many local businesses. She had smiled proudly and enjoyed each heart-warming tale from the audience, inspired by the simple gift of a card from her own children. The stylist held a mirror to the back of her newly toned and treated hair, gloriously loose, glossy, and frizz-free. As she thanked, paid, and tipped the stylist, Hope was fairly sure it would last no further than the first hint of drizzle.

Then she heard the name spoken on the radio. The salon hushed at the sudden change in pace. Hope heard 'that' name three times. There was no mistaking it. Her knees actually trembled, as if they would give way.

She must have walked to her car, she must have driven out of the town but she remembered nothing of it, only becoming aware of her surroundings as she pushed through the door of her in-law's cottage.

Agnes was in the kitchen, "Good Lord, Hope!" she gasped "Whatever has happened?"

Brian, hearing the concern in his wife's voice, hurried into the kitchen. He pulled out a chair. "Here, sit down," he said. "I'll get you a cup of tea."

Agnes asked after Adam and the children, fearing some dreadful news.

"They are all safe and well, nothing's happened," Hope assured her. "I've just had a bit of a shock!"

Brian passed her the tea. "You're as white as a sheet…"

Hope cut across him. "Did you hear Faith's program today?"

"We just caught the tail end of it," he said. "It was a bit of a strange way to end a…"

"Oh, Hope!" Agnes said, covering her mouth in shock and sudden comprehension. It occurred to her then that she had heard the name before. Sarah-Faith Browne...

Agnes and Brian had known Hope's parents well. They had watched Hope grow up and fall in love with their son. The fact of her adoption had never been a secret, and although it rarely came up in conversation, no one felt it was any more than an interesting detail. They had supported Hope when she attempted to trace her birth family after her parent's death. Sarah-Faith Browne had been nothing but a name, a mysterious figure that they had tried – and failed – to track down. Since then, Hope had seemed unworried by her lack of success. They had assumed the matter had been a passing fancy, now laid to rest.

"Is it her?" Agnes breathed. "Are you sure?"

"I'm certain," Hope said. "The name, the date, everything adds up. The trouble is," she said, suddenly tearful, "I've never really been more than curious, if that, about my birth mother. She was just an imaginary teenage girl who couldn't keep me. But now…"

"Now she is a real person, someone you actually know," said Agnes. "It must feel very different."

Brian, finally catching on, went into problem solving 'Dad' mode. "You need time", he said. "I'll pick the kids up from school and take them to your place. You two stay here and talk this through."

Agnes smiled her thanks. "They'll love that," she said.

"And don't worry about cooking," Brian added. "Happy meals all round for tea today!" He grabbed his coat, hat and keys, and was gone.

Agnes sat at the table with Hope. "Where do we go from here, then," she said.

Hope looked at her, bewildered. "I really don't know what to do."

"You don't have to do anything at all," Agnes said, "if that's what is best for *you*, Hope."

"But maybe I owe it to Faith to speak up. She's a nice woman, she has become a friend. It would be dishonest to know and say nothing."

"You don't owe her anything at all. There's a lot to be said for letting sleeping dogs lie."

"But…" Hope's mind whirled in a fog of shock, delight, and indecision.

Agnes interrupted her thoughts. "You both seemed to have survived the adoption. She has success, wealth

208

and a career. You had a happy childhood, and now a happy life with children of your own. It seems to me that is a very positive outcome for you both."

Hope nodded. "It's a strange feeling," she said. "I finally know, at least, who my mother is, but she is nothing like the woman I imagined. The reality is a bit of a shock."

"Faith New is rich, successful, beautiful and appears to be a very genuine person. What more could you have hoped for?"

"Gloria Estefan!" Hope laughed. "I always imagined she looked like Gloria Estefan, and was some wild, cool, rock chick!"

"Are you disappointed?" Agnes asked, seriously.

Hope laughed again, but then became pensive. "Ridiculous as it may seem," she said "you may be right, to a degree. I really didn't think about her much, but when I did, she wasn't anything like Faith New." She thought a little more. "But then Faith New isn't really like Faith New either."

Agnes looked at her, confused. Hope explained. "The woman I have become friendly with, who chats with me at work, is not the hard headed ice-maiden she portrays in the media."

"Maybe," smiled Agnes, "you have become friends with Sarah-Faith Browne, and not Faith New."

They talked and talked. Hope catapulting from making a full, raw declaration, to permanent silence. Agnes simply listened until Hope, caught in a spiral of indecision, looked to her for help. "It seems to me," Agnes said, "that it doesn't need to be all or nothing. I do believe that the truth has a way of coming out in the end, so it's just a question of deciding when, where, and how. So you have some control over it all. Then take it at your own pace – and hers, of course."

Hope shook her head. "Faith has kept it secret all these years, maybe she would rather keep it that way."

"I doubt she had any choice, Hope, she was very young, I believe."

"She was only fifteen," Hope said. "Bryony's age."

"It's hard to describe how much attitudes have changed since then," Agnes said, "being an 'unwed mother' was a total disgrace. I pity her."

"It's strange," said Hope, "I do feel a connection with her, but not as a mother. Is that bad?"

"Not at all, it's realistic," Agnes advised. "You *have* a Mum, and a Dad. She hesitated for a moment, "A wonderful Mum and Dad, who would have supported you whether you decide to speak to Faith or leave things as they are."

Hope looked puzzled. "You mean I shouldn't say anything?"

Agnes was struggling to be neutral, she so wanted to protect Hope from pain. "Before you decide, maybe you should consider the outcome if you do tell her and she wants nothing to do with you."

"I have considered that," Hope said, "and really it would make no change in my life. Except maybe to draw a line under all the speculation. But if she *does* want to know me…"

Agnes took Hope's hand, "There is no right or wrong, love, just be honest with yourself on what you expect."

Hope gave a frustrated groan. "The problem is," she said, "I *know* now, and Faith doesn't. It doesn't seem fair to her." She buried her head in her hands. "What do I *do*?"

"I can only think of one thing to do," Agnes said.

Hope looked up, knowing what her mother-in-law was about to suggest. "As a last resort," she said, "I suppose it might work."

"As a first resort, dear," Agnes insisted, "it will definitely work. Let's pray."

Agnes simply laid the facts out before her Heavenly Father and asked Him, as she always did, to make the right path very clear. Hope, who had not prayed with any conviction for a long time, summoned all the belief she could muster and added, "Please, Lord, help me to see what is the kindest and wisest way."

****

Danny had been aimlessly walking around Applebury for most of the day. It was his day off again. Which for him meant two successive nights in his dark, unheated house, hoping his father would return and put some money on the meter card. It was starting to get dark, with big clouds gathering low in the sky. He decided to stride home before the rain came. As he pushed the door open, he smelled the sour tang of sweat and cheap vodka. His father was in the kitchen, repeatedly flicking the kettle off and on.

"Dad!" he shouted.

"Something wrong with this kettle," his father shouted, becoming more and more angry.

"There's no electricity, Dad. You need to top the card up."

"Course there is!" Kit shouted, throwing the kettle to the floor. "Damn thing's broken!"

"No, Dad," Danny argued, "there's been no electricity for a week. Since you went away."

"You should have called someone," Kit growled, walking through the house and flicking at the light switches.

"What, and tell them I'm on my own here with no heat, no light and no food?" He stood in front of his father. "Last time that happened, I had to go into care. No thanks, Dad, I'll take care of myself."

"Meaning I don't take care of you?"

"Well, do you?" asked Danny. "Where did you go Dad? Are you alright?"

"Friends, Danny, I was with friends, just having a laugh." He walked back into the kitchen, swerving into Danny.

"I wish you would stop, Dad, why don't you stop?"

His dad swore at him. "God forbid I should go out an' have a little drink with some mates. Hell, Dan, you need to lighten up a bit."

"Dad, you've been gone a week! How am I supposed to live here like this?"

His father suddenly turned. Danny knew he had gone too far. "Just get out of my way, Danny boy," he shouted. Shoving Danny aside he grabbed the TV remote and began flicking it. He threw it across the room, muttering.

"It's not broke Dad, there's no electricity. You need to top up the card."

"I don't need you telling me what to do. You could just as easily do it yourself. Pay your own way, for a change."

"How could I, Dad. You stole my money to get drunk, *again*."

"Just get out!" Kit went to strike Danny, as he had many times before. Danny twisted himself out of his father's grasp and escaped through the front door. With only a T-shirt and joggers on, Danny ran through the icy rain back to the garden centre, letting himself in through the side door. Hanging his wet clothes on the old radiator, he changed into his spare work uniform and wrapped himself inside his sleeping bag. Grabbing his gardening book, he prevented any further thoughts of home by immersing himself in the benefits of semi-ripe cuttings over root propagation when farming Christmas trees.

****

At the same time, the last few festival trees of Applebury were being assembled into position. For those unable to transport their decorated tree to the church, Debbie had arranged collection by Pat and Jim in the Taylor's van, and Guy and Adam in the Harvey's courtesy minibus. Hope, Mark and Debbie, with the help of others in the church, placed each tree in its designated place among the nearly 100 entrants to the Applebury Christmas Tree Festival.

Debbie looked up from her checklist. "That's it!" she declared. "That's the last one in place!"

It was impressive. Every wall lined with Christmas trees both natural and artificial, each one ornamented with its own special story. Each row of chairs beside the red-carpeted aisle was finished with a red ribboned Christmas wreath, and the platform stage was fronted by a line of miniature potted trees, covered in silver foil stars.

"I declare Applebury Church Christmas Tree Festival unofficially open!" shouted Mark, pushing the last plug into the very last available socket.

The whole church filled with glorious twinkling lights and someone shouted "Praise the Lord!"

Guy winked at Jim. "Well, let's hope He's paying the electricity bill."

****

Soon afterwards, Jim and Pat were in the van, heading to Taylor's to pick up Pat's car. As Pat unlocked the gate, she saw the light from the scullery window, and jumped back in the van.

"There's a light on. Someone's in there," she whispered.

"There's no need to whisper," Jim whispered loudly, "no one can hear us." He reverted to his usual voice. "I reckon you've left the light on, hurrying to shut up shop." He parked the van near the front door.

"That's the scullery," she hissed. "I checked all the lights before I left, I know I did." As they looked, the bright windows turned dark. "There's definitely someone in there!" Pat pantomime gestured, as she pointed it out to Jim. "Call the police! We're being robbed!"

"What's in there to steal," said Jim, "except a load of plants?" A thought occurred to Jim. "Did you set the alarm, Pat?"

"Yes, I set the alarm," she growled, elbowing him in the ribs, "I've been setting the alarm for ten years or more, why would I forget now?" She took out her phone to call 999.

Jim laid his hand on the phone. "Not yet," he said, "not till I've had a look." He jumped out of the van to her side, took her hand. "Come on, the scullery is the only room in Taylor's that's not wired up to the alarm. There's only one person I can think of who knows that."

Her mouth fell open in horror. "Danny!" she whispered.

"You go in the front door," he said. "Make as much noise as you like, I'll wait over here." He walked to the scullery door as Pat lifted the shutter, disabled the fire alarm, and switched on all the lights as she headed for the 'burglar.'

As Danny had woken to the noise of the van outside, he cursed his own carelessness, as he realised he had fallen asleep reading. He switched off the light, and waited for whoever it was to drive away. Suddenly, he heard the noise of someone opening up. He struggled out of his sleeping bag, unlocked the door and ran outside, straight into the arms of Jim. He struggled and shouted, thinking it was the police, or worse, a gang of thieves. Then, light blazed again.

"Danny!" He looked back at the scullery doorway, where Pat stood, her hand to her face in shock.

He froze. Pat held up his sleeping bag. "Have you been living here?" she asked, furiously. He nodded. "Get in the car," she shouted, "I'm taking you home."

"You lock up!" she shouted at Jim across her shoulder, as she slammed the car door and the car screeched away.

Jim looked on, shaking his head. When Pat was on the warpath, there was no stopping her. The journey was accompanied by a ten-minute tirade from Pat on the merits of honesty and gratefulness. Only stopping as Danny directed her to his home.

"You can drop me here." he said, as they reached the end of his road.

"Oh no you don't, young man, I'm going to speak to your father."

Good luck with that, Danny thought, as he directed her to a parking space outside his home. Pat got out and followed him to his front door, still giving him the benefit of her opinion.

"Well it looks like you're in luck," she said, realising the place was in darkness. "No one's home."

"He might be," said Danny as he opened the door, "the meter's been empty for a couple of weeks."

His father lay sprawled on the couch, half awake, surrounded by several empty cans, a half bottle of vodka on his hand.

"Danny Boy!" he shouted.

"Ruddy heck, Dad, you've sold the telly!"

"Swapped it Dan," Kit said, waving the bottle in his direction, no doubt not his first of the day. "No point in a telly if you can't use it."

Danny smiled sadly. "Oh Dad, look at you." Danny took a sweatshirt from the cold radiator and lovingly helped his father put it on. He looked at Pat, and by way of explanation, began to clear away the empty cans. Then Kit noticed Pat standing at the door.

"Who's that, the social?"

"No Dad, it's my friend from work."

"Bit old for a friend, aren't you love, what are you snooping around for?"

"This is Pat, my boss," Danny explained.

"What do you want," Kit grumbled. "Ruddy social workers."

Pat walked in to the kitchen and began looking through the cupboards, Danny followed her.

"You can't live like this Danny, it's not right. How long has he been like this?"

"He's not always like this, just sometimes he has a...setback," Danny said, trying to explain, if not excuse. "He's only got me and I..."

Kit blocked the doorway. "What are you snooping for, you old witch!" he bellowed, then staggered back to the sofa. "They're gonna take my boy," he wailed. "Danny boy!" He fell into a mumbled, rambling conversation with no one in particular, punctuated with shouted obscenities and sorrowful truth.

Pat knelt beside him, took his hand. "You can get help," she said, "things can get better." Kit looked at her, closed his eyes, and fell back onto the cushion, fast asleep. Danny was sitting on the stairs, his head in his hands. He looked exhausted. "My Dad is not a bad person," he said, "my Dad is ill." He covered his face with his hands. "When he is okay, he doesn't want to be like this. He has an illness."

Pat sat on the step below him. "Danny, it *is* an illness. But it's an illness you didn't cause and you can't control. Your dad needs help." Pat looked at him. "Danny, this disease will kill him, you know that. He has to stop drinking and you can't make that happen. Only he can."

"I can look after him," Danny said, "we always come out alright in the end."

"If and when your Dad comes out of this one," she said, indicating the rambling, skeletal figure on the couch, "he will need a lot of support to deal with the withdrawal alone."

"What do you mean, 'this one,'" Danny asked, suspiciously.

"Let me guess," Pat said. "Months pass and everything's fine, then he starts becoming secretive, hiding bottles, going for 'walks', meeting the same old group of friends. He gets angry if you say anything, so you say nothing and hope he'll see sense. But of course, he can't see sense because the need to drink has taken over completely." Danny nodded, as Pat continued, "It's so powerful, it's more important than his health, his job and the people he loves."

"When he is well, Dad knows he needs help," Danny said, his voice trembling.

Pat put her hand on his. "But you need to keep yourself well, too. You should be warm and well cared for, and at least know where your next meal is coming from. Come on, Danny," she said. "You're coming home with me. We'll get your Dad all the help he needs, but you can't stay here, it's not safe."

He ran upstairs grabbed his meagre clothes and his mother's photo, then, taking one last look at his father, he left the house. They had almost reached Pat's house, driving along in the darkness. Danny had been deep in thought. He looked across at her. "How do you know it so well, Pat," he asked, "how do you know what it's like?"

Keeping her eyes firmly on the road ahead, with a flat, expressionless voice, she answered him. "My name is Pat Taylor, and I am an alcoholic. I have not had a drink for twenty-seven years."

Chapter Sixteen

On Friday morning, Pat and Danny arrived extra early, as they had arranged to meet Jim for breakfast in the café. The night before, with Danny safely sleeping in Pat's spare room, she had called Jim and told him, with remorse, what she had found when she took Danny home. "He is adamant he doesn't want anyone official involved," she said, "he says his Dad has an illness, and he'll get better again, like he has before."

"Well, he's right, Pat, we know he is, in a way."

"He is absolutely not right," Pat insisted, "nothing will change unless this Kit, Danny's Dad, decides it's going to."

Jim was one of the few people living who had known Pat at her lowest. Her addiction had ended her career and her marriage, and had almost killed her. He held her in high regard and had too much respect for her to argue. "So, where do we go from here?" he asked.

Between the two of them, they came up with a plan, which they put to Danny as he feasted on his 'full English' breakfast. "It's not free board and lodging, Danny," Pat stipulated. "You'll have to earn your keep. The garden is more than I can manage these days…"

"Always has been, really," interrupted Jim. Pat silenced him with a glance.

"I will expect you get the garden into shape, properly. Not just a bit of weeding and mowing the lawn.

"And you'll need to keep your place clean and tidy," Jim added, "and pull your weight around the house, too."

Pat began to stack their plates. "Agreed?" she asked sternly.

Danny pressed his eyes with his fingers and thumb, to push back the tears of relief. He nodded, unable to speak. Jim stood. "Come on, lad," he growled, "we've got work to do."

Danny stood, flung his arms around Pat and hugged her hard, then dashed off to top up the winter wonderland displays. Jim looked back at Pat and winked.

****

Faith sat at her desk. Somehow, she continued to function, but almost as if she were watching herself from a distance. She switched on her laptop as Megan arrived with a pile of newspapers and a large coffee. Megan was both concerned and fearful. In the years they had worked together, Faith had seemed indestructible. Always friendly but never familiar, Faith was serene, sophisticated, and in control at all times, the epitome of self-possessed professionalism. Yet, the Faith New in front of her today was little more than a sleepwalker on auto pilot. Megan jumped, startled by Faith's voice. "How bad is it, Megan?"

Meghan passed her the coffee first, then the local paper. Faith inhaled sharply as she read the headline. 'FAKE NEW – the hypocrite at the heart of Christmas.'

"And the rest?" she asked, opening her hand to take the rest of todays red tops.

"Family favourite denies her own father."

"Phoney Faith—too good to be true."

Faith googled her own name. Similar headlines popped up all over social media and the internet, from Facebook to HuffPost.

The harsh familiarity of cyber-malice was enough to heave Faith from her zombie state.

"Oh, heavens," Faith sighed, cradling her head in her hands.

"We've had to stop comments on your page," Megan said, "it's troll central!" Faith went to look. "Really," Megan said, "don't look." She actually grabbed Faith's hand to stop her.

"It's that bad?" Faith asked.

Megan nodded. "Are you able to explain, give your side of the story?" she asked, already aware that had it been possible, it would already have happened.

"I'm not sure I can," Faith said, "there is an innocent party involved..." Megan went to speak... "and it's certainly not my father," Faith added.

Faith got through the program, somehow. With Megan and the rest of the production team screening out any calls to do with her personal life, it was a very stilted, artificially jolly show, heavily reliant on music to fill the lack of content. As the show finished, Megan passed on a message. The director had asked her to see him immediately after the show.

Miles shut the door behind her as she walked into his office. The Christmas scoop that had made the news across the country was now creating headlines for all the wrong reasons. Not only that, but he had been called back from his Christmas holiday to deal with the scandal.

He had been haranguing her from the minute the door closed. "You need to sort it out Faith," he barked, "the press is loving this, Fake New, hypocrite!"

"I have read them," she said quietly.

"You abandoned your family to make a career, and now it's all blown up in your face, is that really it?" He was both incredulous and furious.

Faith shook her head. "Of course not, Miles," she said, shocked at the change in his manner. "It's personal, very personal."

Ignoring her and giving her no chance to speak further, he bulldozed on, "This will undo all the good this Applebury angle has done," he said, "we will haemorrhage listeners. As it is, they are probably only listening now for the scandal."

"We can ride it out," Faith said, "people have short memories."

"Don't be naïve, Faith," he sneered "don't you see, you can't spend the entire run up to Christmas spouting family values, love and forgiveness, when you've got some dirty little secret hidden away in the family closet!"

Those words again. She stumbled back against the door as if he had punched her. Reaching for the door handle, Faith turned and walked out. Megan, of course, was waiting for her.

"Faith, I'm so sorry, I wish it had never happened."

"Me too," Faith replied in a voice filled with suppressed fury, "but it has, and we will deal with it." She put on her coat and strode to the door, at the last minute she turned. "Megan," she said, kindly, "I'm very grateful for everything you do. None of this is your fault." Megan looked as if she were about to cry, which Faith could not bear. She turned to leave. "I've got a meeting," she shouted over her shoulder, "I'll see you Monday."

Faith did indeed have a meeting. She had been asked to open Applebury's Got Talent as guest of honour. Driving to Applebury, she rehearsed her 'I won't be coming after all' speech. Parking outside, Faith checked her appearance in the little Dior compact she carried. She looked pale, old and haggard. "Buck up," she admonished her reflection, then applied the reddest lipstick she possessed, and flung on a pair of sunglasses. "Lights, camera action," she muttered, as she stepped into the church hall, head held high.

The school's carol service had finished. Mark and Debbie were saying their goodbyes to a few lingering parents. Seeing Faith arrive and a few curious heads turn, Mark showed Faith through the connecting door and into the church. "We'll be along in a minute," he said, "make yourself at home."

She chose a spot illuminated by the bright winter sun, then moved, realising it would highlight every wrinkle and blemish. The light in front of the stage was softer, more forgiving. She sat in a row of chairs at the very front of the church. "Seriously," she told herself, "I have been in this game far too long." The church, stuffed with colourful festival trees, yet calm and still, was a peaceful bubble in her current turmoil. Her phone buzzed; it was a text from Megan. 'You might need this for caller ID,' she had written. Faith read her father's name and the number of his mobile phone.

"No!" she shouted, and threw her phone into her bag like a hot brick. She curled over in her chair, elbows on her knees. For a few minutes she allowed herself to feel, cupping her hands over her mouth to suppress a sob. Someone sat beside her, put their arm across the back of her chair. She looked up and there was Guy. He said nothing, just smiled gently, acknowledging her pain. She looked away but leaned in to him, as if to borrow his strength.

"I had a child," she said, "when I was fifteen. My parents 'dealt with the problem.'" She mimed parentheses. "I didn't really understand what was happening, and before I knew it, my child was gone. They just told me to get on with my life and forget about her. I became a different person, with a different name and a different attitude, but I could never forget her, or forgive my parents. Making that decision has overshadowed everything."

"You were fifteen, Faith," Guy said softly, "the decision was made for you, not by you. You've lived with the consequences of that ever since."

"And yesterday, my father pops up, and I feel now exactly as I did then," Faith added. "It was nearly forty years ago, for goodness sake!"

Mark and Debbie walked into the church, a mug of tea in each hand. Guy stood up to take a mug for himself and Faith. "Thank you," said Faith, placing the mug on the seat beside her. "The church looks beautiful," she said, "and reporting on the festival, the friendship and community of Applebury has been a genuine pleasure to me, and, if I'm honest, a godsend for the station." Mark smiled at her unintended irony. Faith continued, her eyes pleading, "I can assure you that I have not done anything illegal, or immoral, but that is not how it looks in the press. So, the big question, with all this scandal is, do you still want me to be a part of your 'Love@Christmas' festival?"

Debbie moved across to sit beside her. "Faith, whatever this is, it is something that you have chosen to keep private. It's hard when people speculate, I know, but there is no reason for you to pull out of the festival. This will blow over and we will be here if you need us, all three of us."

Faith smiled. A tear escaped and threatened to be the first of many. She shut her eyes and took a deep breath, trying hard to detach her own emotions. She continued, "I have not spoken to, or had any contact with my parents, since I graduated from university. The reason for that is…" another tear escaped. "The reason for that decision was that at fifteen, I had…" It was as if an unexpected hand had ripped apart the scar of her pain. Every emotion attached to that decisive year welled up in her soul; panic, fear, disgrace, shame, distrust, fury, rejection, bewilderment, and deep, deep sorrow.

She looked at Guy, hardly able to speak. "Please, tell them." Guy hesitated, honoured to be asked, yet concerned not to add to Faith's distress. "Please," she said, "I can't seem to pull myself together."

Guy repeated the history Faith had entrusted to him. There was a still silence once Guy had finished speaking. Faith, hearing her story told by another, felt an unexpected peace. As she looked up, both men had tears in their eyes, and Debbie was openly weeping.

"Can we pray for you, and this situation?" asked Debbie. Faith agreed, more out of respect for them than any other conviction. Mark and Debbie addressed their Father as if He were right there with them. No pious invocations, no holy histrionics, just a straightforward request for peace, protection and clarity. As they "Amened" their agreement, Guy put his hand on Faith's.

"Look at us two heathens in church, praying," he said. "That's already a miracle!"

****

Jim had promised he would keep Danny busy at Taylor's for at least two hours after closing, long enough to give Pat time to do something Danny could know nothing about.

While Danny was sorting the last of the wreaths and Christmas trees, transporting cyclamens and dead-heading tiny roses, Pat was deep in conversation with his father. She had topped up the card for the meter, restocked his cupboards and cooked him a meal. She spoke to him as an equal, with understanding but no sentiment.

"I am not telling you what to do," she said, "but I am telling you it can be done. Even now I have days when I struggle, but it can be done."

He looked at her, sincerely, as he had looked at many well-meaning 'professionals' and friends over the last ten or so years. "I know I need to change, I will never drink again, from this moment," he said.

"Kit." She looked at him directly in the eyes. "I know it's not that simple, and I know it has to be in your own time. So there's no need to say what you think I want to hear." He sat back, surprised.

"You can't kid a kidder," she smiled. "I really have been there and done that! The fact is," she continued, "Danny is safe and well looked after, for as long as you need. This will give you time and space to get help if you want to. Think about it."

She drove home and was seated in her armchair as usual when Jim and Danny arrived. "All done," Jim said, as much a question as a statement. Pat nodded and Jim smiled back.

"Taylor's looks great now," Danny said, "all ready for the big Christmas weekend."

"I hope you're both hungry," Pat shouted from the kitchen. A few minutes later she was ladling beef stew and dumplings into their bowls, and a treacle tart warmed in the oven.

Chapter Seventeen

The final Saturday before Christmas had always been busy, even for Taylor's, but today was unparalleled. The Applebury Brass Band were playing beside Santa's Workshop, and Brian, at the cash desk, could hardly resist singing along. Rosa, working at the adjoining desk, looked across at her grandfather in his Santa hat and smiled. "It's a good job Grandma can't see you now," she said, as he speed-scanned the purchases of customer after customer.

"It's gentle exercise," he laughed, "wouldn't you agree?"

Rosa smiled. "I'm glad you're here, Grandad."

A tall Christmas elf with artificially pink cheeks walked towards them, carrying a tray of mini gingerbread men, which he offered to the waiting customers.

"Danny!" Rosa giggled, "what *are* you wearing?"

Danny beamed widely, looking down at his green velvet jacket, red knickerbockers and striped socks. "I've been promoted," he said.

"I thought Briony was going to be the elf, what happened?"

Danny gave a mischievous smile. "For some strange reason, she refused," he said, pulling down his fake beard. "I can't imagine why!"

Seeing a pair of children squabbling as they waited in the queue, Danny knelt to hand them a gingerbread man each. "You are being very patient," he said, "I will tell Father Christmas that you have been very good at waiting." The children snapped to attention, their mother smiled her thanks. "You too, Mum," Danny said, offering her the tray.

He saw Rosa staring. "What?"

"You're not usually much of a people person, Danny," she said.

He put on a confused expression. "I don't know who this 'Danny' person is. *I'm* Santa's elf, and I have a job to do." With that, he gave her a cheeky wink, and marched off with his tray of goodies.

Briony was in the café, relieved that the regulation apron was less embarrassing than an elf costume. Pat worked behind the counter, and Jim and Adam covered the rest of the store between them. Meanwhile, Hope was enjoying the luxury of a day off, if a day out with her two youngest children could be considered a day off. She had promised them they could do their Christmas shopping at the festival craft fair. Hope longed to linger at the jewellery and craft stalls, but the children dragged her from one sweet and cake stall to the next, followed by some sort of raffle, where she effectively paid three pounds to win a 99 pence packet of toffees.

"Mum, look!" Callum clapped with excitement. He pulled her to a nearby table, the sign above saying, "Applebury Angels. Supporting the foodbank."

"Look, Mum, the Angel has your name on it!" He pointed to a cone of white-painted, turned wood, with a cheerful little face, and the words 'Faith. Hope. Love.' inscribed underneath each other on the front. A pair of wire wings and a halo in gold completed the decoration.

"It does have my name on it," Hope said. "Clever boy!"

"Grandma!" shouted Lily, as she spotted Agnes and Brian looking at a stall filled with pebble pictures.

The two of them walked to join Hope, exchanging a few words as they did. Lily hugged her Grandma, who lifted Lily to her hip.

Brian took Callum's hand. "I wondered if Callum would like one more practice before tonight?"

"And I thought Lily and I could look for some unicorns," Agnes added, "if it's alright with you?"

"You could have an hour to yourself," Brian said.

Hope could have kissed them both. "Oh, that would be luxury," Hope replied, delighted. "Agnes, before you go, look at this," she said, holding the angel up for their inspection.

"Faith, Hope, Love," Agnes said archly. "Well, I never!"

"Don't read too much into it," Brian warned. "Go careful."

"We'll be off," Agnes said. Leaning in to hug Hope, she whispered, "I'll keep praying."

Hope watched the four of them walk away, turned back to the angel stall and looked at the variety of turned, knitted, crocheted and felted angels for sale. "I really think this is the best one here," she said, offering her angel to the lady behind the stall. "I'll take it."

"Faith, Hope, Love," the lady said, wrapping the gift in tissue. "Hold on," she rummaged under the counter for a second. "This one comes with its own special box."

She placed the carefully wrapped angel in its box and, replacing the lid, passed it to Hope. "Do you need a carrier bag?"

Hope was unable to answer. She hardly heard the question. Carefully inscribed on the lid of the box she read,

"See, I am sending an angel ahead of you to guard you along the way and to bring you to the place I have prepared." (Exodus 23:20)

****

"Is Grace here?" asked Callum, as he and Brian walked from the church hall to the church itself.

"She's waiting at the piano already," said Brian.

Callum ran up the aisle to the piano, as Brian took his guitar from its case and checked it was still in pitch.

"Are you excited for tonight, Callum?" asked Grace.

Callum seemed to notice the sheer beauty of the setting for the first time. "It looks like we're in the forest," he said, "and it smells like a lovely forest, too."

"It is beautiful," agreed Grace.

"Right," Brian announced. "I'm ready to rock and roll."

They had practiced many times before, and Callum was faultless on each occasion, in an empty church with no distractions. They ran through the performance one more time. The gentle simplicity of guitar and solo treble swelling to a crescendo with the piano accompaniment.

"That was spot on, Callum," said Grace.

"Beautiful," agreed Brian, "absolutely beautiful."

Despite Callum's obvious self-assurance, Grace was worried that their spectacular finale relied entirely on a little boy who had never performed in front of an audience before. "There will be lots of people here tonight, Callum," she said.

"Hundreds," Callum replied, with a swagger, and they've all come to hear me sing!"

Brian, catching Grace's concern, said, "If you get a bit nervous, remember, I'll be right here."

"I know, Grandad," Callum said, with an air of weary indulgence.

"Remember what I told you," Brian reminded him, "whatever happens..."

"Just keep going!" they chanted in unison, finishing with a hearty high five.

Grace looked on. "I swear I will be watching you perform at the Albert Hall one day."

"No Mummies allowed!" shouted Callum, as Hope appeared and walked towards them.

"I haven't come to listen, sunshine boy," she said, "I've got you a present." She held up a red waistcoat printed with Christmas trees.

"Wow!" Callum snatched the waistcoat from her hands and put it on. "This is the finest Christmas waistcoat ever," he said. "I love my waistcoat. And I love you, Mum!"

****

Saturday morning for Faith was simply a matter of hiding from the press. She could see the tops of their heads as she looked down from her bedroom window. She seriously considered throwing a bucket of water on them, but that would probably result in headlines of attempted drowning. The doorbell kept ringing. She disconnected it and headed for a shower, but that didn't stop them hammering on the door and shouting through the letter box. As she finished drying her hair, her phone rang. It was Guy.

"Are you okay?" he asked, "you weren't answering your phone."

She apologised. "I had a shower," she said, "it's the only place I can go to get away from the press banging on the door."

"Persistent beggars, aren't they?" he said. "That's why I'm ringing."

The clatter of the door knocker began again and shouts of "Miss New, do you have a comment?" carried up the stairs as she began to apply her make up.

"What are your plans for today?" he asked.

She held the phone out to let him hear the door knocking. "Just lie low and survive," she told him, ruefully, "until they give up or go away."

"Unlikely though," he commented.

"True," she sighed, "and I have to be at the church for the talent show at five-thirty, so I don't know how I'm going to…"

"I'll tell you what," Guy interrupted, "get your walking boots on, pack up your glad rags, and I'll whisk you off for a spot of lunch before the show. Somewhere far away and anonymous."

"That's an offer I can't refuse," she said. "The only problem is getting out of here."

"Can't you use the back door?"

"I can, but I still can't see…" she looked out of the window into her walled back garden. She had been meaning to get that old apple tree pruned for at least the last two years… "As a matter of fact, I can!" She realised the overhanging boughs of the trees led directly from her own garden to the lane behind. She explained her escape plan, and less than an hour later Faith was in Guy's car, travelling into the countryside. After a long restorative walk, they found a welcoming fireside and good food at the County Arms Inn. A few hours' refuge from the gossip and havoc awaiting her 'out there.'

At the church, Debbie, Mark, Grace, and Doug were clearing away the hall after the stall holders had left. There were boxes and boxes of mince pies in the kitchen, teapots open, and tables prepared with cups, saucers and paper napkins, ready for the interval. A little staging area was set up for the next act on the running sheet to wait their turn. The rest of the helpers had left as Mark and Debbie feasted on a hurried meal of fish and chips from the paper.

"Guy and Faith seem to be hitting it off," remarked Debbie, with a conspiratorial smile.

Mark looked at her. "I know what you're thinking," he said. "But it doesn't do to speculate."

"Well, I'm just saying, they make a good pair, and it's probably no coincidence that they've met."

He smiled.

"It could be all part of 'the plan,'" she said, pointing heavenwards.

"You are incorrigible," he said.

Just then, as if on cue, Guy and Faith appeared at the door. "See, it's a sign!" Debbie side-whispered to her husband, as she wiped her hands on her jeans and stood to welcome them.

"We've come a bit early," Guy said. "Evading the press, actually."

"Would you like some?" said Mark, offering his tray of chips to them both.

Faith put her hands on her stomach. "We've already eaten. I'm so full I could burst," she said, "but thank you."

"We escaped to the country," Guy explained. "Now, if you don't mind, ladies and gentlemen, I must just nip home and get my kit for tonight."

"I've left my change of clothes and make-up in your car," said Faith, beginning to walk to the door.

"You stay there," Guy said. "I'll get your bag right now, I'm sure there's a handy place to change somewhere here." He dashed out to the car, returning quickly with a garment bag and cream leather vanity case. He handed them to Faith. "I'll be back," he said, in his best 'Arnie' voice.

"Let me show you where you can change," Debbie said, then, to Mark, over her shoulder, she mimed, "Told you!" She led Faith along the corridor. "Mark and I will be smartening ourselves up in the Pastor's office, so you can change in here," she said, opening a door marked 'Prayer Room.'

Faith smiled. "Very appropriate in my current situation," she said.

"Give it a try," Debbie said, light-heartedly, "you never know!" She switched on the lights. "We'll meet you back in the church."

Once dressed and ready for the big event, Faith had chosen to remain in the church while the audience and acts arrived. Far from the original plan of a 'celebrity welcome' appearance and opening speech, Faith's only hope was that she could remain as anonymous as possible. Mark and Debbie were doing the welcoming and Guy had agreed to do the speech.

She was seated in the front row. The seat beside her, nearest the aisle, was reserved. On the other side, Mark discussed final details with Doug and Grace, who were providing the accompaniment for several acts. She was beginning to wonder whether Guy was coming back at all, when he appeared from the edge of the stage.

"Oh my!" she breathed before she could stop herself. Guy, in his tuxedo, looked like he had stepped out of a Bond movie.

Pleased by her reaction, he sat beside her. "How do you like the bling?" he asked, pointing to his Mayoral chain of office.

"I don't know," she said, "it's a bit gangsta!"

The lights went down. "That's my cue," he said, stepping up on to the platform.

In his welcoming speech, Guy thanked all those who needed thanking, and handed over to Pastor Mark who introduced the first act.

'Tanya's Dancing Dogs' closely followed the dance school's 'Boogie Woogie Elves,' then a variety of acts from the banal to the bizarre, until Frances and Francesca's bendy balloons took their final bow.

Guy handed Faith his gangsta bling, as Mark, with great enthusiasm, called on The Four Pops to come to the stage. They finished the first half with a Rat Pack Christmas. The applause seemed to make the building shake. As Guy and his group left the stage, the house lights came up for the interval. Seeing the crowds, Faith decided to stay where she was, simply to avoid any more unwanted conversation.

Just then, a little boy in a red waistcoat, about eight years old, stood boldly in front of her. "Hello."

"Hello," Faith answered.

"I'm singing last," he said, "and I've got this waistcoat and Mister Harvey said wait here."

"Thank you for letting me know," Faith said, slightly bemused.

Then a familiar face. Hope grabbed the boy's hand. "I'm so sorry."

Faith stood, smiling. "You've no idea how good it is to see a friendly smile," she said, "and Callum is delightful." She looked at the boy. "He had a very important message for me from Mr Harvey." Hope looked surprised. "And," Faith continued, "he did a very good job, very good indeed."

Callum almost burst his waistcoat buttons with pride. "He is a good boy, isn't he?" Hope said.

Faith thought she seemed different, somehow. Her eyes almost pleading. "Faith," the younger woman said, "this might not be the right time but…"

At that moment Guy appeared with two cups of tea. "Nothing stronger, I'm afraid. They can't sell pints of beer in church, apparently. Thank you, young Callum," he said with a wink, handing a cup and saucer over to Faith. "Excellent job!"

Hope, her opportunity gone, made a few moment's polite conversation and left.

Not long afterward, the lights went down for the second half. The second half began with an elderly Elvis tribute singing 'Blue Christmas' and continued through a riotous, eccentric line up, that only a small English town could provide.

Mark took to the stage to introduce the final act. "Ladies and Gentlemen," he began. The Christmas tree lights began to flicker.

"Speak up!" shouted a voice at the back. Mark checked his microphone. "Can't hear you!" shouted another.

Mark smiled inanely, looking with panic at the sound desk. A loud "POP" reverberated around the building as the Christmas tree lights sputtered into darkness, immediately followed by every light in the place. Somewhere, a circuit had blown. Realising this sudden plunge into darkness was not part of the plan, Guy flicked his phone to torch, and shone a thin blue light on Callum in his Christmas waistcoat. Brian began to play the first few chords of introduction, and Callum's clear, pure soprano filled the church.

Silent night, holy night,
All is calm, all is bright,

One by one, phones throughout the audience were held up, illuminating the whole place.

'Round yon virgin Mother and Child,
Holy infant so tender and mild,
Sleep in heavenly peace,
Sleep in heavenly peace.
Silent night, holy night!
Shepherds quake at the sight!
Glories stream from heaven afar;
Heavenly hosts sing Al-le-lu-ia!
Christ the Saviour is born!
Christ the Saviour is born!

As the final verse began, the place burst into light. Mark had pushed the circuit breaker back into place at exactly the right moment. Callum, sensing the drama of the moment, sang louder and stronger than ever as the piano accompaniment swelled

Silent night, holy night,

Son of God, oh, love's pure light,
Radiant beams from Thy holy face,
With the dawn of redeeming grace,
Jesus, Lord at Thy birth,
Jesus, Lord at Thy birth,
Jesus, Lord at Thy birth.

There was a moment of stunned silence. Callum took a bow as if this was his one hundred and first performance, not his first. The audience burst into loud applause, standing and cheering as this final act left the stage. Finally, the stage filled with every act from Applebury's Got Talent. Audience, performers and technicians joined together to sing "Oh, Come, All Ye Faithful!"

At last, the happy crowds had filed out, a cheerful babble punctuated with the occasional shout of 'Merry Christmas!' floated around Faith, as she waited in her seat. Despite the very obvious whispers and side glances from some of the audience, Faith had maintained her poise, and even found an escape in watching the talent show. She watched Guy joking easily with Mark and Brian, his hand on Callum's shoulder. Maria, resplendent in a red tartan cape, linked arms with her."

"So, did you enjoy our Applebury Christmas, dear?" she smiled.

"I really did," Faith answered. "Some of the acts were outstanding." She looked again at Guy.

"Oh, they were?" asked Maria, as Faith looked back at her.

"What?" Faith asked, laughing.

Maria mimed zipping her lip. "I have been told to keep my thoughts to myself," she said, a conspiratorial smile still lingering on her lips.

Guy began walking towards them with Brian and Callum. Faith knelt to speak with Callum. "You were marvellous, Callum."

"And Grandad," the boy reminded her.

"And Grandad, of course," Faith added, looking up at Brian.

She stood to shake Brian's hand. "That was beautiful," she said, "thank you."

Brian took her hand. "I believe it is I who should be thanking you," he said, "your radio show has saved my business and restored my joy in living."

"You give me too much credit, Mr Taylor," she replied. "I think you have your daughter-in-law to thank for the reversal in Taylor's fortunes. She has transformed the place; you really do have a remarkable family."

"Mummy, this lady said you are remarkable," said Callum, as Hope joined them.

"That's very kind of you," Hope said.

"It's true, Hope," Faith replied. "I can't tell you how much I've valued your friendship over the last few weeks." She laid her hand on Hope's arm. "I hope you have a wonderful Christmas."

Adam signalled from the door. "I'd better go, it's way past bedtime," Hope said, looking at Callum, who insisted he was not a bit tired. "See you soon, Faith, and thank you for everything." Again, Faith felt there was more in Hope's eyes than her simple, "Thank you," as the Taylors left the church.

Guy turned to Faith "We'd better get you home," he said. They both headed for the door, only to see

Adam Taylor hurry back inside. He almost ran to them. "Just to warn you," he said, "there are a few reporters outside. They've been asking questions."

"What sort of questions?" Faith asked, "there can't be much scandal at a Christmas Tree Festival."

"Who are you with, for one," said Adam, with an apologetic glance at Guy.

"I have nothing to be ashamed of," Faith declared, "I'll walk out with my head held high!"

"Come on then," Guy said, and they walked out into the car park. There was a surge of reporters, lights, and clicking cameras. To make matters worse, it seemed every member of the audience had stayed in the car park to watch this scandalous sequel to the show.

"Faith New, when did you become aware of your mother's recent death from cancer?"

"Did your parent's separation influence your decision to leave?"

"Can you justify your stance on family against your treatment of your own family?"

Words hit her like bullets: "Abandoned," "Neglected," "Ruthless Ambition," "Cruelty."

Surrounded, jostled and disoriented, Faith was drowning in a sea of ravenous strangers. She began to crumple, then felt herself scooped back into the building.

"You won't be able to get to the car unharmed," Guy said, "and then, no doubt you'll have the same problem when you get home."

Maria stood just behind him, "I have an idea," she said, handing Faith her tartan cape "It has a hood you know."

A few minutes later, a minibus pulled up outside the church hall, bearing the logo 'Edward Henry Court—Luxury Retirement Living.' Sixteen elderly residents, including one shrouded in a tartan cape and hood, climbed aboard and were transported away. At Edward Henry Court, a few minutes later, Guy and Maria pulled up behind the minibus. Faith gave Maria a hug and returned her shawl.

"You're a genius," she said, "thank you." Then leaped into the passenger seat beside Guy. They sat in silence as Guy drove her home, Faith turning over the whole awful situation in her mind.

"I'm sorry you've been dragged into my very public disgrace, Guy," she said, softly.

"Faith," Guy answered, "you have nothing to be ashamed of. If people knew the facts, they would treat you with the respect and understanding you deserve."

"It hardly feels that way," she said. "I'm not sure I can carry on under this shadow. It's not how I saw my career ending."

Guy glanced at her, then back at the road ahead. "So they win, again?" he said.

"I've been exposing lies and self-serving ambition for most of my career," Faith said, "exposing me as a fraud is tabloid gold, so yes, they win."

Guy was silent for a moment. When I said, '*they* win,' I wasn't talking about your colleagues in the gutter press," he said. "I am talking about your parents, the doctor, all the people who took your daughter away from you and shamed you into silence." He paused, "And you are still ashamed to speak up, even now."

She was silent for a moment. "I hadn't seen it that way", she murmured.

"One last thing," he said, "and then I will shut up and stop interfering." She looked sideways at him. "We both know that you are not the only one. There are hundreds, probably thousands of women, who still feel they have to hide what happened to them. I can't even imagine what it's like to live with that pain every day."

She exhaled, "It's too awful to speak about."

"You are a brave, strong-minded, incredibly successful woman, Faith. If you speak out, people will listen. You could turn this all on its head."

"I could just tell the truth."

"Pure and simple," he said, "the facts."

"Well, that would be a shock to them all," she said with a quiet laugh. "I don't know why I didn't figure that out sooner. Sometimes you can't see the wood for the trees, I guess."

As they drove towards her house, Guy could see a cluster of reporters gathered at her door. "Talking about trees," he said, "how do you fancy climbing one for the second time today?" He drove along the lane behind her house and helped her ascend the old apple tree, passing her things across after her.

Once safely indoors, Faith stood at the window, looking at the moon.

"Wherever you are, may you be safe, may you be happy, may you be loved, my Angel," she whispered.

Then, looking past the moon, into the deepest part of the night sky. "And maybe…a miracle?" she asked.

****

Guy drove slowly home. Faith was an unexpected interruption to his life. No longer a husband but a widower, Guy was many things to many people. Father, brother, son, employer, businessman, friend, mayor, entertainer, but he had never been tempted to add spouse or even partner to that list. Until now.

He could see the church up ahead, the lights from the trees outside still shining. He shook his head at the thought of the church's fuel bills, then, as he got closer, he realised the golden glow was not from the trees, but from the church itself. He turned into the car park and screeched to a halt, pulling his phone out to dial 999. He put his hand on the big double doors and pulled it back quickly. The glass was cracking and the door was so hot the paint had begun to blister. As he walked round the building, he could see flames curling from the roof of the church hall.

Guy was calling Mark when the fire crew arrived. He assured them there was no one in the building, and they assured him that the place was too far gone for them to do anything but make it safe. By five am, Guy, along with the church leaders, Brian and Agnes, Doug and Grace, Mark and Debbie, watched as the emergency crews ensured the risk of fire was gone. What had not been destroyed by fire had been drowned in torrents of water. All that remained of the church building was a pile of blackened rubble in a huge dirty puddle.

"We will need to contact the insurers," said Doug, "there's bound to be an investigation."

"Thank goodness we had the place checked out by the fire safety officer before the festival," said Debbie. Mark looked at her. "Didn't we?" she asked, seeing the look of horror on his face.

"Yes," Mark said, "but he advised us on safety for a little festival for twenty trees. "In all the panic I never did think about the increased risk as the festival got bigger and bigger." The Pastor and his wife stared in horror at the ruins of their church, realising that there may be no insurance payment.

"We have a bigger problem than that," Grace reminded them both. "We will have two hundred or more people arriving here at eleven am, expecting a church service and prize giving."

"We will have to cancel the service," Mark said, "there's no alternative."

"We will *not* cancel the service!" Debbie said. "The whole town is looking forward to it. We will just have to all squeeze in the town hall, if Mr Mayor will arrange it.

Guy nodded, "Of course," he said, "it won't be very festive, and there's not a lot of parking, but it's better than nothing."

Mark was in a state of stunned shock. "All my, er, our," he corrected, "all our hard work destroyed."

"There was no way to save anything," Guy said, "the old place was like a furnace with all those trees inside."

Debbie, beside him, said, "We can only be thankful it happened now and not tomorrow."

Mark looked her, irritated. "Must you be so unbearably positive about everything? This is an absolute disaster."

"Mark, tomorrow morning there would have been nearly three hundred people here, mainly children." Debbie said. "Just think about it."

The vision of what could have happened pulled Mark from his puddle of self-pity. Brian and Agnes, who had been whispering together at a distance, walked across to the rest of the group. "Taylor's Country Gardens has space and plenty of parking," he said, "it's not far from here, so people can find it easily. "That can be Applebury Church, for now."

"The big greenhouse will easily hold several hundred people, and the place is already so festive," Agnes added.

It was a perfect solution, they all agreed.

"I'll call Pat and Jim," Brian said to Agnes, "you call Adam."

"But how can we let all the other people know," asked Doug, "there's not a lot of time."

They began discussing signs and nominating marshals and creative ways to let people know the church was gone, but the festival wasn't.

"Hold on," said Guy, "I know someone who can help." He called Faith. Applebury Christmas Tree Festival, for one last time that year was headline news. By seven am, radio and TV crews were at the scene, and the whole world knew that the Church Service would be at Taylor's Country Gardens.

"If you're coming, bring a chair," had been the closing request in Mark's TV interview. Debbie set the phone chain going, ringing two people, who would ring two more, until every church contact had been personally informed of the change of plans. Mark looked at the dead ruins of the church compared to the flurry of friendly, focused activity around him. He cringed as he remembered his oft repeated and pompous assertion that 'only God Himself' could convince him to sell the old building. Inside his head, he made an embarrassed apology to his Maker, followed by a face-to-face apology to his wife.

"Right, gang," said Guy, "we'd better get home and change, unless you are going to address your flock in that interesting get up, Mark."

The pastor, in soot-covered sweatshirt and jeans, with pyjamas poking out at the waist, and flip flops, said with a quizzical smile, "People don't dress up for church these days, Guy."

After they had stopped laughing, the seven of them set off for Taylor's Country Gardens, via home and a change of clothes. The radio news reports brought a TV crew along with the expected, good-natured crowd of churchgoers, festival visitors, and curious shoppers, many with a chair under their arms. It was the stuff of Christmas broadcasters' dreams. A church service in a snow-filled fantasy world, the congregation seated on everything from kitchen chairs to sunbeds, the musicians standing amongst plastic snowmen, and sermon spoken from the back seat of a sleigh. The unintended, spectacular finale to Applebury Christmas Tree Festival, live from Taylors Country Gardens, was trending on social media before the service itself had finished, and featured on every evening news channel across the country.

Chapter Eighteen

It was Christmas Eve, Monday Morning, and Hope's last day cleaning the C2C offices. She had been instructed to leave her keys at the desk once her duties were complete, and by seven am she had finished. "This is it!" she said to herself, standing outside the closed door of Faith's office. Hope knew the office was empty – nevertheless, she hesitated before going in. Looking up at the ceiling, she said, "If this all goes wrong, I'll blame You."

She slipped inside, removed the gift box from her bag, and placed it beside Faith's computer screen. Looking up at the ceiling again she continued, "What I mean is," she closed her eyes and clasped her hands together, "please, please, let this all turn out well for both of us!"

Hope ran out of the office and out of the building, only pausing to drop her keys and a Christmas card with the night porter. At home, Adam greeted her with a hug.

"Did you do it?"

"I did," Hope said, "now we just have to wait and see."

"I love you, Hope," Adam said, "Happy Birthday!"

****

Faith, of course, had not attended the church service at Taylor's. After Guy's call, she had mobilised the news team but had been advised against reporting on the incident herself. Her hidden past, however blameless and private she knew it to be, had already begun to cast a shadow of suspicion over her career. Sunday had been spent weighing up the benefits of dignified silence against media speculation and lies. She had guarded her secret closely to protect the daughter she had lost, but she knew now that it wouldn't be long before some enterprising investigator found her father, and her history would be the subject of scandal magazines and tabloids.

Monday morning, Faith looked at herself in the bathroom mirror. She had hardly slept. Her eyes, smeared with the residue of yesterday's mascara, reflected her torment. "Christmas Eve," Faith said, then, "Happy Birthday," as she had every Christmas Eve since 'that' day.

She gazed at the rumpled pathetic figure in front of her. Even her pyjamas looked defeated. "Oh, no, you don't, Faith New," she shouted. "If you're going down, you are going down fighting." She showered, styled her hair, applied immaculate make up, and dressed in the most powerful of her power outfits. Looking back at herself in the same mirror, she applied a final coat of bright red lipstick. "Here goes," she said, "all or nothing!"

At C2C, she stormed through the lobby, ignoring the waiting press, and went straight to her office. It was almost time for her to go on air. There was a little silver wrapped package on her desk. 'Some Secret Santa candle, no doubt'. Faith thought, sweeping it into her bag and headed to the studio. With a curt good morning to Megan, she took a seat. Speaking to Megan in her producer's booth she said, "I am going to speak after the first record, Megan. I am not sure what the audience reaction will be." She paused, obviously fighting to maintain her resolve.

"I want you to replay my father's call when I give the word, is that possible?"

Megan nodded – the clip, sadly, was readily available online.

Faith took a deep breath. "I have to set the record straight, but," she looked at Megan through the glass, "I am going to need your help to get through today."

Megan smiled at her. "Go for it," she said, "I'm right beside you."

The news and weather finished. "Ready?" Megan asked, as the final notes of Faith's signature jingle died out. Faith nodded, and pulled the microphone a little closer. "There has been a lot of fuss and publicity over the last few days, following a phone call on Friday that, I understand, is doing the rounds of the internet and being broadcast by other stations. If you haven't heard it…" She nodded to Megan who played the clip.

The tragic sounds of her father's call were replayed. "We forgave you," he pleaded, "can't you forgive us?"

Faith continued, "The general feeling seems to be, even here at C2C, that my reputation has been built on a lie, hiding some sort of disgraceful secret." She paused, Megan was looking at her, wide-eyed in horrified anticipation. "Well, that is absolutely true," said Faith, "and the secret *is* shameful, but the shame is not mine. So, for those of you who have been kind enough to say you won't judge until you know the truth behind the gossip, here is my story."

And Faith told it all. Every degrading, ugly, unbearable detail. "So, my listeners, *that* is my dirty little secret. A secret I kept to myself because it's the story my daughter shares but does not know. For all my adult years I have shared a conspiracy of silence and shame, where the grief I felt, and feel to this day, was part of the punishment for what I did. They told me I would forget her and move on with my life, but that is a lie. Losing my child is like a bereavement without a death, and constant, grinding guilt, with no hope of forgiveness. *That* is why I turned my back on the family who turned their back on me when I needed a family most. *That* is why I have never had a successful relationship, because I trust no one. And *that* is why I have never had another child, because I have always believed I don't deserve that privilege." Her voice, which had become loud with intensity of her grief, dropped to a tearful whisper, "and that is why, every year at Christmas, I remember the little girl who was mine for less than a day. Wherever you are, my daughter, happy birthday. I love you, and I hope you can forgive me."

There was a stunned silence in the studio, as Faith put her head in her hands to hide her tears.

'Last Christmas' began to play. Megan ran over and hugged her. "That was so brave," she said, then ran back as her assistant waved frantically from the desk.

****

Guy and Maria were at his kitchen table, listening to the broadcast. Maria was to spend her family Christmas at her eldest son's house as usual. Maria cried openly as Faith laid bare the trauma of her child's birth and adoption.

"Guy," she said, "that could have been me."

Guy nodded, deeply affected. "And now it's happening again, in a way."

Maria looked at him. "Again?"

"Being misjudged, shamed, being forced into a course of action she does not want to take, the threat of losing everything she has. Faith is risking everything in this broadcast."

"Poor girl," said Maria, wiping her eyes, "she needs to know that she is not alone."

"You're right," he said, grabbing his car keys. "I'll see you later!"

****

Within seconds, the calls had begun to come in. Calls from both men and women of all ages and all types. Words of support, words of sympathy, and most powerfully, words of understanding from women with similar stories to tell. Faith could hardly speak. Through sheer strength of will, she pressed on through the show. Thankfully, there were so many callers queueing to comment, Faith's air time was short. Any anticipated gaps were filled with record requests from people reaching out to parents or children they needed to trace. Finally, the end of the show came. Faith thanked her audience, hugged her thanks to Megan, and left the building.

She stopped suddenly as she reached the car park to see Guy's car parked beside hers, and Guy himself standing beside her car. "What are you doing here?" she asked.

"Waiting for you," he said. "I heard your show. I thought you might need some company, or a lift home."

The immense strength she had summoned to lock away her emotion left her. Suddenly weak, she almost fell, leaning against the car to steady herself. "Would you mind?" she said, "I don't think I'm safe to drive."

As they drove away from C2C, Guy said, "No doubt the ladies and gentlemen of the press will be all over your place by now. If you would like a bit of Christmas Eve peace and quiet, we could drive to my place for dinner at about six, and I will drive you back for your car later. She hesitated. "Nothing untoward, I promise," he reassured her. "In fact, Mum's at my place, you can't get much safer than that!"

Faith smiled. "I'd like that," she said softly.

"Mum and I usually have a quiet Christmas Eve, the calm before the storm, you might say. I've got the whole family coming tomorrow, aunts, uncles, cousins, son and daughter-in-law, daughter and partner, and grandchildren – it will be mayhem."

The traffic lights ahead turned red, and Guy pulled the car to a stop. He looked across at her. She looked fragile, almost trembling with the sheer effort of holding herself together. "This time, you are *not* alone, Faith," he said.

As the lights turned green, he followed the road home, Faith weeping silently beside him.

****

TV coverage of the Festival Church Service had created an unexpected late boost to the Christmas trade. Taylor's Country Gardens had been as busy as any Saturday, and, as the last few customers left, Danny was helping to clean the café. He was sweeping crumbs from the floor beneath the tables, when a customer coughed behind him to get his attention. He turned "I'm sorry, sir, but the café is clos…" Danny stopped short, seeing his father in front him. Kit was clean shaven, smartly dressed, and smiling. Danny dropped the broom he held and flung his arms round him.

Pat seemed to appear from nowhere. "Come on, you two," she said, "let's sit here."

Danny was confused. It seemed this meeting was not unexpected to either Pat or Kit. He sat slowly, his confusion very evident on his face.

Pat began "I'm sorry for all the intrigue, Danny," she said. "Your Dad and I have been talking these last few days and we have…"

Kit took over. "Pat has been helping me, Dan. Christmas and New Year is a dangerous time for me, because of the parties, the pubs, all the temptation to drink." Danny must have looked even more bewildered. This was the first time his father had openly acknowledged his addiction. "This time I am getting help, Danny," Kit continued, "I've seen the doctor and I've joined a group that can help me. After Christmas I have a place that will let me stay for a while to get better."

"So, I will be going home?" Danny asked, struggling to keep a tinge of disappointment from his voice.

"Eventually," Pat smiled, "but for Christmas you will be staying with me and so will your Dad."

"It'll get us through the 'festive season,'" Kit said. "I don't have a good record for this time of year, do I?" Danny shook his head in agreement, recalling a succession of ruined or cancelled Christmas days and lonely New Year's Eves.

The two adults looked at Danny. His face both delighted and doubtful. This was not the first time his father had promised to sort things out, and at this point

Danny would not risk believing that it would be the last. But he hoped.

"You saw Dad, Pat," Danny said, "you saw what he can be like," he looked at his father, "and he can get a lot worse than that." Kit looked down, ashamed but not denying the truth of his son's statement. Danny continued, tears in his eyes, "He can be violent, he gets sick, he steals, there's nothing he won't do to get a drink. Nothing." Danny had guarded the secret for so long, he was afraid to let it escape.

"I know that, love," Pat said softly.

"Why would you still want us in your house?" Danny whispered. "Why would you trust him to change?"

"You, Danny," Pat said. "You are the reason I know things can be different."

****

They pulled into the driveway of Guy's home. As Faith stepped out of the car, Maria opened the front door and held out her arms. Faith's tears became a torrent of wracking sobs. Between them, Guy and Maria half-carried Faith to the sofa, where Maria held her close. No words were spoken. No words were needed. These were not tears borne of anger or regret, rather from relief from a heavy, heavy weight of secrecy, shame and guilt. The loss of her child, a hidden grief, could at last be openly mourned. After a while, she wiped her eyes, sat up straight, took a deep breath and apologised for her 'outburst.'

"Faith, if things had been different, I would be in your shoes," Maria said. "If there is one place you can go to, where you are safe and understood, it's here."

Guy, who had disappeared into the kitchen, returned with a mug of tea for each of them. He set it on the table between them. "You can cry, scream, and shout blue murder, if you need to," he said. "No problem!"

Faith laughed, then, suddenly self-conscious, she said, "I must look terrible."

He looked at her, honestly. "Not at all," he said, "you are beautiful…" he paused, "a bit smudgy, but beautiful."

"Oh *Guy!*" Maria objected. She walked to the door. "Come on, Faith, I'll show you where you can wash and brush up."

****

Christmas Eve, Danny and Pat were in the kitchen of her neat little home, washing up the last of the dinner things.

"You're very thoughtful, Danny," Pat said, "what's up?"

For Danny, the evening had been spent in telling his father about his wonderful new job, his college course, his new found vocation, his Taylor's 'family' and the expertise of his hero, Jim.

The transformation of Taylor's and the transformation of Danny's own future seemed to be linked, somehow. It seemed too much to hope that the same could be true for his father.

"I'm so happy, Pat," he said, "but," he pointed to the lounge where his father was making up the sofa bed, "it probably won't last."

Pat understood completely. The bright hope for a sober future, always edged with the practicality of experience. "Whatever happens, Danny," she said, "we will deal with it together."

She had not swept away his cynicism with 'be positive' platitudes. She had not given him a one-size-fits-all plan of action. She had not told him that his beloved father was a hopeless degenerate. He hugged her. Grateful for her recognition of the reality of things, her straightforward honesty.

Kit appeared at the kitchen door. "Bed's all made up, Pat," he said, "now, is there anything I can do to help?"

She flung him a tea towel. "If you two carry on here, I'll go and lay the table in the dining room, ready for the four of us tomorrow."

"Four of us?" asked Danny.

"We can't have Christmas Dinner without Jim, can we?" Pat smiled. "He would have been here this evening, but he had to go somewhere after work.

Danny could have done a cartwheel, instead he scrubbed extra hard at the plate he was washing.

****

Faith, Maria and Guy had spent the rest of the afternoon in friendly conversation. As six pm approached, Faith began to wonder whether she had misunderstood the invitation to dinner, since there was no sign of cooking or preparation from either Maria or Guy. The mystery was solved as the intercom buzzed,

"That'll be dinner," Maria announced. "Guy, would you get the door, and I'll set the table."

"A take-away!" laughed Faith. "I wondered why you weren't basting or baking something!"

"Not my style at all, dear," Maria answered, "I gave all that up a long time ago. No, Christmas Eve, the two of us get a take-away."

257

Guy reappeared with two carriers filled with the very best 'Applebury Spice' had to offer, and the three of them spent a very pleasant, peaceful evening.

It was almost eight pm when Faith, retrieving the shoes she had kicked off earlier, said she ought to be getting home. As she waited for Guy to get their coats, she looked at an array of photos arranged in the hallway.

"That's the family," Maria said, pointing out her children and grandchildren, "and that's where it all started, of course," pointing to a larger framed photo at the centre.

"Your wedding," Faith said, "that's a lovely photo."

"There he is, dear boy, always smiling," said Maria. "Guy was our page boy."

Faith, her focus on putting on the coat Guy held out for her, hardly looked at the image of little boy in the hired suit. "Very sweet," she said politely.

Maria laughed. "Look at my husband," she said, realising that Faith had only given the photo a cursory glance. Faith looked at the smiling groom and then made the connection, catching her breath in surprise.

"Oh, my word!" she exclaimed.

"Exactly!" squealed Maria, "how could he not see it?" Even as a small child, and now even more so as the grown man standing before her, "Guy is the image of his father!" Maria said.

On the journey back to Sparchester for her car, Guy invited Faith to the Christmas morning church service. Mum likes to go," he said, "and by ten o'clock I've had enough of the family to be very glad to take her!"

Faith laughed at his honesty. "Don't they object?" she asked.

"From about five am I'm on grandad duty," he said, "so their Mums and Dads get a decent sleep, while I put the turkey in, supervise fights, and build Lego models. That way I can have a guilt-free snooze after lunch!"

"I'll see how I feel tomorrow," Faith said, as they stood beside her car. "I might not be up to the whole Christmas day church thing; I'm looking forward to a quiet day away from it all."

"Bliss!" Guy lied, since the merriment and mayhem of a family Christmas was all joy to him, from start to finish.

"Well, in case I don't see you," he handed her an envelope. Inside were two tickets to the Boxing Day performance of a West End show. "Of course, you can take who you like," he said, "but I'll pick you up Boxing Day at two pm, if you'd like to…"

"I would love to," she said, reaching up to kiss him on the cheek. Then, getting into her car she said, "Thank you."

As Guy drove home to prepare for the arrival of his daughter, son-in-law, and their two very tired little ones, Faith was pouring herself a glass of wine at home. Pulling the envelope of Guy's tickets, from her bag, she saw the little Secret Santa gift, and placed the two gifts beside each other on the coffee table in front of her. Faith watched the flames flicker in the log burner, allowing herself to process this morning's momentous disclosure. Having shed the initial shock of stripping bare her past, Faith found she could look peacefully into an uncertain future. No doubt the 'scandal' was the stuff of media gossip for the time being, but she knew that would be momentary. Some celebrity divorce, indiscretion, or death, would soon kick her story into yesterday's news, and she would be free to carry on, one way or another.

Exhausted, spinning thought after thought over in her mind, Faith fell asleep in her armchair.

Chapter Nineteen

Christmas Morning, and Danny and Kit were already in the kitchen when Pat came downstairs to prepare the Christmas meal before church. Instead, she found the cooker top filled with pans of neatly peeled and prepared vegetables, a tray of pigs in blankets ready to roast, and the turkey already stuffed and in the oven. Her two guests looked at her beaming.

"Take a seat," Kit said, "let *us* look after *you* today."

Danny, carrying a tray of tea and toast, led her to the lounge, where Kit's sofa bed was already tidied away, the cushions on her chair were plumped, and a little pile of presents lay under the Christmas tree.

"Well, this is an unexpected treat!" Pat exclaimed. "I'm not used to all this fuss."

Pat had the rather uncomfortable experience of having to eat her breakfast under close scrutiny, her tea being topped up after every sip, and offers of alternative flavours of jam, honey, or other spreads, at every bite of her toast. As soon as she had finished, her tray was whipped away and she was passed one gift after another, to be duly opened and admired. The haul of hand creams, bubble bath, slippers and scented candles were evidently inspired by a google search of 'gifts for middle aged women' and she found it hard not to laugh out loud at the 'age defying body scrub.' Thankfully there was a loud rap at the door.

"Can you get that Danny, love, while I tidy up all this paper?" Pat asked. Danny ran to the door and Pat signalled Kit, who had begun to tidy up, to sit down and watch.

"It's Jim!" Danny yelled, with enormous joy, hugging the breath out of Jim, who stood smiling on the doorstep. Danny stepped into the lounge, grinning from ear to ear, with Jim right behind him.

"Come and take a seat," Pat said, "we're nearly ready."

"You've started Christmas already, I see," said Jim.

Danny and Kit looked on proudly as Pat showed Jim her 'thoughtful' gifts.

Suddenly Jim slapped his hand to his forehead. "Oh my word! he cried, "I've left something in the van. Dan, would you do me a favour, it's in the back, you can't miss it." He passed Danny the keys.

Jim and Pat leapt to their feet and looked through the window, as Danny went to the van. "Come on Kit, quick," Pat said, beckoning him to the window. "You don't want to miss this!"

As they looked on, Danny opened the van doors, appeared to hesitate for a moment, then jumped inside the van. He re-appeared moments later, proudly lifting a brand new, top of the range push bike onto the ground. Decorated with a large tinsel bow, the label read, "To Danny, With much love and respect from all of us at Taylor's Country Gardens."

It was signed by Adam, Hope, Jim, Pat, and Rosa.

He looked back at the house where Jim, Pat and Kit were all beaming at him from the window. Pat wiping her eyes between smiles.

****

Faith woke with a start; Maria's words had been turning over and over in her head as she slept. "The image of his *father*!" she shouted.

The image of his father!

She allowed herself to think back across the decades, to her 'holiday romance.' He was probably only eighteen years old, but had seemed like a dashing, older man to her. Bronze skinned, dark eyed and tall with thick curly black hair, Faith realised she had not even known his last name. "The image of his *father*," she said again, picturing Hope. Surely…Her eye fell on the little gift-wrapped box. She leaned forward and drew it to her, absently unwrapping it.

Inside, a little hand turned wooden angel with the words 'Faith, Hope, Love,' smiled up at her. Lifting it from the box, a tightly folded wad of paper fell out onto the floor. Faith knelt to retrieve it from underneath the coffee table. It was a photocopied document. Unfolding it she saw a brightly scrawled message at the bottom, but it was the title that took her breath away.

"Adoption order," she read. For a moment, Faith became word blind, her brain and emotions split apart in astonished disbelief. She tried to read again.

"Adoption order in respect of an infant named Hope Lilian Thomas, an infant of the female sex formerly known as — the child of Sarah-Faith Browne…

Faith, dumbfounded, fell back against the sofa, flipping the note over and back again, as if the words she had read could not possibly be there on a second look.

"…and it is ordered that the applicants be authorised to adopt the infant 'Hope Lillian Thomas' and shall be entered the date of birth of the infant as 24th day of December 1980… and shall cause the aforesaid entry in the register of births to be marked with 'Adopted.'"

Faith trembled as she realised she held the copy of her daughter's adoption certificate in her hand. And it was her own daughter who had written,

Dear Faith,

Christmas is a time for giving and forgiving.
This angel is for you, there is nothing to forgive.

With love,

Your daughter,

Hope

PS, please come to the Christmas Day Service at Taylor's at 10.00 am.

She had underlined the last sentence three times. Faith looked at the clock, it was already 9.00 am – and it was half an hour drive to Applebury. She got ready quickly.

"What do you wear to meet your daughter officially for the first time?" she thought, changing from formal to casual twice over, then settling for somewhere between the two.

She drove in a state of fear and excitement. Her sensible self knew that these reunions should be cautious, measured and with a strict understanding of boundaries. Her heart wanted to fly to her daughter and dance with joy at having found her safe, happy and loved, as she had hoped, and even prayed, so many times. Faith entered the garden centre and heard her name called. It was Hope, standing a little way back from the door.

"Let's have a few minutes without an audience," she whispered. Taking Faith's arm, Hope led her to the orangery, where they sat together on a bench. Snow falling lightly outside, surrounded by twinkling lights and swathes of early narcissi and hyacinth – the setting was almost magical. Mother and daughter sat face to face, just looking at each other.

"How long have you known?" Faith asked.

"I suspected," Hope replied. "I even hoped. But really it was your Dad phoning in to the radio station that did it."

Faith shook her head, not understanding.

"Remember I told you my original documents had no information. I didn't even have a name?" Faith nodded. "You see it only had my mother's name, a name I have never been able to trace."

"Sarah-Faith Browne," breathed Faith.

Hope nodded. She took Faith's hand. "Then I was sure. But I wasn't sure how you would feel about it. Until I heard your broadcast yesterday."

"That's why, at the talent show, you were so…"

"Weird?" added Hope. They laughed.

"When did *you* finally realise?" asked Hope.

"An old photograph, would you believe?" Over the next few minutes, she explained, the first of many times, the tale of how she found her daughter.

A festive piano began to play 'O Come, All Ye Faithful.'

Faith began to stand, "We'd better go in," she said, wanting exactly the opposite.

"I say we go for a walk," Hope replied. "We need time to get used to all this."

"It is all a bit of a shock," Faith agreed, "good shocking, but shocking nevertheless."

Faith and her daughter did not attend church that Christmas morning, instead they spent a good hour celebrating their existing friendship, and exploring possibilities of the far deeper bond they shared.

"Do the family know?" Faith asked, as they returned to Taylor's Country Gardens.

"Adam, Agnes and Brian know, of course, but no one else." Hope replied. "I couldn't just presume you wanted this shared far and wide."

Faith said turning to face her "I am very, very glad that we have met and even more glad and proud to find that you are," she paused, almost afraid to say the words, "you are my daughter. Will you tell them, ever?" Faith asked, looking at Hope's children through the glass door of the newly designated church.

"Of course," Hope replied, "but don't expect much of a reaction if I tell them today." Faith looked at her in surprise. "I'm afraid the miraculous appearance of my long-lost Mum doesn't even come close to Father Christmas squeezing down the chimney with a sack full of toys."

"Long-lost Mum," Faith repeated, softly.

"Oh, I'm sorry," stumbled Hope, "is that okay?"

"Okay? It's wonderful. And it is miraculous," Faith agreed.

"I realise this might be too much, too soon, but," Hope asked, "I wondered if you would like to join us for Christmas lunch?" She saw Faith's hesitation. "I do understand if it's too much," Hope said, "but you are very welcome if you would like to meet the family. And you don't have to stay for lunch," she added. "Stay for ten minutes, or an hour, or all afternoon…"

At the doorway, Lily, who had been keeping watch, ran down the aisle towards them. "Come on," she said, "church is over, and you missed it!"

Hope leaned down and picked her daughter up. "Thank you, Miss Cheeky."

"Hello," said Lily, her chin lifted to emphasize her confident, accusatory gaze of her deep brown eyes. "You made Mummy miss church."

Faith froze, the direct, fearless gaze, the heart shaped face, lightly freckled skin, and white blonde hair. She was looking at a tiny version of herself. She looked at Hope, who nodded.

"It's uncanny," Hope said, "apart from your blue eyes, and…"

Callum squeezed between his mother and Faith, looking up at Faith. "And Callum has those!"

Faith huffed out a choking tearful breath, her hand over her mouth, as she looked into saw the boy's eyes of deepest blue.

Hope set Lily down. "Go and find Daddy, you two," she ordered.

Turning to Faith, "I'm sorry. It was selfish of me to put you in this position. I don't know what I was thinking."

Faith, dabbing her eyes with a tissue and trying hard to stop herself dancing with joy, merely said, "I'm fine, truly."

Maria spotted them from a distance, and muttered something to Guy beside her. Soon they were both at her side, looking ready for a fight, should Faith need protecting.

"Is everything alright?" Guy asked, looking aggressively at Hope.

Faith laughed, "Hope," she said, "I think you know my dear friends, Guy and Maria."

Hope nodded, a smile spreading across her face.

"Guy and Maria," Faith continued, formally, "I would like to introduce you to my daughter."

Many of the remaining church goers turned to look as a whoop of joy went up from the little group by the door. Agnes with a swift touch on the arm, stopped Brian from joining the group. "Give her a minute," she said. Then, looking at Adam in exasperation, "But you can go." She wagged her head as if to shoo him away. "We'll take the little ones back to your place."

As Faith followed Hope and Adam out into the carpark, Guy caught up with her. "You know my number," he said. "If it all gets too much, or if you need me for anything at all, call me."

She looked up at him, his eyes filled with concern. "Guy Harvey," she said, reaching up and placing her hands either side of his face, "you really are a true friend and a gentleman."

****

Danny, of course, had cycled to church ahead of them all and had set off for Pat's house after the service. Jim, Pat, and Kit were squeezed into the front seats of the Taylor's van.

"That was a lovely service," Pat said, climbing into her seat. "Thank you for agreeing to come."

"No problem," the two men replied in unison, as they waited for her to click her seat belt into place.

"Not you, Jim, you daft thing, I meant Kit," she said. "I know it's not your 'thing.'"

Kit smiled. "Well, it can't do any harm, and it might even have done me some good. I liked the bit about 'giving and forgiving' and you can't beat belting out a few carols on Christmas day."

Jim started the engine and began to pull out of the car park. "One bit of advice about church, Kit," he said, as they headed home. "You need to go regularly like me. Otherwise you don't get the benefit."

Pat looked across at him. "Regularly?"

"Absolutely," Jim growled. "Once a year, regular as clockwork!"

****

Planning for a quick getaway later, Faith parked in the street outside Hope's house. She sat in the car for a moment, watching Hope and Adam park their vehicles. Then Adam turned and beckoned her in. "This is it!" she muttered to herself, and she joined Adam at the door.

"What a wonderful Christmas this is," he said, "I'm so glad you and Hope have found each other."

"You are?"

"Yes," he said, "it's like a missing piece has been found."

She felt ridiculously pleased, and more so as the afternoon progressed. She was welcome, but not overwhelmed, and felt as much a part of the family as any good friend could. Faith stayed, she shared, she savoured the first of many a Taylor family Christmas.

Later than she expected, Faith pulled into her drive, pleased to see there were no reporters hungry for a last shot at her reputation. She poured herself a glass of wine, and sinking back into the thickly cushioned sofa, she took the little gift box from her bag.

As she removed the angel from its box, Hope's note fell into her lap. *Christmas is a time for giving and forgiving…*

She pulled out her phone and scrolled through Megan's texts, pressing her finger to the number on the screen.

"Hello Dad," she said, "it's Sarah-Faith."

The End

Notes

Until 1983 private adoptions were legal in England. These were placements arranged through private individuals, often doctors, nurses, lawyers, local vicar, etc. In such cases there was no Adoption Agency involved in the placement of the child with prospective adoptive parents. For people who were adopted privately it can be a much harder to find information about their adoption. In these situations, it is possible that the court records will have some background information.

Though this tale is purely fiction, the following sites have been used to ensure accuracy and may be of help if you are affected by the subjects covered in this book.

Forced Adoption and Reunion

http://www.adoptionsearchreunion.org.uk

This website provides information for adopted people, birth relatives and also adoptive parents in England and Wales. The information available on this website applies to adoptions that were made before the 30th December 2005.

https://www.pac-uk.org

Independent advice and counselling for anyone who has been affected by adoption or other forms of permanent care, as well as the professionals who support them, https://www.gov.uk/adoption-records/the-adoption-contact-register

Addiction and Recovery

https://www.alcoholics-anonymous.org.uk

SECOND CHANCE

Jill Debra Green

Catherine had not planned a fresh start. She had spent the last twenty odd years of marriage apologising for herself, excusing her husband's infidelities and making the best of things for the sake of everyone but herself.

Her grown-up children, one a gentle man of faith and the other a ruthless business owner, despise her resigned compliance, while her 'best friend' exploits it.

An impulsive purchase and a chance meeting at a mobile cafe at an antiques fair, launches Catherine on a journey that leads to a second chance of happiness, an independent livelihood, and eventually true love...

Coming Spring 2022

Treasure in Port Petroc